Single Ladies 2

Single Ladies 2

Blake Karrington

www.urbanbooks.net

Urban Books, LLC
300 Farmingdale Road, NY-Route 109
Farmingdale, NY 11735

Single Ladies 2 Copyright © 2017 Blake Karrington

ISBN 13: 978-1-62286-455-3
ISBN 10: 1-62286-455-7

First Mass Market Printing May 2017
First Trade Paperback Printing February 2017
Printed in the United States of America

10 9 8 7 6 5 4 3 2 1

This is a work of fiction. Any references or similarities to actual events, real people, living or dead, or to real locales are intended to give the novel a sense of reality. Any similarity in other names, characters, places, and incidents is entirely coincidental.

Distributed by Kensington Publishing Corp.
Submit orders to:
Customer Service
400 Hahn Road
Westminster, MD 21157-4627
Phone: 1-800-733-3000
Fax: 1-800-659-2436

Chapter 1

Tammy sat at the kitchen table rubbing the corners of her eyes in frustration. With the wedding swiftly approaching, and not even having the guest list complete, she had more than enough on her plate. To top things off, rumor had it that Chris was supposed to be on his way home sometime this year. The only problem with that was nobody knew when. The Federal Bureau of Prison's Web site had a release date for him about three years from now, which only made things more confusing.

"Are you okay?" Darious asked, walking into the kitchen. "You look stressed out right now."

"Yeah, it's this wedding. I didn't think planning it was going to be so hard. I'm trying to find the right catering company, a DJ, a suit for Anthony, my two bridesmaid's dresses, a dress for me . . ." Tammy sighed. "And look," she said, passing Darious the white notepad she'd been writing in all day. "Aside from Falisha, Lisa, Kim, my mom, and my uncle, I really don't have anybody coming. You got like sixty people so far, and counting. This is supposed to be my—"

"Baby, calm down," Darious said, taking the notepad and tossing it onto the table. "Take a deep breath and relax," he continued as he held her hands. "It's not that deep."

It might not have been that deep to him, but this wedding meant everything to her. She wanted it to be perfect, and her not having but a few family members there on her behalf seemed sad. Thinking about it actually made Tammy realize just how displaced her family was. She had two brothers and three sisters, all on her father's side of the family, but she hadn't seen them since she was six or seven years old. She couldn't even remember the last time she'd seen her dad, and neither she nor her mom knew if he was dead or alive. Tammy's family situation was a total mess.

"I don't know if this means anything to you, but my family is your family now, and they are going to love you without limit. You wanna know why?" Darious said, raising Tammy's hand up and kissing the back of it. "Because I love you, and after that, nothing else matters," he said, and kissed her hand again gently.

His words were believable because Darious's mom had been nothing less than an angel. The whole family welcomed not only Tammy, but also her two kids into their lives with open arms. She never had to ask them for anything, but if Tammy did need something, it seemed that they would be there for her with no problem. They made her feel like she was important and that she mattered in this world. Darious was right, and being a part of this family was one of the many things Tammy was grateful for. Marrying Darious, her knight in shining armor, was the ultimate gift, one that made planning this wedding worth all the stress and frustration Tammy was going to have to go through.

Lisa sat on the edge of Nate's bed getting dressed, hoping he didn't wake up before she left. She didn't feel like talking, and this definitely wasn't a cuddling session. She came to his place, they had sex, and now she was on her way out the door. That's the agreement they had, and Lisa was going to stick to the "sex with no strings attached" deal they had made.

"Damn, you leaving already?" Nate asked, waking up from his little catnap. "You know you can stay awhile, right?"

That's the exact reason why Lisa wanted to leave. Nate couldn't see it, but Lisa was trying to save him from getting hurt. He made the deal, but he really didn't understand the lines that weren't meant to be crossed. Lying up, pillow talking, cuddling, spending time, getting to know each other, were like a gateway drug. Those were the things that led up to something more serious, and before that happened, Lisa was going to secure those border lines by all means.

"Nate, we been through this before. You know I can't stay," she said, glancing over her shoulder.

"Yeah, you told me that, but I thought maybe we—"

"You thought wrong," she said, cutting him off. She turned around to face him because what she had to say next was important, and he needed to see the sincere look in her eyes when she said it. "Look, Nate, I like having sex with you, and to be honest, I think you're very talented in bed, but this bedroom is as far as we'll ever go. I thought we established that from the beginning," she said.

Nate was offended by the way she was talking to him, but he stayed cool. The sex they had was great, and the last thing he wanted to do was end it.

"We did establish that from the beginning, and you know what? That's my fault," Nate said, lying back down in the bed.

"Are you sure? Because if you can't handle what we got going on, just let me know," Lisa spoke.

"Nah, we good, just lock the bottom lock on your way out," he said before grabbing the remote control off the nightstand and turning the TV on.

Lisa turned back around, finished getting dressed, got up, and left without even saying good-bye. This was how she wanted it to be. No relationships, no cares, no worries, no stress, and most importantly, no love. She didn't want, or desire, these things from a man right now, and given what she'd been through, Lisa may not ever want to open up to anybody again. That's just the way she felt, and she found that it was easier being the way she was.

The sun was shining bright, and there had to be at least twenty kids outside running around on the small street. Tammy sat on her steps between Darious's legs, smoking a blunt and periodically yelling at Anthony, who was playing a little too rough with the other kids.

"Anthony, get ya behind out of that street!" Tammy yelled, seeing a car turn down the street.

The car crept down the street slowly, and all of the kids stopped and watched the spaceship of a car pass by. The all-white 2013 Bentley Continental GT slowed down, but didn't come to a complete stop as the kids had hoped. It simply drove down the street and made a right at the corner.

Everyone was so focused on the car passing by that nobody paid attention to the man walking up the street from the opposite direction. Darious was the first person to turn around and see him. The hateful look in the man's eyes prompted Darious to pull the compact .45 from his waist and set it on his lap. He was still doing his thing from time to time, and he had been robbed before, so this time, he wasn't taking any chances. It was about to be a shoot first, ask questions last type of situation.

"You know him?" Darious asked, nudging Tammy to get her attention. "Do you?" he asked again, clutching the gun a little tighter and taking the safety off.

Tammy finally turned around, and it was right in the nick of time, because Darious was ready to fire his weapon. It was like Tammy had seen a ghost, the way she jumped up from between

Darious's legs. For a moment, she couldn't believe the father of her kids was standing right before her.

"Chris?" she asked in shock, curious as to when and how he got out of prison this early.

She'd heard the rumors, but she didn't think they had much truth to them. She definitely wasn't aware that the new crack laws had gotten him released way before his time was up.

"I see you got ya'self a li'l wannabe thug," Chris said, not fazed at all by the gun Darious had sitting on his lap. "These are the kind of niggaz you got around my kids?" he asked, giving Tammy a look that would have killed her if she hadn't put her head down. "I been gone for four years, and you said you was trying to better your life, and this the *best* you can come up with? Wow. And you smoke weed now?" Chris spoke quickly firing verbal shots at both Tammy and Darious like a machine gun.

You must have lost ya mind questioning me! Tammy wanted to scream, but her mouth wouldn't move.

Chris looked over and gave Darious a hard stare. He wasn't a threat in Chris's eyes, and if he knew who he was pulling a gun out on, Darious would have never done it. Chris was a killer for real, plus, he was a little crazy, and just about everybody knew it. Well . . . except for Darious.

Tammy just sat there wanting to read Chris for his insult, but her heart was pounding so hard that she was sitting there with a dumb look on her face. Darious got mad at how humble and submissive she seemed to have become in Chris's presence. He started to say something, but decided against it, seeing Li'l Anthony running down the street toward them.

"Dad! Dad!" Anthony yelled, running up and throwing his arms around his dad. "You're home! You're home!" he yelled, holding Chris tightly.

Chris embraced his son with loads of kisses to the top of his head. Tears started to fill his eyes, but he quickly got control, remembering that Darious was looking on. He had missed being able to hug and kiss his kids. The prison never let him have physical contact, and the emotion of being able to fully express his love for them was overwhelming. Anthony had grown up so fast in the past four years, and although the prison bars had separated them, Chris's kids still loved him as if he had never left.

Tammy stood there, watching Chris and Anthony embrace. She could feel the emotion of their reunion, and all the love that she had suppressed for Chris seemed to pour out of her at rapid speeds. She had deep feelings for

Darious, and even loved him very much, but the truth was, there wasn't anyone in this world she'd rather be with than Chris. The love they shared was different from any other. Also, Chris had the nerve to be standing there looking as good as ever. His hair was cut low, so his waves complemented his rich, flawless, dark chocolate skin, and his beard was well groomed. She could smell the Frankincense oil coming off his skin, and the prostration mark on the center of his head proved that he'd been praying for this day to come.

"Where's my daughter?" Chris asked.

"She's with ya mom. Do you want me to call them?"

"Nah, that's cool. I gotta get ready to leave. I'm in the halfway house over off Remount Road right now, and I got like an hour to get back before those people start trippin'," Chris said. "I'll come back another time."

Darious wasn't feeling this little family reunion, but he understood that Chris was the father of Tammy's children. Before things escalated, he figured he would give them some privacy for Tammy to let Chris know what the real was. Darious stood up and put his gun back in his waist, all the while not taking his eyes off Chris.

He tapped Tammy on her ass. "Yo, I'm going to go make a quick call," he said before walking off down the street. The tap on the ass was to let Chris know that Tammy was his girl now.

Tammy gave Chris a look that pretty much begged him not to react to Darious's antics. Chris couldn't help but to smile, knowing that Darious had no idea what he was capable of doing to him. Not only that, but Chris didn't even want to be with Tammy after what he'd been through with her during the time that he was locked up.

"So, how did you get down here, and who told you where I lived?" Tammy asked.

"Come on, Tammy, you think I don't know where my kids rest their heads?" Chris said. "And if you must know, I got down here on the bus. I'm still trying to enjoy my freedom."

"You need a ride back?" she blurted, not knowing what in the hell had made her offer him a ride.

"I'm good, thanks for the offer, though."

Tammy was so glad he had declined her offer. There was no way in hell she could have explained to Darious that she was giving Chris a ride back to the halfway house.

Tammy wasn't sure what to say next. The fact of the matter was that Chris had just come back and made her life a little more confusing and difficult. She was happy that he was home, and almost instantly after seeing him, her feelings for Darious started to decrease, and her feelings for Chris had increased. The connection was unreal, so much so, that it sent chills down her spine, along with a tingling sensation between her legs.

"So, where are you going to stay after they let you out of the halfway house?" she asked, peeling off a couple of dollars so Anthony could get something from the approaching ice-cream truck.

Chris put his head down and began scratching the top of it in frustration. Reality had set in, and the thought of not having a house to come home to weighed heavy on him. This was something that in his mind, Tammy had taken away from him.

"I guess I'ma check into a shelter until I get a job or something," Chris answered, somewhat ashamed of how low his situation had become. "I'll be all right, though."

That sent a sharp pain through Tammy's chest, feeling like she was partly responsible for his hardship. He was supposed to be coming home to his family, but Tammy was living a different life now.

"Why do you have to go into a shelter? Why can't you just stay at ya mom's house until you find a place?"

"Tammy, I'm a man, and real men stand on their own two feet. Trust and believe that I won't be making the shelter my permanent home. One thing you should know about me by now is that I'm a go-getter, and failure is not an option. I'll be on my feet in a couple of months, and when I do get right, I'ma help you out with the kids," he answered.

"Look at me, Chris," Tammy said, trying to get some eye contact. "All you gotta do is give me the word; you know I'll help you in any way that I can," she said with sincerity in her eyes.

Chris searched to see where Darious had walked off to before responding. "Yo, you still crazy. I appreciate the offer," he said and chuckled. "But, you go ahead and keep doin' ya thing. I'ma be a'ight, I promise you that."

The bus would be coming soon, so there wasn't much more time to talk. As badly as he wanted to burn Tammy's ears up, he had to leave it alone for right now. He only had enough time to hug and kiss Anthony before getting to the bus stop. As he was about to walk off, he reached out and grabbed her hand, hoping he could at least get a hug from her.

Tammy had wanted one herself, ever since she laid eyes on him, but with Darious around, she thought it best to refuse him. She hesitantly pulled away.

Chris just smiled, understanding her dilemma. He turned and headed toward the bus stop. It hurt Tammy that she wasn't able to show Chris the love she still had for him, but she knew she would have a lot of explaining already to do to Darious.

Gay Ernie and Carol were sitting on Carol's steps, smoking a blunt when the sound of a car door slamming caught both of their attention. They looked up the street and saw Falisha walking away from a silver Jaguar, which pulled right off in a hurry. Falisha looked like she had just finished having sex. Her hair was all over the place, and her shorts were zipped up, but unbuttoned.

"Who da hell is you creepin' wit', bitch?" Gay Ernie yelled with a snap of his neck. "And don't be lying, neither."

"Boy, ain't nobody creepin', and that was Fox," Falisha admitted, knowing Carol already knew his car.

"Lamar gon' break ya whole neck," Carol spoke. "I hope you used a condom," she said with her face turned up like Fox was the nastiest nigga in the world.

"Bye, girl," Falisha responded, putting her hand in Carol's face. "And y'all need to mind all y'all's own business. Me and Fox is still cool. He just be looking out for me."

"I bet y'all are," Gay Ernie laughed, smacking his butt. "And I bet he do be looking out." Ernie snapped a circle. "You know what they say, it ain't trickin' if you got it."

"Shit, somebody gotta pay the bills around here," Falisha mumbled, taking a seat on the steps.

With the stripping business in his rearview, and a new, less-paying job on deck, Lamar and Falisha weren't living the luxurious lifestyle they were accustomed to. Lamar was paid every two weeks, and before he did anything, he had to make sure the bills were paid. After that, he broke down the rest of his check with Falisha, who, most of the time, spent it on going out and getting drunk just about every night. Even the things baby Jordan needed had to come out of Lamar's portion of his pay. He didn't mind, because Falisha and Jordan were his family, and taking care of them was his responsibility.

Sometimes, he wished Falisha would get a job so she could help. He never said anything, though, because when she was home, she did a great job taking care of Jordan.

"A'ight, y'all, it was fun, but I gotta run," Falisha said, taking one last pull of the weed. "And don't forget, we're going to Flake's tomorrow night. All drinks are two dollars," she said before disappearing into the house, and leaving Carol and Ernie on the steps.

Lisa picked up Naomi from school, went straight home, and got into the shower. She sat there, allowing the water to rain down on her head, thinking about how Nate always hit the spot when she paid him a visit. She also wondered if she was being too hard on him for not entertaining the thought of them spending a little time together, or maybe even trying to start some type of friendship.

It had been well over a year since Ralphy's death, and many of her friends and family members told Lisa that it was time for her to move on. But the truth was, she wasn't ready. That's why her outer shell was so hard, making it impossible for Nate to get through. She didn't just love Ralphy, she was still in love with him. Hell, even having sex with Nate was hard at times, but Lisa kept going back because it was the only thing that made her feel human. It made her feel like a woman, and that's all she wanted to feel.

Lamar looked down at his son, Jordan, resting ever so peacefully in his playpen. It had been seven months since Falisha gave birth to him, and Lamar was still in awe about having a miniversion of himself existing in this world. He never got tired of spending time with his son, and he loved Jordan more than anything and anybody, especially his son's crazy-ass mother.

"Come on, Falisha," Lamar mumbled to himself as he looked down at the watch on his wrist.

She knew he had to be at work in less than two hours, and these weren't like the days when he worked at the strip club, where his hours were flexible. Lamar had a real 9 to 5, so being late could cost him his job, and as of late, it seemed like Falisha couldn't care less. Her main priority was going out to the bar and getting drunk every night with her girlfriends. That was just one of the many problems in their relationship.

"Bitch, we goin' to Max's tomorrow," Falisha told her girlfriend, Carol, as they both came stumbling through the front door, loud and drunk.

Lamar could hear them from upstairs, and if they got any louder, they would be sure to wake up Jordan. He stormed downstairs, and it was apparent he had an attitude for more than one reason.

"Damn, Falisha, keep it down before you wake my son up," he said when he got to the kitchen. "And how da fuck do you plan on watching Jordan while you're drunk?" he snapped. "Damn, who does that?"

He could tell that both Falisha and Carol were way over their limit. Falisha's hair looked sweated out, her clothes were stained with God knows what, and her speech was so slurred that Lamar could barely understand what she was saying. Carol had passed out at the kitchen table almost immediately after she sat down.

"Don't worry about me and my son. All you need to do is go to that dumb-ass job you got," she said, all the while trying not to laugh. "Come on, you wanna strip for Mama tonight?"

Falisha danced her way over to where Lamar was standing. She thought that it was cute and funny, but Lamar wasn't laughing one bit. No way in hell was he going to leave Jordan in the house with Falisha while she was like this, and it was too late to find a last-minute babysitter.

His only option was to call out of work, something that he hated doing, but he knew was necessary. When it came down to his son, nothing else mattered to him, including his job.

Chapter 2

Tammy lay in the bed next to Darious watching TV, trying to enjoy some alone time with him while the kids were gone. Chris's mom had taken them down to the halfway house to see him, and after that, they were going to stay with her for the weekend. Tammy had some free time on her hands, but unfortunately, it really hadn't been all good at home ever since Chris's visit. Things were changing, and Darious was starting to feel the slight wedge that was coming between him and Tammy. Instead of the normal laughing and joking that occurred during the day, things had been quiet, and the talking was to a minimum. In the past week, even the sex had changed. It wasn't as wild and passionate as it used to be, and the back-shot position was the only way Tammy could get off.

When Darious tried to make love to her, he saw nothing but emptiness when he looked into her eyes. Tammy wasn't into it like before, and Darious could see it plain as day.

"Yo, we need to talk," he said, rolling over to face Tammy.

"Wassup, boo?" she responded, not taking her eyes off the TV.

"So, is this the way it's gonna be now? We don't talk, we don't go anywhere, and every time I go to hug you or kiss you, you twitch as though I'm not supposed to be touching you or something."

"Baby, you trippin'. We are good," Tammy said, turning to face him. "Everything's fine." She hardly believed the words she'd just uttered.

Ever since Chris had walked up on her, Tammy couldn't stop thinking about him. He had thrown a monkey wrench in the game with his untimely arrival. Although she and Darious were about to get married in less than a month, she still wondered what her life would be like if she was back with Chris.

"You still love him, don't you?" Darious asked, looking Tammy in her eyes. "And please don't lie to me."

The question caught Tammy off guard; she was surprised he would ask her something like that. She knew that Darious loved her, and until now, she thought that she loved him the same way, but the truth was, she didn't. The love that she had for Chris was different from the love she had for Darious. Chris was the father of her children and the person who practically raised her since the age of fifteen. The love she had for him was stronger and more powerful than any love she could have for anybody. She just didn't want to hurt Darious by telling him that.

"Why would you ask me something like that?" Tammy asked, hoping that Darious would change the topic.

He wasn't about to let up. "Come on, Tammy, just be real with me," he shot back.

Tammy shook her head. "Look, Darious, I'm in love with you, and I hope that you feel the same way. But, truthfully, when it comes to my kids' father, I'm always going to have love for him. We got a lot of history together, including two children. What kind of woman would I be if I sat here and told you I didn't have love for him? We broke up on the account of him going to jail, and not because of the way he treated me, which, by the way, was good."

Darious started to say something about her last comment, but Tammy stopped him so she could finish. "But in four years, a lot has changed, and we grew apart. I found out he had another baby out here, which means he cheated on me at some point in our relationship, and then his family disowned me. I was at a messed up time in my life, then out of nowhere, you showed up." Tammy smiled. "We are about to get married, and if that's not enough to prove my heart belongs to you, I guess this would be the perfect time to tell you that I'm pregnant," she said, climbing on top of him.

"You're pregnant?" he asked, excited and visualizing Tammy having his first child.

"It's kind of early on, so I didn't want to tell you yet. I had an early miscarriage before, and I wanted to make sure I would be able to carry it this time."

"Damn," Darious said, reaching out to rub Tammy's stomach.

"Are you ready to be a daddy?" she asked, leaning in to kiss him. "It's a big responsibility."

"Promise me that you'll never leave me." He cupped the sides of her stomach. "I don't want to lose you."

"Babe," she said, looking him in his eyes, "I love you, and I promise you that I'm not going anywhere."

Darious rolled Tammy onto her back, positioning himself between her legs. This called for a celebration, and a few kisses to her soft lips did the trick in making his dick hard. Before Tammy knew it, her night shorts and panties were off, and Darious was pulling his dick through his boxers and pushing it right into her pussy.

Normally, Darious would lick the pussy a little to make it wet, but today, there wasn't any need to. Although it was Darious inside of her right now, Tammy's mind had once again drifted off, and this time she was imagining that it was Chris on top of her instead of her soon-to-be husband. That alone made her box overflow with the sweet nectar that was only produced when Chris was at the forefront. She knew she was out of pocket and down out wrong, but in that moment, it felt so good.

"You all ready for bed, Naomi?" Lisa asked, walking down the hallway toward her room.

Her cell phone ringing in the bathroom got Lisa's attention. When she reached it, she threw her head back in frustration as Nate's number popped up on the screen. He knew that there were selected times he could call, and at night wasn't one of them. He was really trying his hand today, but just like before, Lisa had to enforce the rules upon him. She decided not to answer the phone, and just in case he decided to call right back or shoot her a text, she turned the phone off altogether. Nate was going to learn one way or another, and Lisa was going to make sure of it.

***

"Damn, boy, give it to me," Kim moaned, looking back at her ass clapping against Brian's lower abdomen.

She was taking his long, deep thrusts, but Brian had stamina, and that's where he was getting the best of her. Kim was tired, holding on to the headboard and trying her best to throw it back at him. Her doing so only intensified his strokes, and by this time, she wasn't even concerned about coming. She just wanted this young sex maniac to come from out of her.

"Take it like a big girl," Brian said, grabbing a handful of Kim's hair and pulling her head back. "Damn, this pussy is good," he uttered, feeling himself about to come.

Kim couldn't take it anymore. She'd been in the doggie-style position for the past twenty minutes and could barely feel her legs. Not wanting to be the one to give in first, she held her ground, but tried a different tactic in trying to make him come.

"Oh my God, I'm coming. Come with me," Kim screamed, reaching back and spreading one of her ass cheeks apart so he could go in deeper.

It worked, because in seconds, he reached his peak. His thick, creamy come squirted into the condom until there was nothing left inside of him. When he finally pulled out, Kim was relieved and flopped down onto the bed. She was so worn out that she couldn't even talk, nor did she have enough energy to roll over and check to make sure the condom didn't break. All she wanted to do was lie there for a minute to get herself together, but from the looks of how hard Brian's dick remained, and him grabbing another condom from the nightstand drawer, round two was right around the corner.

"Hey, bitch," Falisha greeted when Lisa exited her house. "You know Tammy wants us to go and get fitted for our dresses tomorrow."

"Yeah, I know," Lisa said, walking across the street. "What are you doing out here by yourself, and where is my godson?" Lisa asked, taking a seat on the steps.

"Ya godson is in the house with his daddy. I just came outside to get some air," Falisha replied. "Oh, did you hear Chris was home? And, did you know him and Darious had some words? I'm not sure about this upcoming wedding. You know how Chris got that girl wrapped around his finger," Falisha spoke, fired up and ready to gossip about everything she'd heard.

"Girl, Chris ain't gon' want that girl after what she did to him while he was locked up. You know men have a memory like elephants when it comes to their hearts being broken. I just hope he doesn't do anything stupid," Lisa said as she put her hair in a ponytail.

Right in the middle of their conversation, a black SUV turned onto the block. Lisa looked at it, and then put her head down, furious, because Nate had been bold enough to come to where she lived. He had definitely crossed the lines with this one, and it might be the final straw.

"I can't believe this nigga," Lisa said as Nate's Yukon Denali stopped right in front of Falisha's house.

"Who da hell is this?" Falisha asked. "It better be for you," she joked.

Little did Falisha know, it was for Lisa. Nate climbed out of the truck looking rather handsome, rocking a pair of 501 jeans, a short sleeved button-up Polo shirt, and some Jordans. He had a fresh set of dreads, with a nice line-up, and on his wrist was a watch that almost blinded Falisha when the sun hit it.

"Damn, he can get it," Falisha whispered out of the corner of her mouth, giving Lisa a little nudge.

Nate shut his door, and then leaned against it, standing a few feet away. "Wassup, Lisa?" he spoke, not at all concerned about the angry look in her eyes.

"Oh shit, he is here for you," Falisha laughed. "Damn, girl, he fine."

"Falisha, shut up and go check on Jordan," Lisa said, shooing her away so she could talk to Nate alone.

Falisha got up and went in the house, but she didn't go far, crouching down by the front window so she could see and hear what was going on. It was in her nature to be nosy, and she didn't care one bit.

"How da fuck do you know where I live? And what possessed you to just stop by like I gave you—"

"First off, you need to watch how you talk to me. I didn't disrespect you, so don't—"

"You *did* disrespect me by coming to my house," Lisa snapped, cutting him off. "You all the way outta pocket."

Nate looked off and shook his head. "You know what? You're 100 percent right," he said, digging into his pocket.

Lisa's heart dropped to her stomach when Nate pulled out her wedding ring. "I tried to call you, and I even texted you several times to let you know that you had dropped this in my bedroom," he said, passing her the ring. "And while I'm here," he said, right before he got back into the truck, "you might wanna find ya'self another boy toy, because I'm moving in a couple of weeks. This thing that we had is over. I'm done wit' you." Nate hopped back into his truck without giving Lisa a chance to say anything.

She looked down at her ring, wondering how she could have been so foolish and careless. This whole time, she thought the ring was in her Michael Kors bag. The ring meant everything to her, and by the time she picked her head up to at least thank Nate for bringing it, he had pulled off. If she'd had her phone with her, she would have called him, but she didn't, and the effort to run and get it wasn't worth it. Nate was gone, and that was that.

"You can come back out, Falisha," Lisa called out, knowing she was close by the door.

She came outside with a big smile on her face, rubbing her hands together, ready and excited about the scoop she was about to get. Today, Lisa would provide all the gossip Falisha needed.

"I'm flying back out to Charlotte," Kim told Brian as they lay naked in his bed. "I'm staying for about a month. After my girlfriend's wedding,

I'ma chill with the family for a minute," she explained.

"I thought you had that big trial coming up," Brian responded. "Plus, you got the bar exam."

"Well, the bar is three months out, and I already turned in my three motions for the trial. My boss can handle it from there; plus, if he needs me, he can always call me," Kim told him.

Brian was, and always had been, supportive of Kim's career. They had been dating for five months now, and everything seemed to be going fine. She never thought that she would have moved to Philly and fell for a thug, especially one whom her law firm had represented in a homicide case. In any event, she was happy. Although they weren't using words like *boyfriend*, *girlfriend* and *love,* their relationship worked. He had his own place, and so did Kim, so they gave each other space, and on occasion, time apart.

"Well, just make sure you bring ya ass back. Don't go down there and get caught up wit' one of those country boys," he joked, tickling Kim's side.

"Stopppp," she laughed, trying to get away from him.

Brian wrapped her up in his arms, holding her tightly as if he never wanted to let her go. He didn't have to say anything in order for her to feel the vibe. She could tell that he didn't want her to leave.

"You don't have to worry, I don't think a country boy can do for me what you've done thus far. Best believe, I'm coming back for you," she smiled, leaning in to kiss him on his chest, then his lips.

They lay there for a while longer, enjoying the moment. A moment was all that Kim had anyway, because, not only did she have to finish researching several new cases, she also had to study for the bar exam.

It was another day in the struggle for Chris. The streets of Charlotte had gotten worse since he'd been gone, and finding a job was even harder. He'd been home for over a week, and it seemed like everywhere he went, nobody was hiring. Chris had better chances of getting himself pregnant than somebody offering him a job, it seemed. His criminal background was killing him every time.

After the visit with his mom and his kids, Chris headed back to the halfway house. Seeing his kids was the highlight of his day. It seemed like they had grown up so fast. He walked into his dorm room, which he shared with three other parolees, Bizz, Ish, and Malcolm, some of the hardest criminals the feds had been forced to let go due to the new laws that were being passed yearly. To his surprise, Bizz and Malcolm were sitting in the middle of the room, breaking down slabs of cocaine, and bagging them up. Ish stood by the door, watching out for the police in the event they decided to do rounds. There had to be more than three bricks of powder on the small table they were operating from, and off to the side, sitting on Malcolm's bunk, were two fully loaded, semiautomatic handguns.

These niggas is going back to jail, Chris thought to himself, grabbing his workout clothes from under his bed. The last thing he needed was to be caught up in some nonsense that would land him right back in prison. He surely wasn't in a rush to get back to USP Pollock, B4 pod, cell 405, and by the looks of things, that's exactly where his roommates were heading.

"Damn, playa, you find a job today?" Bizz asked, all the while not taking his eyes off the scale.

"Nah, homie, it's hard out there for a nigga. I been to, like, seven different places, and ain't nobody hiring."

"Well, you know I always got room for you over here, playa. We doin' good out here, and I sure could use some brains in my operation," Bizz responded.

Bizz wasn't lying when he said they were doing well. He'd been home for a little more than a month, and he had already purchased a house on the West Side. Malcolm had just got to the halfway house three weeks ago, and he was already looking at a storefront he wanted to turn into a barbershop. Ish had only been there three days, and first thing this morning, he went to the car lot and bought a Dodge Charger. Bizz had a sweet operation going on, and the money he was making was enough to feed a couple of families. Chris couldn't lie, it was tempting as a mother.

"Nah, homie, I'm cool right now. I'm trying to stay out here with my kids, ya dig?" he replied.

"Okay, playa, I see you trying to do the right thing. I hope everything work out for you," Bizz said, finally picking his head up to look at Chris. "But, let me tell you this, when I first came home from prison, didn't nobody give me shit. I couldn't get a dime from nobody, and I put in over twenty applications for a job my first two weeks being out. Not one person hired me, not even the ones my parole officer hooked me up with."

"So you just gave up?" Chris interrupted, not really feeling Bizz's many excuses.

"Naw, playa, I'm not saying that. It ain't like I didn't try. I gotta get it the best way I know how. I'm not gonna starve out here . . . man, you're just gonna have to see for yourself," Bizz said, shifting his attention back to the scale. "Come fuck with me when you're ready."

Chris got up and exited the room. Malcolm and Ish heard the whole conversation, but didn't pay it any mind, especially the part when they started talking about doing the right thing, and getting jobs. Right now, it was all about getting money, and Bizz was feeding them too good to stop right now. He was making their lives comfortable, and that was more than enough, given their current circumstances.

Chapter 3

Doctor Keller stepped out into the waiting area and called Falisha's name. She wasn't doing much today but getting a routine checkup, along with trying to find out why she'd been having a little discharge in her panties for the last week. She was hoping that it wasn't because she was pregnant again; she didn't want to have another child, at least not at this time in her life.

"Well, I have a bit of bad news, Falisha," Doctor Keller spoke, looking down at his chart. "You have contracted an STD."

Falisha's heart sank into her stomach, and she started crying instantly. She thought that it was the big one, HIV, but thankfully, it wasn't. "You have gonorrhea," the doctor told her. "The good news is we can treat it with a simple shot of penicillin." Falisha was so embarrassed, she hardly wanted to get undressed to get the needle. The process of elimination began immediately, and that was easy because the only two people she was having sex with were Lamar, and just recently, Fox. She didn't use a condom with either of them, but she knew beyond a shadow of a doubt that Lamar wasn't sleeping around. She couldn't say the same for Fox, who she knew was a whore.

"Okay, Falisha, no sex for a week," the doctor said, pulling the needle out of her ass. "And tell your partner that he needs to be checked out as well, or it will be very easy for him to give it right back to you," the doctor instructed.

Telling Lamar that she had given him an STD was out of the question. She was more worried about her own image than his health, and this was probably the only time in their relationship that Falisha hoped Lamar had cheated on her, so that the blame could be directed elsewhere. The chances of that were slim to none, so another route had to be sought. For now, Fox was about to get an earful, and there was no way he was going to wiggle himself out of this one.

Carol stood up on her steps, looking down the street to see if Ernie was coming. He had called ten minutes ago and said that he was on his way with some weed and Patrón. It was a little too early in the day for liquor, but Carol could smoke weed any time.

"Damn, bitch, hurry up!" Carol yelled at Ernie, who was taking his sweet time walking up the street. "If some dicks was here waiting for you, yo' ass would be running!" she shouted.

Ernie sped up his stride, only hearing the words "some dicks" come from Carol's mouth. Ernie was as gay as they come. He looked, walked, talked, and dressed just like a woman. The only way one could tell that he wasn't a woman was if he didn't shave for a week. That, and the obvious bulge he got in his pants when he saw a good-looking man that he liked.

"You are such a fucking diva," Carol said, watching as Ernie struggled to crack the blunt open. "Give it to me."

"I don't wanna mess my nail up," he shot back, putting his hands on his hips. "And don't use too much spit," he added.

"Shut up, Ernie. And why don't you go knock on Falisha's door and tell her to come smoke with us," Carol instructed him.

"I would, but Falisha ain't home. I called her right after I called you, and she said that she was out," Ernie spoke.

"That translation meant, she's creeping. That girl swear she has all the sense. Lamar gon' kill her when he catches her."

Ernie looked at Carol in shock. He normally was up on his gossip, but somehow, Falisha sleeping around had yet to reach him. "Oh no, bitch, you never told me she was doing her thing," Ernie said, popping his neck and sucking his teeth.

"Bye, boy!" Carol said, raising her hand up to his face. "That girl been messin' around with Fox for a minute now. You know that used to be her old boo," Carol informed.

"You talking about sugar daddy Fox?" Ernie asked.

"Yeah, I used to fuck around wit' Fox. He used to make me suck his dick for an hour at a time," Carol told him.

Ernie blushed at the notion of sucking some dick for an hour. He wanted more details on that part of the story alone, but Carol refused to go in on it. It wasn't like Ernie didn't know she was a whore. Hell, everybody in Charlotte knew Carol was a whore. A good whore at that. She's been sexually connected to some of the biggest ballers Charlotte had to offer, and the thing she was known for the most was her dick-sucking skills. Well, that and the fact that she had the nerve to be a cute whore. By her looks, she could have been wifey material, but her reputation made that only the reality with someone who wasn't from Charlotte.

"Well, that's news to my ears," Ernie said, reaching out for the blunt.

"Yes, it's going to be news to Lamar's ears soon, if she don't be careful. Once that happens, all hell is going to break loose."

"So, how do you feel?" Lisa asked, bringing Ms. D some hot tea into the living room where she sat watching TV.

"I feel good. I got one more round of this chemo shit, and then I'll be through. Next week can't get here fast enough," she responded.

Over the past year, Ms. D had been in and out of the hospital, going through several rounds of intense chemotherapy. For a moment, she had almost given up, but family and friends, like Lisa, Tammy, Lamar, and Falisha, gave her the strength to keep fighting. It was a blessing too because doctors predicted that one more round of chemo and a light surgery would dead the cancer all the way. Everybody was excited for her and was going to be there until the very end.

"Now, what about you and that boy you're seeing? How's that working out for you?" Ms. D asked, cutting her eyes over at Lisa.

"What boy, Ms. D?" Lisa asked, trying to play stupid.

"Don't make me kick yo' ass, girl. You been walking around here with that extra pep in your step for the past couple of weeks. You think Ms. D don't know when somebody's turkey getting stuffed?" She laughed.

Lisa couldn't keep lying to Ms. D if she wanted to, and she probably felt more comfortable talking to Ms. D than anybody.

"It's just sex, Ms. D. He's a nice guy, but I'm not looking for anything more than just that," she explained. "It happens at his house most of the time. Sometimes we go to a hotel, but never do we do it in my house. He doesn't even know about Naomi."

"Well, that's good for you. Everybody need some dick in their lives. Do he got a daddy who can come knock the dust off of this ole' pussy?" Ms. D joked, laughing so hard she almost choked.

Lisa had to laugh at that one too. Ms. D was terrible, and she always knew how to make somebody smile or have a good day. That's why Lisa loved her so much and looked at her like a second mom. She was a good person, and had an even bigger heart, but the best part about Ms. D was that through all her trials and tribulations, she kept her head held high. For Lisa, that was pure inspiration; the very thing she needed.

***

Falisha swerved, punched on the gas, and shot right through traffic like a speed demon. She ran red lights, stop signs, and even caught a hit-n-run on a cat. Her car came to a screeching halt, damn near crashing into the barbershop where Fox hung out. He saw her coming from a mile away and knew that she was steaming hot. He had to run outside and grip her up before she came into the barbershop and embarrassed him.

"You nasty muthafucka," Falisha snapped, swinging on him.

Fox blocked the punch and slipped two more before grabbing her.

"Calm da fuck down!" he yelled, pulling her around to the side of the building where nobody could see them.

Falisha stayed calm, looking around for something to bust him in his head with once he let her go.

"Falisha, look at me," Fox said, shaking her a little. "My bad, shawty. I just found out yesterday, and I just was about to call you and tell you," he lied. He had been to the doctors and treated almost a week ago. "I beat da bitch up and everything," he told her, which was actually the truth.

"Get da fuck off me!" Falisha demanded. "Now."

"You better not hit me either," Fox said, loosening his grip on her.

When he let her go, Falisha looked down at a stick she'd been eying since she got there. She was on her way to pick it up and crack him in his head with it, but stopped when Fox started digging in his pocket.

"I know this don't make things any better, but you need to take a chill pill," he said, pulling out a healthy wad of money. "Go get ya hair done, feet done, nails done, hit the spa wit' a friend, then go burn the mall down," he told her, not even counting the money he peeled off and held out.

It was all fifty-dollar bills, so it had to be at least forty-five hundred he was trying to give her. Falisha looked at him, then looked at the money. She was mad as hell, but also broke, and she thought about all she could do with the money. When she reached out for the money, Fox pulled it back.

"First, you gotta forgive me tho," he said with a sad look.

Falisha snatched the money out of his hand with lightning speed. "I'll fuckin' forgive you when I please," she snapped.

She folded the money, then tucked it into her back pocket before walking off. Fox didn't want to push his luck, so he just let her go. One thing he knew about Falisha very well was that she loved money, and as long as that kept being pumped into her pockets, she would eventually forgive and forget.

"Ernie, I bet you got a big ol' dick," Carol said as she sat back on her steps feeling the effects of the weed.

"If you mean this useless organ my mother cursed me with at birth," Ernie replied, "yeah, it's big. Sometimes I wish I could cut it off and use it on my damn self," he said with a smile.

"Damn, Ernie, you should let me sample some of that. I'll fuck da shit out of ya gay ass," Carol teased, looking at him with lustful eyes. "My pussy good too."

"Oh no, baby, I don't do fish. I'm strictly dickly over here," Ernie said, snapping his fingers at Carol and rolling his eyes.

The weed had Carol horny as hell, and right now, anybody could get it. The mailman, paper-boy, dope boys, young, old, short, tall, money, or broke. When Carol wanted to fuck, she was going to make something happen, and if Ernie stuck around much longer, he might find himself a victim. She was too high to move right now, but as soon as she came down a little, somebody was getting fucked.

Chapter 4

Tammy, Lisa, and Falisha walked through the mall, hitting up every store they passed. They were supposed to be there for their dress fitting, but that was the last thing on their agenda. It had been awhile since they had all been out together, so making a full day of it was the plan.

"Come on, y'all, let's sit right here," Falisha said, waving the other girls over to a table by the food court.

Bags from different stores were all over the place. "I still can't believe that you're about to get married," Lisa spoke as she sipped on her smoothie.

"Yeah, and what did Chris have to say about you meeting somebody else at the altar?" Falisha chimed in, getting straight to the meat and bones.

Tammy put her head down. "He don't know, yet," she said in a low tone. "I wanted to tell him, but he—"

"Girl, that man is going to kill you," Falisha said, throwing one hand in the air.

"Shut up, Falisha. Chris ain't gonna do shit," Lisa shot back.

Lisa looked over at Tammy, who had a very familiar look in her eyes. Lisa knew it all too well; it was the same look she had when Dre was released from prison. "You still love Chris?" Lisa asked, pretty much knowing the answer already.

"Girl, dat nigga look so good," Tammy spoke. "Damn, he made a bitch wanna give it up on the spot."

"That's right, girl. That's ya baby daddy," Falisha said, raising her hand for a high five.

"No no no, Tammy, you can't do that," Lisa cut in. "Didn't y'all bitches learn anything from my situation?"

Lisa could see Tammy easily going down the same path she went down, and the one thing, if anything, Lisa learned from her experiences, was to never play with a man's heart. Almost every time, both parties end up being hurt, and sometimes things could become deadly. Lisa didn't want to see Tammy go through what she'd been through, and having two men like Chris and Darious go at it would end with the same unfortunate results.

"Tammy, you need to tell Chris that you're getting married. You say you love Darious, right?" Lisa asked.

"Yes, of course, I love him," Tammy responded. "He's good to me, and my kids like him. We been talking about having a baby and moving into a bigger house," she said.

"Well, be with him. Show that man the respect that he deserves and don't give Chris any indication that there's a chance that y'all two will get back together."

"Yeah, but it ain't nothin' wrong with givin' him some pussy, right?" Falisha playfully asked.

"Falisha, shut up," Lisa said. "Tammy, listen to me, and listen to me good. Under no circumstances, whatsoever, do you have sex with Chris. First off, it's cheating, and second, it will ruin everything," Lisa said emphatically. "Please trust me on this one."

"Okay, okay, okay," Tammy buckled, taking in a deep breath as she thought about the great sex they used to have.

Lisa was 100 percent right, and hearing her advice made Tammy realize that she couldn't be selfish. Too much was at stake, and the price of losing Darious was too high. Tammy needed to be honest with Chris.

"All right, since we're all here and everybody's all up in my business, why don't we get on yo' ass," Tammy said, smiling at Lisa. "Who da hell is Nate, and why haven't I met him?"

Lisa looked over at Falisha, who stuck her tongue out at her. "I knew ya ass couldn't hold water," Lisa told Falisha. "Girl, he's nobody, just some guy that I talk to."

"Like hell. That's her boyfriend, but she's in denial."

"Falisha, I'ma kick ya ass. That man is not my boyfriend. My husband is probably rolling over in his grave, right now, God rest his soul," Lisa smiled, crossing her chest.

"You know it's nothing wrong with you having somebody. Eventually, you're gonna have to move on," Tammy told her, getting a little more serious about the situation.

"Yeah, I know. I'm just not ready for no relationship right now. I couldn't possibly love somebody else."

"Who said anything about love?" Tammy corrected. "This is gonna be a process for you, and at this stage in ya life, you need to start off slow. Take baby steps, but don't rule out the possibility of one day allowing yourself to be with someone again."

Everything Tammy said ran through Lisa's mind, from the time that she woke up until she went to bed at night. A part of her wanted to move on, but then guilt set in, and she thought about how two men had died because of her selfish desires. It was something that she could never forget, and as long as she had that on her soul, moving on would forever be difficult.

"Yo, you got a visitor," Malcolm walked into the room and told Chris, who was getting ready to take a shower. "Shawty look nice too," he added.

A visitor? Chris wondered to himself, already having seen his kids two days ago.

The only person who he thought it could have been was his second baby's mom, whom he hadn't seen since he had been home. Whoever it was, they were here early, and since it was Friday, they were cutting into his religious pass to go outside.

Chris walked down the steps toward the living-room area where the visits took place, slowly taking his time in putting on his T-shirt. To his surprise, it was Tammy sitting there with a huge smile on her face. She had on a pair of 7 For All Mankind jeans, a white halter top, and some

Christian Dior sandals. Her hair was slicked back into a ponytail, and it looked like she had just stepped out of the nail salon. Her sweet-scented body wash lit up the whole downstairs, and the sounds of her cracking chewing gum in her mouth vibrated throughout the room.

"You can leave it off," Tammy joked, catching a glimpse of Chris's lower abs before he got the shirt on.

Chris couldn't lie. Tammy looked good from head to toe, and it didn't seem like she had aged a day since he'd been gone. She really took good care of herself, and for a split second, the urge to get a hug, or maybe even steal a kiss crossed his mind. It had been some time since he had enjoyed the touch of a woman, and if he remembered correctly, that last touch had come from Tammy. Temptation was a mutha, especially feeling that at any given time, Tammy would give him some pussy.

"What's good with you, Tammy?" Chris greeted, walking right past her, and taking a seat on the couch.

"You must really hate me," she said, taking a seat right next to him on the couch.

"Nah, what makes you think that?"

"'Cause, I can see it in your eyes. I haven't seen you in years, and it seems like you can't stand the sight of me. Shit, you didn't even give me a hug."

"Tammy, you telling me that you came all the way down here for a hug?" Chris said and laughed.

"Yeah," she joked, but was serious at the same time.

Chris shook his head. "Yeah, you still crazy, I'll give you that. So, wassup? Are the kids OK?"

"Yeah, the kids is cool. I just came down here because I needed to talk to you about something, and I'm sure you may have some stuff you wanna get off your chest as well," she said.

Chris did have a lot on his mind, and a lot of questions he needed answers to, but now wasn't the time, nor the place for that. He'd spent the last four years of his life living in hell, and the things that transpired between them was enough to send any sane man to the nuthouse. All Chris wanted to do right now was enjoy the fact that he was home.

"I really don't have a lot of time, because I have to go to Jumu'ah," Chris said.

Tammy had heard that Chris had gone full-fledged Muslim while finishing out his prison stint, but she figured all that would go away once he was home.

"Please don't be mad at me," she began. She then paused for a couple of seconds. "I'm getting married in a few weeks," she continued, before putting her head down to avoid any eye contact with Chris. "I'm sorry, and I know I should have told you, but I . . ."

Chris looked over at her and didn't say a word. He simply got up from the couch and walked out of the room. Tammy called out his name a couple of times, but Chris kept walking. Tammy teared up immediately, knowing that once again, she had hurt the man whom she still loved. She was starting to regret even telling him as she stood there in sorrow. The only thing left for her to do was leave.

Lamar walked into the bedroom where Falisha was putting Jordan to sleep. After she had the baby, she had become super thick all over. Her thighs were thicker, her ass was fatter, and her breasts went up at least one cup size. Her stomach wasn't flat like it used to be, but Lamar liked it the way it was.

"Come on and put Jordan in his playpen so we can do us," he said, climbing onto the bed.

Jordan was dead asleep, but Falisha wasn't up for having sex right then. "I don't feel like it. Maybe later," she said, not budging one bit.

Lamar wasn't trying to hear that. He rolled
Falisha onto her back, and then got on top of her.
"Stop playin' with me, Falisha," he said, leaning
in, trying to kiss her. "Open up," he smiled,
thinking she was joking.

"I said no," Falisha replied, turning her head
so Lamar's kiss missed her lips.

He kissed and bit down on her neck anyway
and reached down to pull off her house shorts.

"So, you gon' rape me?" she said, getting
Lamar's attention.

"Whoa!" He picked his head up and looked
down at her. "Are you fucking serious?"

"What part of no don't you understand?" she
shot back with a stern look. "Get off of me."

She didn't have to tell Lamar twice. He practically jumped out of the bed when he saw that she
wasn't playing. "What da fuck is yo' problem?"
he snapped.

"I told you, I didn't feel like it," she answered,
rolling back over next to him. "And I don't feel
like talking about it, so could you please just
leave it alone."

Falisha felt bad denying him that which was
his, but there was no way in hell she could
indulge him at that time. The doctor had told her
not to have sex for at least a week, and since she
had just received the penicillin shot two days

ago, Lamar could still contract gonorrhea from her. He may already have it, but just in case he didn't, Falisha wanted to be STD free so she could deny that he received it from her. She'd like to have killed Fox, but she was also mad at herself for even having sex with him, especially without a condom. She had made a horrible mistake, but in the end, only Lamar would suffer.

Lisa sat in the house, thinking about everything Tammy had said to her at the mall. It somehow coincided with everything the rest of her friends and family had been telling her over the past few months. On days like today, she totally agreed with the notion of having a male friend in her life. It was Friday evening, Naomi was at her grandmother's house for the weekend, and all Lisa had planned was to wash clothes and clean up the house for the rest of the night. This would have been one of those days when she'd call Nate and get a dose of her "medication," but he wasn't answering her calls. Tammy was busy, Falisha was looking after Jordan, and Kim was over 500 miles away. In a nutshell, Lisa was lonely.

"Come on, Nate," Lisa mumbled to herself as she dialed his number. "Shit," she yelled when his phone went straight to voice mail.

She couldn't believe that she'd been dumped by a man who she wasn't even dating. Nate had dropped her like a bad habit, and it seemed he wasn't going back on his decision. The conversation she had with Tammy just kept playing back in her head. Lisa became so frustrated that she jumped up, grabbed her car keys off the dresser, and headed for the door. The only thing she could think about was getting some air, and given her current circumstances, it looked like she was going to be getting plenty of it . . . all by herself.

"Why ya face so long, my nigga?" Bizz asked, seeing that something was bothering Chris.

Chris just shook his head. "I'm good, homie," he responded, lying in his bunk and staring at the ceiling.

Bizz chuckled while he counted his money. "You worried about ya baby mom. I already know. I been there too. All I can tell you is that you're home now. It's plenty of bitches out here for the pickings. It ain't no need to stress over one."

Chris heard Bizz, but he just wasn't feeling him at the moment. It was one thing for Tammy to step off on him while he was in prison, but now she was talking about getting married.

When she told Chris that, it was like getting smacked with a ton of bricks. Even though she did what she did, Chris had always kept it in the back of his mind that one day they would get back together. He thought that in a couple of years, perhaps they would tie the knot and maybe even have another kid. All that had gone straight out the window, and now he was about to get on some other stuff.

"Yo, Bizz, do that offer to join ya crew still stand?" Chris asked, sitting in his bunk.

Bizz was crazy enough to sell cocaine out of the halfway house, but he did have morals and respected a man who had good character. The crack game wasn't for everybody, and even though Chris used to be in the streets real heavy, Bizz knew that this wasn't what he really wanted.

"So, what do you got going on tomorrow?" Bizz asked, stuffing some money inside an envelope and tossing it up to Chris.

"Nothing, why? What do you need me to do with this?" Chris asked, taking the bills out of the envelope.

Bizz sat back on his bunk and began twirling his thumbs. Anytime he did that, he was in thinking mode. "Homie, you been here for about three weeks now, and you haven't fell into the street life yet. You wasn't worried about clothes, you're not eating takeout every night with us, you're not doing any drugs or drinking any liquor, nor do you mind riding the bus. I know you don't have any money because you're too damn stubborn to ask ya family, and even though you put in a million applications, you still don't have a job. Hell, I'm not even sure if you got a shot of pussy yet, and still, every time I see you, you always got something positive to say. Through all of your hardships, you still get down on ya hands and knees and pray to Allah. You're really trying to stick to the religion and stay away from the foolishness. From one brother to another, I respect you for that."

"Yeah, I respect you too, homie," Malcolm yelled out from under the blankets.

"You love Allah, and a part of me envies you for that, but in a good way," Bizz continued. "Look, it's like ten grand in that envelope. Do whatever you want with it, but just leave the streets to niggas like me and Malcolm. You're better than us," Bizz finished.

Bizz lay back on the bed and flipped out his cell phone, not really wanting to give Chris a chance to reject the gift. He had really taken a liking to Chris and the way he was living his life, and in some crazy way, it inspired Bizz to want to do better for himself. The only problem with that was, the streets were all Bizz knew, and the drug game was his life.

Nate sat in the parking lot of his apartment complex looking at his phone. He could see that while he was at work, Lisa had called him a couple of times, probably to see if she could get one last booty call in. He was more than tempted to call her back, but as a man, he had to stand his ground. The sex was great, but Nate needed more. For him, pussy was easy to get, and he had a whole list of chicks he could call to get right, but Nate wanted more out of life. He wanted a female who was about her business and who could stand by his side, not only when the sun was shining, but also when the storm came. He wanted somebody to come home to after a long day's work, and for that same someone to have a hot meal waiting for him. He wanted someone who he could give his all to. Nate wanted to fall in love, and for some odd reason, he thought that Lisa could have been the one.

"Let her go," he said, as he got out of his car.

He stared at his phone the whole three flights up to his apartment, and as he walked down his hallway, he couldn't believe his eyes. Lisa was standing in front of his door, leaning against the wall, waiting for him. She didn't look like herself though. It looked like she had been crying, and her sassy and aggressive demeanor was more humbled. Nate didn't know what to think, but what he did know was that sex was out of the question with her looking like this.

"Are you okay?" he asked, leaning against the wall directly across from her.

Lisa picked her head up and looked into Nate's eyes. She was going against her better judgment, but she wanted to see for herself whether opening up to someone was in her best interest. She wanted to see how it felt to have more than just meaningless sex, and although she was galaxies away from being ready for a relationship, Lisa wanted to see if she could have a male as a friend. These were the baby steps Tammy was talking about.

"I've been a dental assistant for five years now," Lisa began.

Nate was all ears. "Tell me about it."

Chapter 5

"Ahhhh, shhitt," Lamar yelled, standing over the toilet holding his dick. "Ouch, ouch, ouch!" he said every time he let a little pee come out. "What da fuck is goin' on?" he questioned, feeling like he was pissing out fire. "Ouch, ouch, ouch!"

Lamar had never had an STD in his life, so it was kind of freaking him out. He had noticed some fluid coming out of his dick the other day, but he didn't pay it any mind, thinking it might have been precome or something. He didn't know that it was the beginning stages of gonorrhea.

"Oh, you son of a bitch," he yelled, tapping his feet on the floor as he let a long stream of urine out at one time. "Ouch, ouch, ouch, ouch!"

By the time Lamar finished urinating, he was sweating and exhausted. It took the life out of him. He knew exactly what type of STD he had, and it wasn't from his own personal experience. Working in a strip club, he'd seen it all. Two of his boys caught the disease during ladies' night a couple of years back. They ended up giving a female a threesome backstage during a private show. Lamar now remembered as clear as day the symptoms they'd described a couple of days later.

How da fuck? Lamar thought to himself as he stood in the bathroom, looking at himself in the mirror.

Since he and Falisha had been together, he hadn't cheated on her, not one time. There could only be one other explanation, and given the fact that Falisha was unwilling to have sex with him, Lamar quickly put two and two together.

"I'ma kill dis bitch," he said as he stormed toward the bedroom.

Fortunately for Falisha, she wasn't home, because if she was, Lamar would have tried to do exactly what he said he was going to do to her. Not only had she cheated on him, but she had given him a vicious sexually transmitted disease, which meant that she also let a dirty-dick nigga hit it raw. Lamar was so mad his blood pressure shot through the roof, so much so, that he lost his sight for a second and had to sit down.

He got himself together, and then tried to call her. Of course, she wasn't answering, but Lamar kept trying. After about twenty attempts, the phone just went to voice mail, indicating that

Falisha had either turned the phone off, or her battery died. He called across the street to her mom's house, but her mom said that she wasn't there. She couldn't have been far, because she had Jordan with her, and her car was still parked out front. Knowing that eventually she was going to walk through the front door, Lamar sat downstairs in the living room and waited for her. Only God could save her from what he was about to do.

Chris pulled the hood over his head as he exited the halfway house. He only had a five-hour pass, but that was more than enough time to go and check out a couple of apartments he was looking to rent. Once he had a place to stay, his probation officer was willing to let him leave the halfway house and be on home confinement, which was pretty much freedom, compared to what he had already endured. Chris and several other parolees walked toward the bus stop, then out of nowhere, a Chrysler 300 pulled up alongside them. Chris didn't know who it was until Tammy rolled her window down.

"Come on and get in," she stated.

Chris turned around and kept walking, not really in the mood to talk to her. Tammy drove alongside him, continuously asking him to stop, but he wouldn't. She threw the car in park, jumped out, and ran up to him.

"Chris, can we talk?" she said, trying to block his path.

Chris ignored her and kept moving her out of his way. She wasn't taking no for an answer and kept pulling at him, trying to get him to stop.

"Stop acting like a kid," she screamed. "You a man. Be a man about the situation."

Chris had heard enough. He stopped in his tracks and looked Tammy directly in her eyes. If she really wanted to talk, it was time he let her know exactly how he felt.

"You ain't shit. Fuck you, Tammy," he snapped, pointing at her face.

Tammy jumped a little, thinking maybe Chris was going to hit her, and after hearing what he said, she wished he would have hit her instead of saying those words, because they hurt more than a slap or a punch. She couldn't believe he had the nerve to say that to her after everything she'd been through.

"I ain't shit? Fuck me?" Tammy asked, her voice rising. "*Fuck me?*" she said again.

She was enraged, but more hurt than anything. Tears filled her eyes, and all of her feelings concerning their relationship were about to pour out of her like a river, whether or not Chris liked it.

"You left me out here by myself, Chris," she snapped as she shoved him. "You know how fucking hard it was with two kids, no job, and no money?" Tammy yelled. "What else was I supposed to do? What else was I supposed to do?" she cried, beating his chest.

Tammy couldn't stop crying, and as Chris shamelessly tried to walk off, she pulled and punched on him. One thing he couldn't do was watch Tammy cry like this. She was letting him have it.

"I was faithful to you. I was loyal, but you cheated on me and had a baby on me," she screamed at the top of her lungs. She was crying so hard, she could barely get her words out.

Even through the heavy rain, Chris could see the tears falling down her face. He knew that he'd hurt her by going to jail, but not as much as Tammy was displaying. He could sense the hardships she went through by her words, and he felt bad that she had to go through what she'd been through. Her situation was so deep, Chris couldn't even fix his mouth to complain about his little heartbreak from when Tammy left him. It just didn't even out to what she had experienced. Chris was starting to see that now.

"Come here, Tammy," he said as he reached out for her. "Stop and come here."

She resisted at first, but eventually succumbed
to his touch. He held her tightly in his arms,
knowing that he could never hate her, even if he
wanted to. This time was for Tammy, and finally
getting it all out of her system was exactly what
she needed.

Falisha walked through the door with Jordan
in her arms. She had been next door with Carol
for a few hours, gossiping and wrapping up
Tammy's wedding gifts. Lamar was sitting on
the couch, waiting for her the whole time.

"Hey, I was next door. My phone was in
Jordan's bag, so that's why I didn't answer it,"
she said, walking over and handing Jordan over
to Lamar.

"Damn, you wanna know the crazy part about
it?" Lamar said, walking the baby over and
placing him in his playpen. "You wasn't even
going to tell me." He followed her to the kitchen.

"Tell you what, boo?" she asked, trying to
play it off as she stood at the sink washing out
Jordan's bottles.

By the time she turned around, Lamar's hand
was already in motion, striking the side of her
face with force.

Lamar smacked spit out of her mouth, and before she came to from that blow, he back-handed her with the same hand.

"You dirty bitch, you burnt me," Lamar said through clenched teeth.

Falisha tried to swing back, but Lamar blocked it, and then hit her with a closed fist, dropping her to the ground immediately. His attack didn't stop there. He reached down and grabbed a handful of her hair, lifting her back up to her feet. Her legs felt like spaghetti noodles, and she could hardly see out of one eye. He put his hands around her neck and started choking her against the sink. She frantically clawed at his hands trying to get him off her, but the more she put up a fight, the darker it got for her.

"I should fuckin' kill you, bitch," he yelled, shaking her neck back and forth violently until her eyes started to roll in the back of her head. "Dumb bitch."

Little Jordan crying was the only thing that snapped Lamar out of his trance. If it wasn't for him, he probably would have killed Falisha. He let her go right at the moment she started to pass out. Falisha fell to the floor, knocking the kitchen chairs over with her. She was hurt pretty badly, but alive. Lamar squatted over the top of her and spoke.

"I want yo' ass out of my fuckin' house. It's over," he said and spit in her face before walking off.

Falisha lay there bleeding from her mouth. She wanted to get up, but she couldn't. Her body was too weak to do anything. All she could see through her blurry vision was Lamar walking out of the front door with Jordan in his arms. This surely was the worst day of her life . . . and the drama was far from over.

Lisa wrapped her hands around Nate's back, digging into it with her nails as he dug his dick deep inside of her. He stroked slow and hard, taking his time to make sure he hit every diameter of Lisa's love box. His dick was touching places it had never touched before, and Lisa couldn't believe how good it felt.

"Go deeper," she whispered, then bit down on his chest.

Nate did go deeper, so much so that the condom popped. He almost busted a nut when he felt how soft her insides were.

"Hold on," he told her as he pulled out. "I got another one."

Nate reached in the nightstand and grabbed another condom. He took the broken condom off and was about to put the fresh one on when Lisa stopped him. She grabbed the condom out of his hand and placed it on the bed next to her.

"I wanna feel you," she said, pulling Nate back down on her.

"Are you sure?"

Lisa nodded. "Just don't come inside me," she said, spreading her legs farther apart.

Nate entered her, cramming every inch of his hardness into her softness. Lisa moaned, digging her claws into his back again. It seemed like without the condom, Nate went even deeper. He looked down at her, and for the first time ever, he kissed Lisa. His full, thick lips softly pressed against hers, and after getting over the initial shock of it, Lisa kissed him back. It'd been almost two years since she'd kissed a man, but with Nate, it all came back to her, just like remembering how to ride a bike. His tongue became her tongue's play toy.

Heavy breathing and grunts from Lisa was all that could be heard in the room. She was at the point where she wanted to come, but not in this position. It was a little too personal for her.

She pushed Nate's body up, and then rolled over onto her stomach, spreading her legs slightly apart for him. He slid his dick inside her, while lying on her back. He grinded upward while biting and kissing her shoulder. Lisa tooted her ass up a little and could feel his girth rubbing against her G-spot every time he went into her.

"Don't stop," she panted, grinding her hips to his motion. "Right there. Oh yes, right there."

Her pussy tightened around Nate's dick, and as she came all over his dick, he too was at his point. He pulled out as previously instructed, and then jerked his dick the rest of the way. His come shot out onto the bed, but looking down at Lisa's sexy body, he wanted so bad to push his dick back inside of her. Respecting her wishes, he restrained himself. He was happy and satisfied that he had made it this far, and for Lisa, this was more than a baby step. Today, she took more like a test drive around the block.

Chris's five-hour pass turned into a visit at the halfway house. After Tammy spazzed out on him, he really didn't feel like going anywhere. They sat in the visiting hall in silence, watching the rain through one of the windows. Tammy had cried her eyes out and got the bulk of what she had buried inside of her out on the table. She felt a little better, but Chris still had plenty of issues to deal with.

"So, what are we going to do?" Tammy asked, breaking the silence. "I'm so confused right now."

"Well, as of right now, you got a fiancé at home waiting for you. To be honest wit' you, I don't even like him. I'm trying to give him a pass, because I know he doesn't know any better," Chris said.

Darious was another issue in itself. He was very disrespectful in his actions the day Chris stopped by. It may have been the whole territorial thing men have, but it was a bad move on Darious's part, especially dealing with somebody like Chris. With Darious, it was like he wanted to establish his position in his household, which was respected to a certain extent, but with Chris, it was like a lion who left his pride, only to come back and find another weaker lion there.

It kind of shocked Tammy that Chris hadn't done something to Darious by now. She could see a big change in Chris and the way he carried himself. Jail had not only preserved him, but it had matured him also.

"The one thing I can say is that I think ya dude really do love you. I remember I used to be like him when it came down to you. So, for that reason alone, I'm going to respect his boundaries and limit my visits to your house. I'll send my

mom to get the kids when I wanna see them."
Chris stood up, indicating that the visit was over.

"Why are you leaving?" Tammy asked, getting
up from the couch as well.

"Visiting hours are over," Chris said, pointing
to the clock on the wall. "We'll talk again soon."

"Well, here, take these," she said, digging in
her bag and pulling out a set of keys. "The house
is the same exact way it was when you left. I
couldn't sleep with another man in that house.
After I moved, I kept paying the rent, so I'd
always have a place to go if times ever got rough,"
Tammy said, passing him the keys.

She refused to leave without getting a real
hug from him, so she just stood in front of Chris,
blocking the exit.

"I guess you want a hug," he said with a smile
on his face. "You got issues." He shook his head.

"Please," she begged with a sad, puppy dog
face.

She stepped into his body, hoping that he
wouldn't reject her. Chris looked into Tammy's
eyes and could see more than just the beauty in
them. He could see the look of a woman who had
once loved him more than anything in the world.
He saw the eyes of a woman who was in pain and
whose heart cried out for him.

Chris grabbed the sides of Tammy's waist and pulled her closer to him. She wrapped her arms around his neck and laid her head on his chest. His natural body scent was like pheromones, drawing her in. Chris wrapped his arms around her body, bear-hugging her gently. Her body fit snug inside of his, and for a moment, neither of them wanted to let go.

They stood there holding each other for almost two minutes, and when Chris tried to let go, Tammy held on tighter. She didn't want to let go, and she wished that this moment would last forever. The tears started to fill her eyes again. She wanted Chris back so bad. She needed him in more ways than one, and the regret of stepping off on him while he was in prison weighed heavily on her.

Nate looked over at Lisa, who was asleep with her head sunk into the pillow. He didn't realize just how beautiful she was until he saw her in this fashion. She had a natural beauty, one that didn't require any makeup at all. Her body was flawless, despite the bullet wound to her gut. Even that, Nate found to be somewhat sexy, but he couldn't help but to wonder how she got it. There were many things he wanted to know about Lisa, but that was only going to

come with time. Her wounds were deep, and
if Nate wanted to get into that portion of her
life, he was going to have to work extra hard
and be very patient.

Aside from waking up on the kitchen floor with
a cut in her mouth, the side of her face a little red,
and a splitting headache, Falisha was okay. Her
self-esteem was battered and pretty low at this
point. She felt that she had to be the worst type
of female to have cheated on her man, caught
an STD, and then gave it to him. On top of that,
she had been cured and wasn't even going to tell
him about it. As she sat there on the edge of her
bed, she realized that it actually was worse than
it sounded. How reckless! There was no way she
could deny it, nor could she try to clean it up.
Lamar wasn't trying to hear anything from her,
except that all of her stuff was out of his house.

Falisha sat there and cried, seeing how serious the mistake was. She was about to lose
more than just her man; she was about to lose
her family too. It didn't seem like she cared
when she was out doing her thing, but the truth
was, she really did love Lamar and Jordan.
They meant everything to her, and losing them
was a devastating blow.

Chapter 6

Chris came back to the halfway house to see several police cars and a marshal's van sitting out front. Normally, it meant that somebody had violated the rules and regulations of the halfway house and was about to be sent back to jail. It happened every couple of weeks, so Chris really didn't think anything of it until he got inside, and one of the correctional officers tried to put him in handcuffs.

"Hold up, what's goin' on?" Chris asked as he pulled his hands away from the guard.

Several U.S. Marshals came from upstairs carrying two large trash bags and a couple of scales. Two more detectives escorted Bizz and Malcom down the stairs in handcuffs. Bizz had a sick look on his face. He knew he wasn't going to be able to get out of a life sentence this time, no matter what. Malcom had the same look. Chris just knew that he was about to go right back to jail with them, but to his surprise, the marshal spoke up.

"He's good to go," the marshal said, pointing to Chris.

The only real reason Chris wasn't going to jail was because when the marshals ran down on Bizz and Malcom, they took their own beef and said that Chris didn't know what was going on. A search of Chris's belongings inside the dorm turned up clean. He didn't have anything that would suggest he was involved in the drug ring. No paraphernalia, no drugs, no guns of any sort. All they found was clothes and his hygiene products.

"A'ight, homie, keep ya head up out here," Bizz said as he was escorted out. "And don't forget what I said," he yelled.

"Yeah, stay up, homie," Malcom added as he walked out of the building with his head down.

"Damn, shorty, you better learn how to bob and weave," Fox joked when Falisha got into his car.

Her lip was still a little fat, and the force from the punch had left a little bruise on her chin. Falisha was not in the mood for jokes, especially since Fox was part of the reason things had gotten so ugly in the first place.

"I need to stay with you for a couple of weeks," Falisha said, looking at her face in the sun visor mirror. "Just until I get my own place, which shouldn't take long."

"Come on, shorty, you know you can stay with me for as long as you want," Fox told her. "And on some serious shit, I'm sorry about what happened. I should have strapped up wit' these dirty-ass hood rats. But trust me when I tell you that it's a lesson learned."

"Yeah, well, you're not getting none of this pussy for a while. Got me running around wit' some damn gonorrhea."

"Hell, it's ya fault I caught dat shit in the first place," Fox smiled, poking her in the side.

"*My* fault? How in the hell is it *my* fault?"

"Because you left me. If you was my girl, I wouldn't have to be out here looking for a quick nut. Yo' ass up there playin' house wit' a nigga that don't give a fuck about you," Fox shot back.

"That's not true. He do care about me," Falisha tried to defend. "Well . . . I know he used to care. I don't know about now."

"Oh yeah? Well, if he cared about you so damn much, why in the hell is you and ya son still living on Walton Street? He should have been got y'all up out of there. Look at ya girlfriend. You know who I'm talking about. The one that's about to get married," Fox said referring to Tammy. "She's out of the hood, and she's getting married to the nigga."

Falisha thought about it. Lamar did have plenty of opportunities to move them to a better neighborhood, but for his own personal reasons, he chose to stay. And when it came to marriage, he had mentioned it once or twice, but never followed through with anything, and that was eight months ago. It seemed like once he got Jordan, all the love that he used to show Falisha went to him.

"Yeah, I hear you, Fox. So what are you saying? Things would have been different if I would have stayed with you?" she asked. "And don't be lying either."

"You know I keep it 100 wit' you at all times. If you was my girl, I would have changed ya whole life around. You would have been in a position where you would have been able to take care of you and your son on ya own. You smart as hell, Falisha. The first thing I would have done was encourage you to go back to school and pick up some type of trade. I could picture you being like a nurse's assistant or maybe even a registered nurse if you wanted to. Or maybe running ya own hair salon. You know you can do some hair. You could have done anything, and I would have supported you and backed you up financially. I tell you this one thing, you wouldn't have been on ya desperate housewife shit like you are right now," Fox said with a straight face.

It sounded good, but Falisha knew that she needed to be very careful messing around with Fox. She'd been here with him before, plenty of times, and she knew that he was the master of manipulating women into doing whatever he wanted them to do. Although he'd never treated Falisha like he treated the rest, she was well aware of the games he played, and how sometimes he would use his wealth to get what he wanted. Falisha wasn't better than anybody else when it came to that, because she too found herself caught up with his money. Fox was vicious too. He was the type of nigga that knew how to buy love, and if it wasn't love, it was damn close.

Her life had been turned upside down, and she really couldn't afford to be getting caught up with Fox. But as she sat in the passenger side of his brand-new Jaguar, she reflected on her life and came to the conclusion that she really didn't have anything else to lose if she did start messing back with him. In her mind, she would rather have something than nothing at all, and maybe this time around, she could be the one who did all the manipulating. She was in survival mode now.

Tammy felt bad about telling Darious that she was pregnant when she really wasn't. At that time, she only said it on the spur-of-the-moment to make him happy and to take his mind off Chris. It had worked, but now Tammy was in a dilemma, because about twenty minutes ago, her period came. She was sitting in the bathroom trying to debate how she was going to tell him that she had miscarried the baby. When lying at this level, she needed to be sure that all her *i*'s were dotted and her *t*'s were crossed. It had to seem so real and convincing, that Tammy had to believe it herself. That's the only way it was going to work.

The first thing she needed to do was come up with some fake tears, which was relatively easy, considering all she had to do was think of not ever being with Chris again. Her eyes watered immediately, and she genuinely became sad. The next thing she needed to do was get Darious to come into the bathroom without her calling him. She needed the shock effect.

"Tammy, you ain't shit," she mumbled to herself, picking up a water vase next to the toilet and throwing it against the bathroom door.

The sound was loud enough to get Darious's attention in the bedroom. He jumped out of bed and shot down the hallway toward the bathroom. Tammy put her game face on. Darious knocked on the door, then eased his way in.

"Damn, Tammy," he said, stepping over the glass. "What happened?" he asked kneeling down next to her on the toilet.

Tammy wiped her face with the tissue she had in her hand, faking like she had to get herself together. "I lost the baby," she said, then began to cry again.

Darious put his head down. He was sick but didn't want to show how much. Tammy was his number one concern right now and being strong for her was what he wanted to be. "Babe, I know you're upset, but don't worry about it. When the time is right, we'll try again," he said, lifting her chin up. "We got the rest of our lives to have a baby. But, babe, you can't keep breaking up our shit." He chuckled, looking around the bathroom at the broken glass.

That made Tammy smile. She looked into his eyes and started crying again, only this time it was for a different reason, and the tears were actually real. She hated what she was doing to him, when all Darious ever did was try to love her. He was a good man, and he deserved better treatment than this. The love he had for Tammy made her want to be stronger and to do right by him. It was the wake-up call she needed, and from that day forward, she was going to do her best to be the wife that he needed.

"So, are you ready for the workweek?" Nate asked Lisa as he cradled the phone between his ear and his shoulder, while doing the dishes in his sink. "'Cause I'm not."

Lisa was home folding the last load of clothes while she talked to Nate. She was enjoying the conversations they'd been having lately. It was another step forward. "I'm definitely not ready. I got three twelve-hour shifts, plus I work eight hours on Friday. Hell, I'm not even thinking about the weekend, because I might be too tired to do anything."

"Oh, did you have plans for this weekend?" Nate inquired.

"A whole lot, actually. I'll probably go out with the girls on Friday. It's my girlfriend's bachelor-ette party. It's going to be at a strip club, so you know it's gonna be turned up," Lisa laughed.

"You know, I'll never get tired of hearing you do that."

"Do what?" Lisa asked, tossing the rolled up pair of socks onto the table.

"Hearing you laugh like that," he answered, leaning against the kitchen sink.

Lisa smiled, and was about to say something, but was interrupted by the doorbell. "Who da hell is at my door?" she said, keeping him on the line.

"It better not be ya other boyfriend," Nate joked.

"Shut up, boy," she replied, pulling the curtains back to see who it was. "Aaaahhhhhh!" Lisa screamed and rushed to the door. "Heyyy, bitch!" she greeted, swinging the front door open for Kim.

"Heyyy, bitch," Kim responded, dropping her bags and giving Lisa a big hug.

"Why didn't you call me? I would have come and picked you up from the airport."

Lisa had forgotten that Nate was still on the line, but Kim's nosy self reminded her. "Who you talkin' to?" she asked, pointing to Lisa's phone.

"Oh shit. Damn, I'm sorry, Nate, are you still there? I'm going to have to call you back."

"Yeah, I'm here. Go ahead and holla at ya folks. Call me later," he said, then let her go.

"So, who da hell is Nate?" Kim asked as she headed up the steps. "Does he have a brother?"

Lisa followed her upstairs to the guest room. It was established months ago that when Kim came back for the wedding, she would stay with Lisa instead of checking into a hotel. Lisa wouldn't dare have that, especially since she had an extra room.

"Girl, don't worry about Nate. I'm about to call up the girls so we can go out," Lisa said walking toward her bedroom.

"Where's Naomi? I miss my pie face," Kim said, pulling out the stuffed animal she had bought her.

"She's with Ralphy's mom. But since you're here, I'm going to pick her up in the morning," Lisa answered, coming back into the room with the phone up to her ear. She put it on speaker so Kim could hear.

"Heyyy, bitch," Tammy yelled through the phone. "You don't know how to call no damn body."

It felt good to be back home with friends and family. Up North was cool, but down South was where it was at. Everything was different. The food, the people, the Southern accent, and the warm hospitality; even the air smelled different.

"We gotta get together," Tammy said.

"Girl, I'm getting dressed right now," Lisa shot back. "Tell Darious that yo' ass is coming with us tonight."

"Shut up, old lady. Give me about an hour," Tammy said before hanging up the phone.

It was Sunday, and no spots were open, but the girls definitely were going to make it a fun night out. The only person that was missing was Falisha, and there was no telling where she could be, messing around with Fox. With or without her, the girls were going to have a good time. There was a whole lot of catching up to do.

Chapter 7

Though the United States Marshals were on the scene, the Charlotte Drug Task Force made the arrest on Bizz and Malcom. The case was sure to be adopted by the feds, but for now, Bizz had to sit in the county jail until he saw a judge and was formally charged with numerous drug offenses.

Chris entered the front doors of the Charlotte county jail on a mission to visit Bizz. The first and only phone call Bizz made was to Chris, and he told him that he needed to see him as soon as possible. At first, Chris was a little skeptical about it, wondering what Bizz could possibly want. The last thing Chris needed was to get caught up in his case. He had already dodged a major bullet when he wasn't arrested with them.

"Damn, homie, I didn't think that you was going to come," Bizz said, walking into the visiting room. "Shit is crazy right now, li'l bro."

Chris stood up and gave Bizz a handshake and a thug hug before sitting back down. "Yeah, well keep ya head up, and if you need me to do anything for you, just let me know," Chris told him.

"I really appreciate that, homie. And since you said that, there is something I need you to do for me."

Chris thought to himself that he had offered too much too fast. "Yeah, well, just as long as it don't end up having me up in here wit' you," Chris spoke, looking around the visiting room.

Bizz smiled. "Nah, homie, I wouldn't do no shit like that to you. In fact, I need you to be out there. What good are you to anybody if you sittin' up in here wit' me?"

Bizz looked around the room to make sure people weren't being nosy, then leaned in closer to Chris. "The police didn't take everything from me. I still got some money stashed away in the halfway house," he whispered.

"How much money are you talking about, and what do you want me to do with it?" Chris asked in a low voice.

"I got like 150K stuffed in a cubby hole behind one of the boilers in the basement. Look, brah, I'ma be in here for a minute. I just need you to hold me and my daughter down. The lawyer

he got to the door and opened it, Kim and Lisa were standing on the porch.

"Wassup, nigga?" Kim greeted, opening the screen.

Lamar had little Jordan in his arms, and he looked so cute, Kim almost started crying. This was the first time she'd seen the baby in person. "Oh my goodness! Let me hold him," she said, reaching out for the baby.

"Yup, that's my godson," Lisa bragged, kissing Jordan's head.

Jordan was adorable. Light skinned like Falisha, but with all of Lamar's features. He had dark curly hair, thick eyebrows, and some fat cheeks. His big brown eyes could make anybody melt. It looked like Lamar spit the boy out himself.

"When did you get in town?" Lamar asked Kim.

"Yesterday. You know me and my girls had to go out last night. Speaking of, where is ya baby mom? I haven't seen her, and she's not answering the phone."

"And she's supposed to be doing my hair today," Lisa added.

Lamar took a seat on the edge of the porch and shook his head at the thought of Falisha's foolishness.

"Falisha don't live here anymore. We broke up the other day," he told them.

Both Kim and Lisa's jaws dropped. Especially Lisa's because she lived right across the street from them and never knew anything was going on. They just knew Lamar had to be lying.

"Lamar, stop playing," Lisa said, playfully punching his arm.

The serious look on his face made it clear that he wasn't playing.

"What da hell happened?" Lisa asked in shock.

Kim stood there rocking baby Jordan, looking at Lamar while shaking her head. It was the kind of headshake that spoke volumes, without a single word uttered.

"She's about to come and pick Jordan up, so you can ask her when she gets here," he said, not really wanting to be the one to put Falisha's business in the streets.

Kim hadn't been back in Charlotte for twenty-four hours, and she had already gotten an earful of gossip. So much had happened since she'd been gone. She still wasn't up on Lisa and her little sexcapades with Nate. Getting caught up was going to be fun, and Kim had thirty whole days to do it.

***

"Oh God, I've never seen water that looks so blue," Tammy said, looking down at one of the resorts in a brochure for vacation destinations.

She and Darious had been in the travel agency for the past several hours trying to solidify where they were going for their honeymoon. They looked at resorts in Mexico, Jamaica, Dominican Republic, Hawaii, Puerto Rico, Miami, and other places Tammy had never been to or even heard of. They were all so beautiful, and had so much to offer.

"So, what do you think, babe?" Tammy asked.

"I don't know. The one thing that I'm certain of is that I'm not going anyplace where I need a passport. My probation officer won't let me leave the country on such short notice."

"Well, that's good, babe, because now we can narrow it down to a couple of places. So that leaves us with Puerto Rico, Hawaii, Miami, and I saw a nice place in California you would love."

Darious didn't want to fly on an airplane at all, and he damn sure wasn't trying to be driving to California, so that left one spot: Miami. With hundreds of resorts to choose from, Tammy was sure to find the ideal place. Darious really didn't care where he spent his honeymoon, just as long as it was with the love of his life. Anything to make Tammy happy. That was the sole purpose for just about everything he did. He just wanted to maintain that smile on her face.

The white F-type Jaguar sped down Walton Street, kicking up dust in the process. It came to complete stop right in front of Lamar's house. No one knew whose car it was, so Lamar, Kim, and Lisa all looked and waited for the driver to do something. Everyone was shocked when Falisha stepped out of the car looking like a bag of money. She had on a floral, thigh-high wrap-around dress, and a pair of St. Laurent sandals. Her hair was tossed up nice too, draping down one side of her face, which covered up the almost healed bruise on her chin. On her face was a pair of Victoria Beckham shades and a cute Michael Kors watch lay right on her wrist.

"Damn, bitch, you ridin' nice," Lisa said, looking at the car.

Falisha had a straight attitude though and didn't feel like doing any talking, not even to Kim. She spoke, but that was about it before she walked over and took Jordan from Kim's arms.

"Where's the car seat and his bag? I told you to have his stuff ready by the time I got here," Falisha snapped.

Lamar was seconds away from spazzing out on her, but he didn't want to make a scene in front of company, so he bit his tongue, reached in the doorway, and grabbed Jordan's overnight bag. One thing Lamar wasn't going to do was let Falisha leave without telling him where his son was staying and when she was bringing him back.

"When I feel like bringing him back. And don't worry about where I'm staying. It's not here with you, remember?" Falisha based.

Lamar came down off the porch and walked up on Falisha, who was trying to strap Jordan in. Kim reached out and grabbed his arm before he got to her, and Lisa helped by standing between him and Falisha.

Falisha picked her head up and saw the look of the devil in Lamar's eyes. He never played any games when it came down to his son.

"Whacha gonna do, hit me, Lamar?"

They stood there staring at each other with the evil eye. "What da fuck is goin' on wit' you two?" Lisa yelled, breaking the silence.

"Nothing at all," Falisha answered. "Look, I will bring our son back in a couple of days," she said, walking around to the driver side of the car and getting in.

As soon as she got her seat belt on, Falisha pulled off, leaving Kim, Lisa, and Lamar's asses in the middle of the street. It was official now. Falisha and Lamar hated each other. The love and respect for each other was gone, and they were so caught up in their feelings that they didn't realize that the only person their madness was going to hurt . . . was Jordan.

Chris sat on his bunk looking down at $150,000 in cash. Even when he used to sell drugs, he had never touched this much money at once. The money was broken down into tens, twenties, and fifty-dollar bills. Mostly tens and twenties, so 150,000 looked like 500,000. He was rather fascinated by it and kind of nervous to have it in the halfway house with him. If the staff was to walk in on him and see all that money, he was going back to jail.

"Damn, that's a lot of money," Mohamed said, staring at the cash as well. "You paid, brah."

Mohamed was a good Muslim brother who was on the same type time as Chris. All he wanted to do was find a job and stay out of jail. Chris had taken a liking to him from the first day he moved into the dorm.

"So, what are you going to do with it?" Mohamed asked.

"I'm not sure yet. I think I might start a business or something."

"Like what? I mean, you can do whatever you want."

After taking care of what Bizz asked him to do, Chris would have 100,000 left. That was more than enough to start any kind of business. He just needed to be smart and make good decisions, because not all legal businesses were successful. At this stage in his life, losing wasn't an option, and he was going to make the money do what it do.

Chapter 8

"Can I ask you something?" Nate said as he and Lisa lay in the bed naked. "You don't have to answer it if you don't feel comfortable. I mean, I would like to know—"

"Boy, would you just ask the question," Lisa said, cutting him off. "And no, we ain't having a threesome," she said and laughed.

Nate had to laugh at that one himself. However, at the same time, something had been bothering him over the past couple of weeks, and now that they were getting a little closer, he figured he'd ask about the bullet wound.

"What happened to you right here?" he said, rubbing his finger over the bullet wound.

Lisa flinched as an initial reaction. Then out of nowhere, memories of that day rushed through her head. Visions of Ralphy being shot also popped up in her head. She could literally taste the gunpowder that was left in the air. Her heart began to race, and then thoughts of her and Ralphy being together rushed her as well.

"I gotta go," Lisa said, jumping up from the bed like she had just seen a ghost.

"Hold up, Lisa, what's going on? You don't have to answer it," he pleaded, trying to get her to stay.

Lisa made record-breaking time and was out the door before Nate could get his pants on. She didn't have to say anything for Nate to know that he had messed up big this time. This time it was really bad, because he'd hit a very sensitive spot. It was like taking four steps backward, and Nate didn't know how he was going to climb out of this hole. It may have been too much this time.

Lamar sat on the couch rubbing his hands together, mad as hell that Falisha hadn't brought baby Jordan back yet. It had been three days already, and not only didn't she bring him back, she wasn't answering the phone. In fact, she had turned her phone off altogether for the last two days. Her mom didn't even know where she was . . . so she said. Lamar was hot. He jumped up and went outside to try to get some fresh air. He could give a fuck about Falisha and what she was up to. All he wanted was his son.

"Hey, Lamar," Carol greeted from the upstairs window. "What are you looking so mean for?"

"Have you seen Falisha?" he asked, hoping she knew something. "I'm trying to find my son."

"Hold on, I'll be down in a minute."

It took a couple of minutes, but eventually, Carol came downstairs, opened the front door, and waved Lamar in. Carol could see how vulnerable he was and played on his weakness.

"So you looking for your son, huh?" she said, taking a seat on the steps.

"Yeah, where is she?"

Carol licked her lips and gave him a seductive glance from head to toe. "If I tell you, what are you going to do for me?" she asked as she continued giving him that look.

"Come on, Carol, stop playing. I really don't feel like that shit right now."

"Boy, ain't nobody playin' wit' you. You gotta at least let me suck it," she said, looking at his crotch area.

Lamar couldn't believe Carol. He always knew that she was a whore, but he never thought she would stoop this low for some dick, and the bad part about it was he knew she wasn't joking. Lamar's dick was probably the only dick she hadn't sucked in the neighborhood.

She curled her finger, motioning for him to come over to where she was. He didn't want to, but if it meant finding out where his son was, he had no other choice but to entertain Carol's crazy ass. He was hoping she'd change her mind once he pulled his dick out, but she didn't. Seeing it only made her thirst for it even greater.

"Boy, stop playing. You gon' love this dick suck," she said, reaching for it.

She didn't have the slightest idea that she was about to suck a postgonorrhea dick, which may still be infected. Gonorrhea of the mouth was highly possible to contract. Lamar felt like if she did get it, hell, she deserved it.

She scooted down on the steps to be on the same level as his dick was. It wasn't even semi-hard at that point, but that quickly changed once she put his soft dick, along with his balls, into her mouth. It took seconds for him to rock up.

"I been thinking about doing this for a long time," Carol said, taking his dick out of her mouth and kissing the sides of it.

She twirled her tongue around his head, then grabbed his long black dick from the base. She pulled his skin back, making it stretch out even longer, then once she saw that he was as hard as he was going to get, she took him into her mouth. Her gag reflex was on 100, because she made his whole ten-inch monster disappear like it was nothing.

With both her hands holding on to his waist, Carol began to suck his dick from the base to the tip at a nice pace. The inside of her mouth felt like some good pussy. It was feeling so good that Lamar was starting to enjoy it. He had to stay focused though.

"Tell me where she's at," Lamar demanded, looking down at Carol doing her thing. "Come on, Carol, where's Falisha?"

Just hearing him say her name made Carol go even crazier. She kept sucking his dick, even harder now, pushing his manhood all the way to the back of her throat with every thrust. She looked up at Lamar and could tell that he was loving it. Precome oozed out into her mouth, and when she got a taste of it, she wanted to chase the rest. She pulled his dick out of her mouth and licked around the tip again.

"Come on, Carol," Lamar said looking down at Carol French-kissing his dick.

"She's with Fox now," she said without taking her focus off his dick. "I thought you knew."

Lamar hadn't heard Fox's name in a long time, and now that he thought about it, it all started to make sense. The nice car, the extra money she's been having, going out every night getting drunk. Lamar felt like a nut. She'd been playing him for a fool this whole time, and Lamar didn't know a thing. It was over between them, but he still felt resentful.

"I guess you about to go running after her?" Carol said, attempting to get up.

"Hold up, you gotta finish what you started," Lamar shot back grabbing the back of her head before she could move.

He was mad as hell, but at the same time, he was turned on by Carol's dick suck. She did it like a pro, and at this moment, thoughts of busting a nut in her mouth was all Lamar could think of. Carol didn't have a problem with it either. She took the length of Lamar's dick back into her mouth with a smile on her face.

Chris had agreed to meet up with Tammy and the kids at a park near her house. He had an eight-hour pass, so he wanted to spend as much time with the children as he could before he had to leave to take care of some other business. The halfway house was about to let him go on home confinement, so he had to get things situated at the house on Walton Street for the probation officer's visit.

"You lookin' nice today," Tammy said as Chris walked up. He had on a pair of Capri khaki shorts, a V-neck white Polo tee shirt, and some

Gucci sneakers. A pair of Ray Ban shades covered his eyes, and surprisingly, around his neck was a stomach length white gold chain with a large diamond-crusted C hanging from it. He smelled like Creed, and it looked like he was fresh out of the barbershop.

"How did you get here?" Tammy asked, wondering if he was driving, and if so, what kind of car.

"I bought a li'l lemon," Chris smiled.

Their conversation was cut short when Anthony and Sinniyyah ran over from the jungle gyms. They were as happy to see their dad as he was to see them.

"Dad, can I ask you something?" Anthony said.

"Yeah, son, you can ask me anything," he answered.

Little Anthony climbed up on the picnic table to be face-to-face with his dad. "When can we come home with you, so we can be a family again?"

The question took both Chris and Tammy by surprise, and neither one of them wanted to be the one to answer the question. Anthony had shot the question right out of left field and sat there waiting for an answer. Tammy decided that she was going to take the lead on this one.

"Anthony, we are still a family. Just because we don't live together doesn't mean that we are not a family," she tried to explain.

"Well, why can't you and my dad get married instead of you and Darious? And do you still love my daddy?" he asked, hitting Tammy with another blow.

Anthony had laid it out nice and thick today, and Tammy stumbled over her words, trying to get the best answer out. Chris decided to step up to the plate on this one.

"Me and ya mom love each other very much, but we aren't together right now. Darious is a good man, and he and your mom are together for the time being. And who knows? Maybe one day in the future, me and ya mom will get married. And guess who's going to be my best man?" Chris said, putting his hand in the air for a high five. "You. And ya sister will be the flower girl."

Anthony gave Chris a big high five, then jumped off the table and ran back over to the swings. Chris picked Sinniyyah up and started kissing and making fart noises with her cheeks. She was cracking up with laughter.

Tammy's eyes watered to the point that she had to get up and walk off. It was moments like this when she wished that she could go back in time and do it all over again. Surely, this time, she would have waited for Chris, and more than likely, it would have been him she was marrying next week. Darious was a good man all the way around, but at the end of the day, there was nothing like being bonded by family.

Lisa never made it out of Nate's apartment complex parking lot. She really didn't want to leave. She just needed to get some air. She sat in her car looking at pictures of Ralphy she had stored on her phone. It made her even more depressed to where she rested her head on the steering wheel. As much as she tried to move on, she still found it to be the hardest thing she ever had to do. It was always the little things that made her think about Ralphy and how happy they used to be. A part of her also felt like she was responsible for Ralphy's death, and to a certain degree—she was. It was her infidelities that made Ralphy kill, and caused another man to retaliate. It was something Lisa would never be able to forget, nor will she ever forgive herself for the part she played. This was part of the reason she didn't want to be in a relationship at all. She didn't want to hurt the next person the same way she had hurt Ralphy.

A tap at the window got Lisa's attention, causing her to pick her head up from the steering wheel. When she looked over and saw Nate standing there looking worried, she wiped her tears and unlocked the door. Nate was right there to help her out of the car.

"I'm sorry for just leaving. I was—"

"You don't have to explain," Nate said, cutting her off. "I know that you are going through a lot right now. I just want you to know that no matter what's going on in ya life, I'm here for you when you need to talk. You gotta understand that I'm not here to hurt you, Lisa," he concluded and reached out to take her hand.

Lisa didn't know why, but for some odd reason, she believed what he was saying. His words were genuine and comforting. She didn't know how much of her life she was willing to share with him, but what she did know was that she needed a hug right now.

Without her even asking, Nate was on top of it. He grabbed Lisa, pulled her into his arms, and held her tightly; exactly the thing that she needed and wanted.

As Lamar was leaving Carol's house, Kim was coming out of Ms. D's house at the same time.

She'd been home for a few days and really hadn't had a chance to sit down and talk to him the way that she wanted to. Their relationship had ended on a messed up note, but on Kim's part, it was water under the bridge.

"Why you lookin' so mean?" Kim smiled, coming down the steps and walking over to Lamar. "I see you got straight baby mama drama."

Lamar shook his head. "Yeah, if it ain't one thing, it's another," he said, leaning against the ear of one of the neighbors. "Right now, I'm trying to find this crazy chick so I can get my son back. It's been a few days, and she's not even answering the phone. Got me pissed the fuck off right now."

The love he had for his son was obvious to Kim, and nowadays, it was rare for men to step up and care for their children the way that Lamar did. Kim respected him for that, among other things.

"What in da hell happened with y'all two?" she asked, thinking that this whole time, Lamar and Falisha were happy.

He still didn't feel like putting their business out there, but Kim was a good friend and could be trusted not to go run her mouth about the situation.

"Yo, between me and you, K, ya girl is foul. She cheated on me and gave me gonorrhea last week—and wasn't even going to tell me. She was burning like a furnace," Lamar vented.

"You lying!"

"Bitch gave me an STD, then started messing around wit' dat cat Fox again."

"Oh, God, I can't believe she would do something like that to you. And where's the baby?"

"I don't know where dis bitch got my son. Probably ova dat nigga house right now," he answered, shaking his head.

Kim had come back to all kinds of mess going on. It was a lot to digest, and this was nothing compared to what she was in store for. She had been gone for over a year, but she wasn't totally in the clear yet. Lamar had some stuff he wanted to get off his chest with her too.

"Why da fuck did you have to leave me?" he semisnapped at her, really getting Kim's attention.

"*Excuse me?*" she responded with a frown. "Why da fuck did I leave you? Did you forget that we was supposed to move to Philly together? Wasn't you the one who decided that you was going to stay with Falisha and the baby? Nigga, I wish you would try to blame this shit on me. This is ya drama," she spazzed.

"Yeah, but you didn't even put up a fight. You knew how stressed out and confused I was. You know I wanted to go with you."

"Yeah, but the fact is that you didn't . . . You know what? We're not gonna do this shit right now. You made ya bed, now lay in it," Kim said, rolling her eyes at him before walking off.

She stopped at the rental car, which was only a few cars down from where Lamar was. "Don't forget that at one point you had the best part of me. So if you wanna place the blame on somebody for your relationship not working out, then you need to take a look in the mirror, because it was *you* who fucked up," she concluded.

She got into her rental car without giving him a chance to respond, and in the blink of an eye, she was pulling off down the street, leaving Lamar looking stupid with even more to think about. Her words were cold, but they were the God's honest truth, and as much as Lamar hated to, he agreed with her 100 percent.

"Hey, babe, can you tell ya sister to drop my son off at my mom's house tonight?" Falisha asked Fox, while staring at Lamar. "Thank you, and can you come pick me up right now? I just wanna come home," she said, then hung up when Fox said that he'd be there in twenty minutes.

"Go pick him up from my mom's house some-time in the next hour," Falisha told Lamar. "And I'll be back to pick him up in a few days." she finished, then grabbed her things and headed for the door.

Lamar wanted to break her jaw for the way she was talking so reckless. Calling Fox, "babe," and talking about going "home" to him and hav-ing his sister watch Jordan. Lamar and Falisha hadn't been broken up for two weeks, and she was already in another relationship. Lamar was hot, but he couldn't focus on that right now. All he wanted to do was go pick up his son and take him home, which he immediately left and was on his way to do.

Chapter 9

Chris woke up at 1:00 a.m. in a cold sweat. He looked over and saw Amy lying there asleep along with Najjiyyah in peaceful bliss. He thought that he would be happy with his new family, but actually, he wasn't. Amy was a good woman. Beautiful, smart, business oriented, and had some of the best pussy he'd ever had, but she lacked in an area where Tammy had excelled. Tammy had captured his heart in so many ways that couldn't be explained, and although he had love for Amy and his daughter, his heart was still caught up somewhere else. It was impossible for him to allow Tammy to get married without letting her know how much he still loved her.

Chris grabbed his phone from the nightstand, climbed out of bed, and headed downstairs. He wasn't sure if Tammy would answer the phone with it being so late at night, but Chris was going to try anyway. It rang twice before she picked up.

"Who's calling?" she asked with a groggy voice.

"It's me, Tam, can you talk?" Chris asked, walking out onto the back deck.

Tammy looked over at Darious, who was lying there snoring like a grizzly bear. A freight train could have driven through the bedroom blowing its horn, and he wouldn't have rolled over. That's just how hard he slept at night.

"Give me a minute," she said, putting Chris on hold while she got up and used the bathroom.

Chris sat down, looking up into the sky and noticing how beautiful the night was. The sky was clear, and the stars were out, along with half of the moon lighting up the earth. The weather was great too. Warm enough that Chris didn't need a tee shirt on.

"Hello," Tammy said coming back to the phone.

"I hope I'm not getting you in trouble or any-thing," he began. "I just needed to talk to you about something."

"At one o'clock in the morning, Chris?" Tammy asked, opening the refrigerator door. "You sure pick a fine time to wanna talk."

"Yeah, I know. Sometimes a nigga wake up when he realize he's 'bout to lose something. Tammy, I know that this might sound crazy coming from me wit' ya wedding already here, but you can't marry that guy," he said, waking Tammy all the way up.

"What? What are you talking about? I'm getting married on Sunday, Chris. What do you mean, I can't marry him?" she said in a low tone, trying not to be heard by Darious if he woke up.

"You don't really love him. Ya heart is in the same place mine—"

"No no no, Chris. You can't do this to me," she spoke. "I do love him, and it may not be with the same amount of love I had for you, but I'm okay with that."

"So, you telling me that you don't want us to be together? You don't want us to be a family again?" Chris asked.

"I did want us to be a family, and I gave you plenty of chances to marry me before, and when you was locked up. You turned me down when I begged you."

"I know, Tammy, I know."

"No, you don't know, Chris. That's ya fuckin problem right now. You play all these little mind games thinking this shit is cute."

"I love you, Tam Tam," he said, cutting her off.

Tammy wasn't trying to hear it. She wanted to keep blasting him. "And I can almost bet anything you laid up over that bitch's house right now. The same bitch you cheated on me with and had a baby with. Since when did you start liking white girls anyway? Dis bitch cool with your mom and everything. What you think, we about to be one big happy family? You got Tammy fucked up. I'm not the young girl you used to know, Chris. I'm grown now, and I do grown woman shit," she blanked.

"You don't love me no more? Tell me, Tammy, you don't love me no more!" Chris yelled into the phone getting a little mad at the way she was talking to him like he wasn't a factor.

Tammy got quiet. She could hear the seriousness in his voice and knew that he was upset. But Tammy was upset too, and she was tired of playing Ping-Pong with her heart. What she was about to say may have been the hardest thing she ever had to do, but in her eyes, it was the right thing.

"I got love for you, Chris, but I'm not in love with you," she said, and then hung up.

Carol walked into the bar slinging her ass from side to side while sucking on a blow pop. She knew she wouldn't have to pay for one drink tonight. Half the bar was looking forward to a dick suck from her to cap their night off, but what they failed to realize was that Carol had one target in mind.

"Heyyy, Fox," she sang, walking up to the bar where he was having a few drinks with some friends.

He turned around, and all he saw was Carol taking the blow pop out of her mouth. She licked the corners of her mouth just to show him how wet her tongue was. Fox immediately got turned on, remembering the last time Carol sucked his dick in his car.

"Damn, yo, get the lady a drink," Fox told the bartender. "Who done let you off the leash tonight?" he joked, sizing her up.

"You know I'm a bitch without an owner," Carol shot back as she licked her soft, wet lips. "So am I riding wit' you tonight, or are you going to let me roam the streets until somebody else pick me up?"

Fox looked down at Carol's sexy body. He wasn't trying to pass up the opportunity to get the best blow job in the city tonight. He could see himself now riding around the city all night getting head from her.

"The quicker you finish ya drink, the quicker we can get up out of here," he told her, grabbing a handful of his dick.

Fox had told Falisha that he wasn't going to be fuckin' the hood rats, but he didn't say anything about getting his dick sucked. He just knew he was being slick, but if he had any idea that Carol had gonorrhea in the mouth and didn't even know it, he would have thought twice about letting her give him some head. He was going to learn the hard way.

Tammy couldn't go back to sleep for nothing. Chris, with his nonsense, kept her awake, thinking about all the what-if's. Him talking about them getting married and being a family really had her questioning whether she was making the right choice. On one hand, she had the opportunity to marry and start a family with Darious, but then, on the other hand, Tammy was capable of reestablishing and bringing back her old family.

Darious didn't have any kids, and he was going to adore Tammy for giving him his first, where Chris had a kid by someone else, and was more than likely to bring that drama Tammy's way. Darious's family welcomed her and her kids. Chris's family hated Tammy, and had disowned her years ago. After clear thoughts, the scale tipped heavily in favor of Darious. There was no question as to whether Tammy still loved Chris. She did, and was probably still in love with him to a certain degree, but the reality of the situation was that she had to move on and leave the past behind her.

After Lamar finally got baby Jordan to fall asleep, he stepped outside on the porch for a little fresh air. It was a good thing he had the next two nights off work, because Jordan was giving him hell lately. It was times like this when he needed Falisha around, because she always knew how to soothe him in the middle of the night when he got cranky. Lamar was starting to think that he may have bitten off more than he could chew in his pursuit of getting custody of Jordan.

Lisa's car coming down the block made him pick his head up. She drove right past his house, then parked toward the corner of the block. It was funny that Kim was with her, because he had been thinking about her all day.

"I see y'all gon' party every night," Lamar said as Lisa and Kim walked by. "Y'all bring me some food?"

"Shut up, boy. And where is my li'l man?" Lisa asked, walking across the street to where Lamar was. "He better be asleep."

"Finally," Lamar answered with nothing but stress in his eyes. "I think I might have to quit my job. It's hard as hell trying to find a night sitter, especially when the nights belong to him," Lamar said, nodding toward the house. "He's liable to wake up any minute now."

"Oh, well, let me get my ass in the house. I'm through with getting up in the middle of the night." Lisa laughed as she headed back across the street toward her house.

Kim started to follow suit, but Lamar grabbed her hand. "You gon' leave me too?" he asked, holding on to only her finger.

"Not if you really need me to stay," Kim shot back, looking in Lamar's eyes. "I'm not that good with babies."

"Nah, I just need you to sit and talk to me for a little while. It's been a long time since we did that."

Kim smiled and took a seat on the steps. "So what do you wanna talk about? I see you got a lot on your mind," she spoke. Lamar couldn't lie. She knew him too well for that. He did get quiet for a second until he got his thoughts together.

"Man, I dropped the ball back then," Lamar started. "I had something special, and I let it go." He shook his head. "Do you know how many nights I bumped my head against the wall thinking about what my life would have been like if I had moved out to Philly wit' you? That decision might have been the biggest mistake of my life."

Kim felt his pain. She too had some regrets from when she and Lamar were together.

"You wanna know what my biggest mistake was?" Kim said, looking into Lamar's eyes. "The day I got that abortion." Tears rose to the surface, but she fought them back. "I was scared and didn't know if you even wanted to be a dad. When I see how much you love Jordan and the things you would go through for him, it makes me wish that I had kept our baby," she admitted, unable to hold back the two tears that fell down her face.

Not a day passed by that Kim didn't think about it. It always seemed like a part of her was missing. Like that innocent baby took a piece of her soul with it, and even if she had a million kids in the future, she would never be able to forget her first.

Lamar put his arm around Kim, giving her a shoulder to lean on. "Can I ask you something?" he said, needing to know for his own self. "Is it too late for me and you?"

"What do you mean, Lamar? How can that even work?" she asked.

"What if I told you we could run away together? Me, you, and Jordan could take off and go anywhere. We could move out west. We can move to Philly, find jobs and start over."

"You would move off of this street?" Kim said in a sarcastic way. "You will *never* leave Charlotte. You love it here."

"I would move with you to the other side of this world if I had the chance to again," Lamar said with certainty.

"What about Falisha? She's not gonna let you just take Jordan."

"I'll find a way, just trust me," Lamar assured.

As good as it sounded, Kim couldn't give him an answer right then. She still had a lot to think about, and other issues of her own she needed to deal with. Lamar had definitely laid it on thick, and Kim could tell that he was sincere. With more than enough on her plate, she decided to take it down for the night.

Chapter 10

Wanting to spend a little time with Darious before they got married, Tammy decided to drop the kids off at Chris's. She had the whole day planned, including an early lunch, a movie, a walk in the park, dinner, and maybe even visit each other's family members. Darious was all for it.

"Give me ten minutes," Tammy told Darious when they pulled up to Chris's house on Walton Street.

She got out of the car and got the kids and their overnight bag situated before walking up and knocking on the door. It took a minute, but eventually the door swung open, and to Tammy's surprise, Amy was standing there with a tank top, shorts, and a pair of house slippers on. She had the nerve to be looking good.

"Oh, you want Chris?" Amy said, turning around to call him. "Come on in, if you like."

The kids were already through the door when she said that, so her comment was basically aimed at Tammy, who just stood there with a dumb look on her face. She had to dig deep in order not to keep from lashing out like she wanted to. It wouldn't have been a good look on her behalf, especially with her fiancé sitting in the car. She had to stay cool, but she moved from the outside steps to the indoor porch, just in case Darious was watching her.

Chris came down the steps while Amy went back up to the room. He could see the anger in Tammy's eyes the moment he walked up to her.

"Why you got dis bitch in our house?" Tammy asked through clinched teeth. "You know you dead wrong."

"I know, that's my bad. We went out last night and didn't feel like driving out to the county," Chris explained.

Tammy wasn't buying it. She was really offended and wanted to run upstairs and beat the hell out of Amy for being so disrespectful. Again, Darious was sitting out in the car, so Tammy didn't want to make a scene. The one thing she couldn't do was stand there looking at Chris.

"I'll come pick them up tomorrow. Anthony needs to be fitted for his suit, and I got some last-minute running around to do. But me and you will have a talk about this," Tammy said in a low voice before turning and walking out the front door.

Chris couldn't help but to smile, knowing how hot under the skin Tammy was. He had achieved the desired effect. The fact that she was mad let him know she still cared about him. Tammy wasn't aware of it yet, but Chris wanted to indirectly sabotage her marriage before she walked down that aisle. He wasn't sure if he was ready to marry her, but at the same time, he'd be damned if he was going to let somebody else do it. She was his baby mom, and if it was left up to him, that's the only title she would ever have . . . until he was ready to change it.

Kim adjusted the camera on top of the computer screen for her 2:30 p.m. Skype appointment with Brian. Since having that conversation with Lamar the other day, she was confused and needed to know a few things before she made the official choice to try to work something out with him.

"I'ma go meet up with Nate for lunch. Do you need anything?" Lisa asked as she passed Kim's room on her way out.

"Yeah, I have to ask you something real quick," Kim answered, waving Lisa into the room. "I know you tryin'a get to ya man, so I'm not gonna hold you up," Kim joked.

Lisa shook her head, smiling at the sound of her having a man. "A'ight, girl, what do you want?" Lisa asked in a playful way, taking a seat next to her on the bed.

Kim put her head down. She was embarrassed to say how she was feeling. She didn't want Lisa to look at her differently. "Would it sound crazy if I told you that I still had love for Lamar?"

Lisa figured that was what this was all about. She knew from the first day Kim was back in town. The first person she asked about was Lamar.

"Nah, girl, it don't sound crazy. One thing I know about love is that no matter how much people think they know about it, love always finds a way to dance to its own beat," Lisa said. "Now, my thing is, do you think that it would be wise trying to rekindle some old flames with him while he and Falisha are going through what they're going through? It looks ugly right now, but it's about to get even messier," she advised before standing up. "Now, if you don't mind, can we talk about this later? I have somewhere to be right now."

"Yeah, girl, go ahead and get out of here. You gave me more than enough to ponder," Kim responded.

Lamar did have a lot of drama going on in his life, and now probably wouldn't be the ideal time to try to get back with him. Even before Kim could even consider trying to get back with him, Lamar needed to clean up the mess he made, then close the book on Falisha, this time for good. Only then would Kim even entertain anything he had said the other night. Kim was damn near ready to call him and tell him just that, but Brian's face popped up on the screen, which, in turn, brought Kim to another realization. She too had some issues to take care of, and she was ready to tackle them, head-on.

Falisha pulled up to Lamar's house in an attempt to pick up baby Jordan, but she was in for a surprise. She honked the horn several times before finally getting out of the car. Her numerous knocks on the door went unanswered, and she knew he had to be there because his car was parked out front. As soon as Falisha was about to pull out her phone and call him, the front door opened. Lamar stepped out onto the porch brushing his waves to the front . . . without baby Jordan with him.

"Come on, dude, bring my son out here," Falisha snapped like she was trying to rush him. "I got somewhere to go."

"I don't know when the last time you been over ya mom house to check the mail, but I think the courts wrote to you and told you that I have primary custody of Jordan now," Lamar said, taking a seat on the ledge of the porch.

"Stop fuckin' playing all the time," Falisha based, slinging the door open and running into the house.

Lamar didn't move from his spot. He sat there and waited while Falisha ran through the house checking every room—every room that she went to and baby Jordan wasn't there. She panicked. She even checked the basement, and still, baby Jordan was nowhere to be found.

"Where da fuck is my son?" she yelled, coming back outside.

"You'll see Jordan when I say it's OK."

Falisha lashed out. She walked up on Lamar and started punching him in his face. He quickly got control of the fight, gripping her up and throwing her against the wall.

"I hate you. I hope you die!" Falisha screamed, charging Lamar with another round of punches. "Gimme my son!" she cried as the tears fell from her eyes while she continued throwing punches. "Let me go. Let me go!" she yelled.

Lamar wrapped her up in his arms to the point where she couldn't do anything. "Nah, shawty. This is what you wanted, right? This was the game you wanted to play," he spoke in a low tone as she tried to wiggle out of his hold.

Jordan had been with Lamar for over a week, and during that time, Lamar went to family court, told the judge Falisha had abandoned their son and that he didn't know where she was living. He said that Falisha was on drugs and alcohol real bad and sometimes went missing for days. On the spot, the court tried to reach Falisha, but was unsuccessful in catching her at her mom's house, the only phone number Lamar gave them for her.

With that, the judge granted Lamar temporary primary custody of Jordan and set a court date of ten working days from that date for Falisha to come forward and challenge custody. If she didn't show, Lamar would get full custody of Jordan indefinitely.

Falisha wasn't just mad, she was hurt. She finally got out of his grasp, then spit in his face. Some went into his eye, blinding him for a second. By the time he got his vision back, Falisha was in the car. Before he could get down the steps, she was pulling off. It's a good thing she did, because Lamar was going to clean the streets with her body after he knocked her out.

She may have gotten away with it now, but Lamar had a whole bag of tricks he was going to use on her. She was going to see once she got into that courtroom.

"Where did you just go?" Brian asked when Kim sat back in front of the computer screen. "And why you breathing so hard?" When Kim heard Falisha yelling and screaming outside, she ran downstairs and watched the whole fight from the window. She thought about intervening, but instead, decided to stay out of it.

"Shut up, boy. I left my food on the stove," Kim lied. "Now where were we? I believe I asked you where you see this thing that we have going."

"To be honest wit' you, Kim, I really don't know. I try not to get caught up with living in the future when it's not even here yet. I think the question that you wanna ask is if me and you are together as a couple right now."

Brian didn't like to cut corners. He was known to get straight to the point. That's one of the things Kim liked about him. "Well, what's the answer to that question then?" she asked.

Brian sat back in his chair and looked into the screen. "I would like to think that me and you were in a relationship, but the truth is,

we're not. We never established that, and I
always thought that you never planned on staying in Philly. You left me with the impression
that you was going back home to stay for good
eventually. I figured you was just using me as
something to do while you were here."

"Aww, don't say that. You mean more to me
than you think. That's why I'm trying to figure
out where we at. I don't wanna do something
stupid, then end up missing out on the chance of
me and you being together."

Kim had only recently realized how much she
cared about Brian. He was hundreds of miles
away, and every time she looked at another man,
or in Lamar's case, she thought about being with
another man, all she could think about is how
Brian would feel about it. If she didn't know any
better, Kim would have thought that she was in
love with him.

"Well, listen, I gotta get ready for work," Brian
spoke. "But I need you to ask yourself one question. Do you really want us to be together right
now? When you come up with that answer, and
you're sure beyond a shadow of doubt, you
let me know. Then I'll tell you exactly where I
see this thing we have going," he said before
shutting down his computer.

Kim flopped back onto the bed and went straight into deep thought. She had been through so much in her life that she didn't know where to begin. The question that Brian told her to ask herself wasn't going to be an easy one to answer. Kim definitely needed time to sort out her mess, and she hoped that Brian would still be around when she got it right. One thing she'd learned about the men in Philly was that they didn't sit around and wait for no chick, and not even she was an exception.

"Mommy, where are we going?" Naomi asked as she and Lisa got out of the car. "I hate surprises," she mumbled, thinking Lisa didn't hear her.

"I thought that we should go out for dinner tonight, and since you don't like surprises, I think I ought to tell you that I invited a friend of mine to come eat with us, if you don't mind."

Naomi was the center of Lisa's world, and she didn't care how nice of a guy Nate was to her. If Naomi didn't like him, it was pretty much a wrap. Lisa wasn't giving him a whole bunch of chances either. If he couldn't hit it off with Naomi on his first try, then it was back to the drawing board with the relationship.

"Who's your friend, Mommy? Is it my godmom, Kim?" she asked as they entered the restaurant. "Where is she? Where is she?"

"No, it's not Kim. He's right over there," Lisa said, pointing to the table where Nate was sitting.

"Hhheee?" Naomi said, placing her hands on her hips and scrunching up her face. "Your friend is a boy?"

Naomi was too much for her own self, looking up at Lisa with a little fake attitude on her face. Lisa could tell that Nate was in for a long night, or maybe short, depending on how he handled himself around Ms. Growny Naomi.

When they finally got to the table, Lisa and Nate hugged, and then Lisa introduced Naomi and Nate. To be dealing with a little girl, Nate was somewhat intimidated by her. She stared at him for a minute, making him feel a little uncomfortable. There was only one thing left for Nate to do, and that's put on his charm. He lowered his head some, then raised his hand a little and waited to be called on.

Naomi kept staring, but found it to be a little funny. She ended up cracking a smile, then pointed to Nate's hand so he could speak.

"Thank you, Princess Naomi. Being as though this is my first time meeting a princess in real life, I wasn't sure what to order for you," Nate playfully spoke. "What do princesses eat?" he asked, looking at the menu in confusion.

Naomi was sort of feeling the princess game, so she played along. "Princesses like cheeseburgers and chili cheese fries," she answered. "And the princess's mommy likes Chicken Alfredo."

"Now, I know the beautiful princess and her mommy are going to need something to wash all that food down with, so what royal drink should I order for you?" Nate continued.

Naomi giggled a little, seeing that he was still referring to her as a princess. Lisa smiled too because Nate had Naomi's full, undivided attention with the princess theme. Lisa was impressed, but she knew that the night was far from over with Naomi. She wasn't the ordinary six-year-old, and winning her over with simply calling her a princess and ordering her a cheeseburger and chili fries wasn't going to be enough. Nate was going to have to step his game up if he intended to make it through dinner.

Chapter 11

The ballroom was transformed into something special once Tammy's mom and Darious's mother came together and brought Tammy's dream wedding to life. White wooden chairs lined the floor on each side, where thousands of white and yellow rose petals covered the aisle Tammy was going to walk down. Crystal doves hung from the ceiling like chandeliers, and the cream-colored walls shimmered with glitter everywhere. A large white piano sat off to the side with a paid professional playing love songs from the '90s. Two tall water fountains sprayed mist into the air several yards away from the altar, making its background look beautiful.

The mothers had really done their thing. Large crowds of people poured into the ballroom, and it turned out to be way more than what was on the guest list. Luckily, there was enough room and chairs to seat everybody that came.

"Damn, dog. You really ready for this?" Lamar asked Darious while he rocked baby Jordan in his arms.

Darious chuckled. "Nah, homie, I'm good right now. I could have chosen anybody, but I didn't. I chose her." He nodded.

"Nigga, that's the best answer you could have come up with. Anything outside of that, we might have been fighting up in dis place," Lamar laughed. "But on a serious note, Tammy is like my little sister, yo. Treat her right, and no matter what, don't ever put ya hands on her," Lamar said, poking Darius in the chest.

Darius respected that coming from him. Lamar wanted him to know that she had men in her family who loved her and weren't going for the abusive spouse relationship. Darius would get touched quick, fast, and in a hurry, and depending on the weather, he might get buried. He understood that quite clear.

"Oh shit, homie, ya folks is here," Darious said, nodding toward Falisha. The hairs on Lamar's neck stood up. He wasn't sure if she was going to show up. Falisha was known for being shaky and undependable, but there she was standing right in front of his face when he turned around.

He looked down at Jordan, fearing she was about to do something stupid, and he would have to ruin the wedding by whooping her ass.

Surprisingly, she showed no signs of a threat; in fact, she looked hurt. She leaned over and kissed Jordan's head, then wiped the single tear that fell down her face. She wanted to hold him, but that would have made what she was about to do even harder.

"I wanted you to know that I'm not going to be at the court hearing on Wednesday," Falisha spoke in a sad tone. "I'm not going to fight you for custody, so you don't have to pay a lawyer. I think our son is better off with you than me, and I give you my word that I will never bother y'all again. Take care of our boy," Falisha said, leaning in to kiss Jordan one last time before turning around and walking away.

Lamar watched Falisha walk away , and his heart dropped. He'd hurt her badly; she didn't even want to be a mother anymore, at least not a mother to his child. It was a tough blow, because despite what they were going through, Lamar did want baby Jordan to have both his mother and his father in his life. His intentions were only to have some legal rights over his son, but he had pushed too hard, and now he'd pushed Falisha right out of both their lives. He just stood there sick, sorry, and confused, but the thing that he began to feel immediately . . . was alone.

***

Lisa's plus two was Naomi and Nate. It seemed like the moment they entered the building all eyes were on them. People who knew Lisa were happy to see her with somebody after all this time. Nate was a catch too and had quite a few ladies huddled up, whispering to each other about how sexy he looked.

"You know all these people?" Nate asked, looking around the room. "They are staring hard."

"I know some of them from the neighborhood."

"Uncle Lamar!" Naomi yelled, running across the lobby.

After hugging and letting Naomi kiss baby Jordan, Lamar walked over to Lisa. He glanced from her to Nate with a curious look on his face. Lisa smiled, then introduced the two.

"A'ight, Lamar, can you keep an eye on Naomi while I go find Tammy?" Lisa asked, looking around for Tammy's dressing room.

"Yeah, I got her. Go and do ya thing," he answered.

Then Lisa did something that Lamar, nor anybody else in the building that knew her, thought they'd ever see again. Right before she left, Lisa gave Nate a peck on his lips. It wasn't a major tongue-twirling, lip-locking French kiss, but it was a kiss nonetheless, in public.

"What did you say ya name was again?" Lamar joked to Nate.

Aside from the wedding, this definitely was going to be the talk of the night, and Nate was in for one hell of an interrogation once Tammy and Kim cornered him.

"Damn, girl, you rocking this dress," Kim told Tammy, who stood in the vanity mirror putting on the finishing touches.

Tammy didn't go with the traditional wedding dress like every other bride. She rocked an all-white pencil dress that came down to the lower part of her thighs. It was form-fitting, showing off all her sexy curves. On her feet was a pair of white Giuseppes with gold buckles, matching the gold trimmings on her dress. Her curly lion mane hair stole the show, making the whole outfit come together something fierce.

"Don't be lying to that bitch," Lisa said, walking into the dressing room. "She's killing that dress." Lisa laughed as she looked Tammy up and down.

She gave Tammy a hug and a quick smooch, trying to avoid messing up her makeup.

"Where's Naomi?" Tammy asked, looking toward the door.

"Oh, she's downstairs with Lamar and Nate," Lisa answered.

"Nate?" Tammy and Kim said at the same time.

"Yes, Nate. I think it's time I start entertaining the notion of having me a little boyfriend. Nothing serious, though. Just somebody to talk to and go out with from time to time," Lisa explained.

"Yeah, well, we need the full skinny on that situation," Kim said.

"Yeah, but not today. Today is *my* day, heyyyyy!!" Tammy said, snapping her finger in their faces.

A knock on the door got all three of their attention, then in walked Chris, shocking everyone. Tammy couldn't believe that he was there, and then had the nerve to look good, rocking a pair of True Religion jeans, a white Polo tee shirt with an oversized black horseman, and a pair of black-and-white Jordans to match the shirt. Louis Vuitton belt, iced out chain, even icier watch, pinky ring, and a nice-size studded earring for accessories made Chris look like he was a rapper on his way to a video shoot. He was thugged out to the core.

"Hi, ladies," he greeted with a pleasant smile. "Y'all look good."

"Hey, Chris," Lisa replied, giving him a hug.

Kim did the same, giving him a hug and a playful punch on the arm.

"Do y'all mind if I talk to my kids' mom for a minute?" Chris asked.

The girls didn't mind. They knew Tammy and Chris needed a moment. But just in case it popped off, they were going to be close by.

"Come on, Kim," Lisa said, walking out of the room.

Before Kim exited, she gave Chris a warning. "Don't start no shit up in here, nigga."

Chris smiled, watching as the door closed. He looked back over at Tammy and shook his head with the same smile on his face.

"You look beautiful," he said, walking over to her. "You know, I always imagined that you would look this beautiful for me on our wedding day. I pictured us having it in a more romantic place than this, but I guess this will do."

"Come on, Chris, don't start. Today is my wedding day," Tammy said.

"Yeah, I know. I just wanted to stop by and show you some love, that's all. Com'ere," he said, reaching out for a hug.

Tammy stepped in, wrapping her arms around him. This really meant a lot coming from him. She didn't expect this much. "Congratulations," he whispered in her ears as he held her tight.

It seemed as if Chris didn't want to let her go, and Tammy kind of felt the same. It felt like this was the last hug they would ever share.

"I love you," Chris said, then placed a small kiss to the side of her cheek.

That kiss was followed by another kiss to the cheek, and then another, each of which got closer and closer to her lips.

They squared off face-to-face. His forehead rested on hers. Her nose rubbed against his, and in a moment of passion, Tammy kissed him. In seconds, they were lip-locked, sharing space with each other's tongues. Chris's hands moved down her back until they reached Tammy's ass, which he immediately palmed.

Tammy's pussy got wet at his touch, and before she knew it, Chris had lifted her up by her ass and carried her over to the futon. He laid her on her back, reached in, and pulled her panties off. Tammy tried to sit up, but Chris pushed her back. He pushed her dress up and over her waist, and wasted no time in planting his face into her pussy. Tammy moaned, feeling his mouth smothering her clit. He licked and sucked on it for almost a minute, making it even wetter than it already was.

"We can't do this," Tammy whined, looking down at Chris's head swaying side to side. "Oh my fuckin' God, boy," she moaned, throwing her head back. "I hate you."

When she opened her eyes, Chris was on top of her. He didn't even get his pants all the way down before he grabbed his stiff dick. With no hesitation, he pushed his long dark flesh inside her. She gasped as it filled her canal. Involuntarily, her arms wrapped around his back.

"Dis daddy pussy," Chris whispered, pushing the tip of his dick up to her back wall. "Say it," he demanded, looking into her eyes.

One stroke, two strokes. "Who pussy is it?" he asked again. Three strokes, four strokes. "Say it," he demanded. Five strokes, six strokes. "Dis daddy pussy. Stop playing and say it," Chris demanded.

Every stroke got deeper and harder, intoxicating Tammy's mind and body. She didn't want him to stop, but she knew he had to before they got caught. Seven strokes, eight strokes. "I love you, Tammy," he whispered. Nine strokes, ten strokes. "Who pussy is it?" he asked again.

Tammy couldn't fight it any longer. She was no longer in control of her thoughts. No longer in control of what her body yearned for. "Dis ya pussy, Chris. Dis daddy pussy," she moaned, trying her best not to scream out his name.

Eleven strokes, twelve strokes, thirteen strokes. "Damn, I love ya, girl."

Chris's come splashed inside of Tammy, causing her to have an orgasm of her own. She bit down on his shoulder as the orgasm rumbled through her whole body. She knew she was wrong, but it felt so good. Having Chris inside of her felt right, and there wasn't anyone who could tell her anything different.

In the midst of enjoying each other's tenderness, bathing in each other's fluids, the front door to the dressing room opened . . . and standing there looking down at Tammy underneath Chris's body, was none other than . . .

Chapter 12

As Luther Vandross's "Here and Now" played through the speakers, Tammy nervously walked down the aisle. Although she was sure the beautiful, elegant, white dress was the reason for all the stares, she couldn't help but feel that all eyes were on her for a different reason. Her uncle, the last living relative on her mother's side of the family, accompanied her. In her hand, she held a colorful bouquet of flowers, and on her face was the fakest smile she'd ever worn in her life. Visions of Chris on top of her, digging his pole deep inside of her only minutes ago, smothered her thoughts. Traces of his sweet saliva was still on her lips. That, along with remnants of his come seeping out of her still-throbbing nectar box was enough to make her want to run and hide.

Guilt was an understatement, and Tammy didn't know what had possessed her to go forward with this marriage after what she'd just done. Selfishness was the only thing that made sense—not wanting to lose out on being Darious's wife, while at the same time, harboring a huge amount of love for Chris. In a nutshell, she wanted to have her cake and eat it too, which had nothing but disaster written all over it. Luther Vandross's crooning interrupted her thoughts,

When I look in your eyes, there I'll see, all that a love should really be. And I need you more and more each day, nothin' can take your love away.

Lisa tried to keep a straight face during Tammy's slow stroll on top of the flower petals that lined the center aisle of the church. Though she truly wanted to yell out, "You ain't shit," she kept her composure.

At one point, Tammy even glanced over at her for approval of what she was doing, but Lisa only lowered her gaze, not wanting to return any eye contact. This was something she couldn't approve of, and she hoped Tammy reconsidered before it was too late. But from the determined look on Tammy's face, she was getting married at all cost.

"You take care of my niece," Uncle Teddy told Darious when they finally arrived at the altar.

Darious smiled and gave him a handshake before Uncle Teddy presented the bride, and then walked off. Mesmerized by her beauty, Darious couldn't take his eyes off of Tammy. She, on the other hand, could barely look at him.

The pastor began, and right in the middle of him quoting a scripture from the Bible, Tammy stepped slightly to the left and turned toward Lisa who had a blank look on her face. She leaned in and tensely whispered so no one else could hear, "Am I making a mistake? Am I wrong for going through with this?"

Everyone in the building looked on, and even Darious had a curious gaze on his face, wondering what was going on with his bride-to-be.

In a low tone, Lisa answered, looking directly in Tammy's eyes. "Only do what you are able to live with for the rest of your life."

They stared at each other for a moment before Tammy turned back around and stood beside Darious.

"You having second thoughts?" he asked in a concerned tone.

Tammy stared into his eyes for the first time that day and saw nothing but pure love. She saw compassion, comfort, care, and concern . . . everything a husband should have for the love of his life. There was no way possible Tammy could turn away now, and the guilt that she felt in the beginning had turned into regret. What happened with Chris was something that should have never occurred, and after today, she knew it would never happen again.

"I'm sure you're the one," Tammy responded with a huge smile. She then turned to the pastor, letting him know that it was okay for him to proceed.

Throughout the service, Kim and Falisha kept looking over at Lisa suspiciously, wanting to know what Tammy had whispered to her and trying to figure out what was going on. Neither was aware of what had happened in the dressing room just moments ago, but both Kim and Falisha were thirsty for something good to gossip about. They were going to remain that way too because Lisa wasn't trying to say a word about what she had seen.

"Congratulations!" friends and family yelled out after the pastor instructed Darious that he may now kiss his bride.

It was official. Tammy was now Mrs. DuPree. Joy and pride consumed her heart, and it felt as if she had a clean slate from this point on. She planned to keep it clean. To the best of her abilities.

***

"Excuse me, Lisa," Darious said when he walked up to the reserved table. "Do you mind if I have a word with you?" he said, not wanting to be rude by just telling Falisha to get up.

Lisa looked over and nodded at Falisha to leave.

Falisha stood, but was reluctant to move, wanting to stay and be nosy.

"Congratulations," Lisa said with a smile. "I know I haven't made it my business to get to know you. I hope that will change, now that you and my girl tied the knot."

"I know this might sound crazy, but you're the closest person to Tammy, and the amount of love and respect she has for you is crazy," Darious began.

Lisa was ten steps ahead of him, and she already knew what he wanted to talk to her about the moment he walked over. "Ask ya question," she smiled, making him smile in the process.

"Do you really think she loves me?" he asked.

"Of course, I do. That girl is crazy about you," she answered.

"But what did she say to you when we were at the altar?"

"She asked me if I thought that she was worthy enough to marry you," Lisa lied. She hated to lie, and she so wanted to tell him the truth, but it wasn't her place to do so. If the truth was going to come out, it wasn't going to be by her. "Enjoy ya marriage and don't hurt my girl," Lisa concluded before getting up from the table to leave.

"Thanks," Darious said. He also got up and headed back to the front where Tammy and the rest of his family were seated.

As he turned around to leave, Darious glanced over and saw Chris leaving the ballroom. He wanted to be sure that it was him, so he walked to the exit door. By the time he got outside, Chris was gone. Darious stood out front looking around, and the only thought in his mind was, *Why the fuck is Chris at my wedding?*

"Hey, Chris," Falisha greeted, seeing him in the parking lot.

"Damn, Falisha, that thing look crazy," he replied, taking in a full-body mental note. "Girl, you thicker than a second-grade crayon," he joked as he checked her out.

"Shut up, boy. And who car you got? It better not be stolen."

The all-black 2012 Chevy Impala sat clean, featuring tinted windows, leather seats, a touch screen TV in the center console, with a wood grain finish throughout. He had a straight-up dope boy car.

"Falisha, if anybody should know me, it should be you, and you know I get at a dollar. I'm doing me right now, minus the trappin'. By the summer, I'ma pull up in something crazy with a V-12 under the hood. You can ride shotgun wit' ya feet up if you want," Chris said, standing there looking like he was about to take a picture.

Falisha couldn't believe that Chris was trying to crack on her. But then again, his baby mom had just got married to another nigga. In any event, she wasn't going to entertain him. He was cute, and she definitely knew what Chris was capable of as far as getting at a dollar, but Tammy was her friend, and she wasn't the type to get involved with her friend's ex.

Chris was a man scorned, and he didn't have any qualms about who he messed with right now. If she was cute with a nice body, Chris was on it. Falisha fit the bill, hands-down.

"I'ma catch you in traffic, youngin'," Chris said.

As soon as Falisha was about to respond, Fox pulled into the parking lot. He drove straight up and stopped right in front of Chris's car. What happened next shocked the hell out of Falisha.

Fox's driver-side window came down, and Chris, who was about to get into his car, stepped back out and closed the door. He walked back around to the front of the Impala and took a seat on the hood.

"You ready to pay that tab?" he asked Fox with a serious look on his face.

"Naw, Cees, I need a couple of more days."

"Come on, Fox. How long do I gotta wait for my bread? It's been almost two weeks already," Chris snapped back.

"Two days. Just give me two days," Fox semi-pleaded.

Falisha stood there looking back and forth from Chris to Fox in total shock. She'd never heard anyone speak to Fox in that manner. On top of that, it was about some money. If it had been anyone else, Fox would have been out of his truck putting his foot in somebody's ass. Not with Chris, though.

"Forty-eight hours, homie, and not a minute later," Chris spoke. "Now move ya' fuckin' car out of my way so I can roll," he said, getting up and walking back to the driver's side.

Fox nodded for Falisha to get in the car.

Chris was on one, and he couldn't resist fucking with Falisha. "Oh, you wit' him?" he asked like he was surprised.

Falisha confirmed it with a nod of the head while she walked toward Fox's car.

"You better stop playin' and get on the winning team," Chris told her before she opened the passenger-side door and sat down.

"Yo, Cees, don't disrespect me like that," Fox spoke up.

"Or what?" Chris shot back, flashing the black Glock .40 sitting on his hip. "You just worry about payin' me my fuckin' money, nigga."

Fox didn't want that kind of trouble right now, so instead of feeding into it, he bowed out gracefully. Plus, he knew Chris wouldn't have a problem lighting his car up like a Christmas tree, in broad daylight, in front of whoever.

"You got it, homie," Fox said, then pulled off.

Falisha sat in the passenger side, wanting to question what had just happened, but the furious look on Fox's face told her that now wasn't a good time. As she sat there, she couldn't help but to play back in her mind the way Chris was talking to her man. It was ugly, but she had to be honest with herself. It was a turn-on. Whenever an alpha male showed his dominance in front of a female, it gets her attention. For that moment in time, that's exactly what Chris had done to Falisha. Not only was he cute, but the nigga went hard.

***

"Ya baby momma looked like she wanted to fight me today," Kim joked as she and Lamar walked through the park after the wedding. "Boy, you definitely got a problem on ya hands."

"Yeah, I know," Lamar agreed, looking to the sky. "Since she's been with that nigga, Fox, she's been a complete bitch."

Lamar was actually understating the issue. Falisha had been more than just bitchy with him. She had been talking to him any kind of way, picking up and dropping off their son when she felt like it, and demanding money whenever she felt like she wanted to put pressure on him.

"Oh shit, this is my boss," Kim said, hearing the special ring tone going off in her bag. "I'm here," she answered.

Lamar took a seat on the park bench and watched Kim pace back and forth while on the phone. She was even more beautiful than the day she left Charlotte for Philly. Kim was adept at captivating Lamar with the simplest things. Curvy body, cute face, and the ability to look sexy as hell in a pair of heels.

"If it ain't one thing, it's another," Kim said, placing her phone back in her bag.

"I hope you don't plan on leaving me already," Lamar responded, getting up from the bench.

"Probably. There was a double homicide in Philly the other day, and my boss wants me on the job. They picked up the case this morning," she explained.

Kim knew from the moment she went on vacation that it wasn't going to last long. Major cases, both state and federal, plagued the city of Philadelphia, so there was always more than enough work to go around.

"I'm not gonna be able to get used to you running in and out of my life like this," he said, reaching for Kim's waist and pulling her close to him. He looked into her eyes. "I missed the hell out of you. You do know that, right?"

"Yeah, right," Kim chuckled as she wrapped her arms around his neck.

For the first time in months, Lamar leaned in and kissed Kim's soft, full lips. It brought back all kinds of memories for her, and she was the first one to pull away. "What are you trying to do to me?" she asked looking into Lamar's eyes.

"I'm trying to win you back. You just don't know how bad I need you in my life. I swear, I don't wanna lose you again," he shot back.

Kim pulled his face back down to hers and kissed him again. She pulled away yet again, but this time she pushed his hands off her waist. She was confused like hell and couldn't figure out for the life of her why she was so attracted to him.

This was the man who had broken her heart. But there was something about the way he touched her, and the way he spoke softly to her, not to mention all the physical attributes he had, which were perfected by God. If all that wasn't enough, then just knowing beyond a shadow of a doubt that Lamar loved her would always draw her near to him.

Kim tried to fight it, but Lamar had his hooks in her, and it had been like that for a while now. Resisting him was almost impossible for Kim.

Chapter 13

"Caught yo' ass," Lisa laughed as she creeped up behind Kim while she was in her room packing her things. "Where the hell are you running off to?" she asked, taking a seat on the bed.

"I have to go back to Philly for a few days."

"What, why?"

"Well, when you're the highest-paid paralegal on the East Coast, there's really no such thing as a vacation," Kim responded with a slight smile. "But best believe that I will be back, and whether or not you like it, you're gonna tell me what the hell happened at that wedding," she said, cutting her eyes over at Lisa with a smirk on her face.

Kim, Tammy, and Lisa had been friends far too long for her not to know that something had gone down by the look Tammy and Lisa had shared at their little conference in the middle of the ceremony.

Truth be told, if Lisa was going to break down and tell anybody, it would have been Kim. But for right now, Lisa didn't see any reason to share that information. It was unfortunate that she had to be the one who walked in on Chris and Tammy, but it was going to take an act of God for anyone to get that out of her, including Kim.

"A'ight, now I need you to help me get this stuff to the car. My flight leaves in less than two hours," Kim said and pushed one of the suitcases across the bed.

"Damn, don't be rushing to get out of here," Lisa barked.

Kim was rushing, not only because she wanted to catch her flight, but she also wanted to avoid having to see Lamar before she left. She told Lisa that she'd be gone for a few days, but the truth was, she really didn't know how long she was going to be gone. Homicide cases were unpredictable, and if Kim wasn't coming back to Charlotte anytime soon, she didn't want to have to face Lamar before she left. Especially since they were in the middle of trying to salvage what was left of their relationship. It was like taking two steps backward.

Fox stood by the window in his bedroom looking out into the backyard, debating whether he should pay Chris the one hundred thousand he owed him. He still couldn't believe Chris had got out of prison this early. Fox could clearly recall the judge giving him a 300-month sentence, which equaled out to twenty-five years.

"Damn," he mumbled to himself as he thought about it. His train of thought was interrupted when Falisha walked into the room.

She could see the stress written all over his face. "Are we still going out tonight?" she asked.

Fox flagged her off without saying anything. Falisha caught an instant attitude, but before she could spazz out on him, he apologized.

"Damn, shawty, my bad," he said, walking over to her. "I got a lot of shit on my mind right now, but yeah, we still goin' out," he said, giving her a kiss.

Falisha had a feeling that whatever was bothering him more than likely had something to do with Chris.

Being as nosy as she was, she couldn't help but inquire, "What was all that about between you and Chris the other day?"

At first, Fox was reluctant to tell her, but eventually he broke down the whole story about how he and Chris were hustling together before Chris was locked up. They were moving a few bricks of cocaine across town when Chris was pulled over by the State Trooper K-9 unit. The dog went crazy in the backseat, which prompted a search of the car they were in. Seven kilograms total was found in a stash spot in the backseat. Not only was Fox on parole at the time, he was a two-time felon. One more strike, whether federal or state, and he was going away for life.

While they sat in a holding cell waiting to be arraigned, Fox begged Chris to take the case. He promised Chris one hundred thousand, plus his lawyer fee if he took the rap. Chris only had one felony on his jacket, so he figured the worst that could happen to him was doing a small stretch upstate. Long story short, Chris took the case. The feds picked up the case, and Fox bailed out on his promise. The lawyer was the only thing Chris had gotten from him.

"Damn, baby," Falisha said after hearing the whole situation.

Fox was a G in the hood and had a lot of respect, but when it came down to gunplay, Chris and his brother, Outlaw, were at the top of the charts. Everyone, including Fox, knew they weren't to be played with.

"Hello, Mrs. DuPree," Darious looked down and greeted Tammy as she rested her head on his bare chest.

"Hey, you," she softly spoke, looking up into his eyes with the hugest smile on her face. Just having her new last name did something to her. She felt happy, at least for a moment.

"Yo, I need to ask you something," Darious began. "I saw ya baby father at the wedding, and I was trying to figure out—"

"Come on, baby, it's our honeymoon. I just wanna enjoy spending this time with my husband," Tammy spoke, cutting him off.

Darious couldn't argue with her request. It would only ruin the mood, and who in their right mind would want to create that type of drama on their honeymoon? The topic of Chris really didn't have a place here and now, so Darious left it alone.

"So what do you wanna do today?" he asked, rolling on top of Tammy. "We are in Jamaica, so we can do the Jet Skis or just go lie on the beach. We could go swimming or get something to eat. It's all up to you, baby."

Tammy reached up and grabbed the side of his face. All of that sounded cool, but maybe for tomorrow's activities. Today, which was the first day of a seven-day, six-night honeymoon vacation, Tammy only had one thing in mind.

"I just want you to make love to me today."

***

"Aye, yo, listen, I'ma need you to take care of something for me," Fox said to Falisha as he drove.

"Yeah, whatever you need," she said, gathering baby Jordan's things.

Fox had been out of the drug game for a few weeks and was trying to take the legal route, but if he intended to pay Chris the money he owed him, he would have to make one more run. Hopefully, this one could be lucrative enough to not only pay Chris off, but to also enhance his chances of successfully going legit.

After hearing Fox run down his plan for what he termed the "ultimate come up," Falisha sat looking out the window in dismay. She was totally against the idea.

"I thought you said you was done with the streets," she said, unsure of what else to say.

"I am out of the game. I just need this last run to get me out of the shit for good. If it's any consolation, I'll give you ten K if you make the run with me," he offered. Fox knew if anything would get Falisha's attention, it was money. And just as he expected, she couldn't deny him.

"One run, Fox, and I want my money up front," she demanded.

That was all he needed to hear, and just like that, Fox was right back at it. But this time he had a fresh new riding partner.

***

Kim looked out the window as her plane took off. She couldn't help but to feel the same way she felt the first time she left Charlotte. It was the feeling that she was leaving behind the most important people in her life. Just being around everyone brought back so many memories for her. Lamar was the same good guy he was when she first left, and it wasn't until recently that Kim took some responsibility for the demise of their relationship.

Getting that abortion without first coming to Lamar was what started it all. Thoughts of what life would have been like if she did have his baby raced through her head and was a constant exercise for her brain. Seeing how active and loving he was with baby Jordan was only proof of how good a father he would have been. Regret started to settle in, and before she knew it, Kim was wiping tears from her eyes.

"Damn, my nigga. That bitch really got married," Outlaw said as he exhaled the thick dark green smoke from his lungs. Chris shot him a quick glance, which made Outlaw change his words.

"My bad, brah, ya baby mom," he cleaned up, taking another puff of the weed.

"Yeah, she did her thing, but it's cool. You know me, tho, it's all about the get back. She played me, and best believe, I'm about to play her."

"Man, fuck dat . . . Man, fuck shawty," Outlaw shot back, disapproving of Chris wasting any more time on Tammy.

Outlaw was too raw and had not experienced getting his heart broken. If he did, he would have known exactly how his brother was feeling at that moment. Hurt mixed with anger was one of the deadliest combinations that a man could have. Nations had been destroyed for those very reasons.

"So what, you wanna kill that nigga?" Outlaw asked, ready and willing to get the job done immediately.

"Nah, li'l nigga. If that nigga get smoked right now, the first person the police is gonna come to is me. I gotta do dis shit another way. I gotta make her feel like I feel right now. Once I do that, then I'll move on," Chris said, waving the weed smoke from in front of his face. "Yo, you need to stop smokin' that shit."

"Shit, nigga, I ain't the one on parole," Outlaw shot back, taking another long, deep pull of the blunt.

Chris looked over and laughed at his brother, seeing that he hadn't changed one bit since the day he left. Just as crazy as he wanted to be.

"Well, you know once I start this publishing company, you gon' have to stop blowin' that tree," Chris said to his little brother.

Chris had been out of the halfway house for a little more than a couple of weeks and had already put some good use to the money Bizz had given him. He had also stuck to his word and made sure Bizz's lawyer was paid off and his daughter was straight. Aside from coming home to the love of his life marrying someone else, things were really looking up for him. The one hundred thousand Fox owed him was really going to put him over the top. Trying his best to live right wasn't the easiest thing to do, but Chris was doing the best that he could with what little he had. It was either this way, or go back to being Cees the neighborhood menace, and the streets wouldn't like it one bit.

Lisa was standing in the kitchen when she heard the doorbell ring. She turned and looked toward the front door. She was expecting Nate to stop by, but it was a little earlier than what she had told him. Naomi had just gone to bed, and Lisa didn't even know if she was all the way asleep yet.

"I know I'm early," Nate said when Lisa opened the door, "but I was already on this side of town, and I didn't want to waste gas going all the way home, and then coming back," he explained briefly.

Lisa had one eyebrow up, and her hand on her hip the whole time. She playfully punched him in the arm as he entered the house. "Damn, it smells good in here," he said, raising his nose in the air. "What in the hell did you cook?"

Lisa had taken a few cooking classes and knew how to create some amazing dishes.

"Well, tonight, we have lemon fried tilapia, mac n' cheese with smoked Gouda, shrimp, and some turkey bacon curly fries," she said, taking his jacket and leading him into the kitchen.

"Oh shit, you really might like me," he joked as he took a seat at the dinner table.

Nate's ability to make her laugh was one of the qualities Lisa loved most about him. He always did it on cue and at the right time.

"So look, I was thinking that I could take you and Naomi out next week. You know, have a little fun for a change."

Lisa smiled, and then shook her head. "And where do you plan on taking us?"

His answer took her by total surprise.

"Disney World," he said. "Naomi don't have to go to school, and . . ." He shrugged with a smile. "Let's face it, you don't have a job right now." He laughed. "No, seriously, it will be good for you."

It didn't dawn on Lisa until that day that she and Naomi hadn't been anywhere special in over a year. Work, school, and home had become the routine. Tammy's wedding was probably the only fun they'd had.

"Disney World?" Lisa asked with her face scrunched up.

Before she could get a word out, Naomi busted into the kitchen with her Dora the Explorer pajamas on.

"Hi, Nate," she greeted, jumping into the chair.

Lisa figured it had not been long enough for her to be asleep yet. "Naomi, you wanna go to Disney World next week?" Lisa asked, almost causing her to fall out of her chair in excitement.

"Yeah!" she yelled, throwing her hands in the air. But then, Naomi paused and got serious for a second. "Can Nate come to Disney World with us?" she asked with a puppy dog face.

"He's the one who wants to take us."

Naomi looked back and forth from Lisa to Nate, and then she leaned in and gave Nate a hug.

"Hi five," Nate said, raising his hand in the air for Naomi to smack it. She did, then climbed out of her chair and ran back to her room in joy.

Lisa stood there, disoriented by Naomi's actions. She had never been this close to a man outside of her father, and for her child to show that type of affection was a shock, especially knowing how much she loved Ralphy. It was scary, but at the same time, a relief. If Naomi didn't have some type of connection with Nate, they weren't going to have much of a future together. Naomi didn't dictate who Lisa was going to be with, but she definitely played a huge role in the selection process. As of right now, Nate had the advantage, and if he continued to play his cards right, there was no telling where this relationship would go.

Chapter 14

The law office of Tim and George was like a madhouse when Kim walked through the door. Everyone was running around yelling out case law, and it sounded like all the phones in the place were ringing at the same time. Kim had almost forgotten what an average day was like at the job. The only way to become acclimated was to be updated on her new case, and then fall right into line.

"I need everything on the Thompson file," Kim yelled as she made her way over to her cubicle. Before she could even get comfortable, a stack of papers dropped on her desk. She glanced down at the four-inch file, then took in a deep breath. Homicides were one of the easiest cases to beat, and most of the time it was due to the lack of witnesses. Unfortunately, this wasn't the case with her current assignment. Several witnesses had come forward with the same account of what happened.

"I need you to work ya magic on this one," George walked up to Kim and instructed. "If anybody can find something wrong with these statements, I'm sure it's you."

Kim picked up the file and scanned through it with her thumb. For it to only contain four statements, the file was pretty thick. But just like George needed her to do, Kim was going to work her magic. Her gift was nothing less than special, and George had all the confidence in the world that Kim would help his client find a way out of his situation.

"Just give me a couple of days, and I'll see what I can do," she said, turning around to her desk and getting right to work.

George hadn't told her yet, but if Kim found a way to win this case, he was going to make her a partner in the law firm right after she passed the bar exam. She had already proven case after case that she was worthy of the opportunity. He also knew that it wouldn't be much longer before somebody else discovered her potential, and he didn't want to risk losing his newfound secret weapon. He was going to make her an offer she couldn't refuse.

Falisha tossed the duffle bag of money into the backseat of the Chrysler 300 Fox had rented and waited for him to come out of the house.

Thinking about baby Jordan at the last minute, she pulled out her phone and flipped through a couple of pictures of him, remembering the main reason why she was taking this risk.

"Come on, you ready?" Fox asked, walking around to the passenger side of the car. "It's better if you drive," he told her.

The drive to Charleston, South Carolina, was going to take a few hours, which was a long time behind the wheel for Falisha. She had never driven this far in her life and was nervous as hell the moment she pulled out of the driveway.

"Listen, we got a lot of money in this car, plus I'm strapped," Fox said, pulling a 9 mm from his waist and sitting it under his leg. "So make sure you do the speed limit," he warned in advance.

The whole way there, Falisha followed his instructions to the tee. At one point, her heart almost jumped out of her chest when a state trooper got behind her. For three whole miles she was sweating bullets, waiting for the red and blue lights to start flashing. Eventually, the trooper switched lanes and got off on one of the exits.

"A'ight, now we in the city, so you can relax," Fox told her as he looked out the window at the familiar streets. "Make a left right here," he instructed while reaching into the backseat and grabbing the money.

He looked inside before zipping the bag back up, then he popped his clip out to make sure he was fully loaded. When he saw that he was heavy, Fox slammed the clip back in and cocked a bullet into the chamber.

Falisha looked over at him in concern. "Are we safe out here?" she asked, looking out of the window.

"Yeah, we good. I'm just cautious when it comes down to doing business. It's better to have one than to be without it," he said, holding the gun up.

His actions only made Falisha more nervous. She had knowledge of the drug game, but this was the deepest she'd ever been in. Her nervousness quickly turned into all-out fear. But as Fox got out of the car, she knew that it was way too late to turn around.

"Stay right here. I'll be right back," he said before slamming the door behind him.

R&B blasted through the speakers as Lisa walked around the house doing her spring cleaning. Every time she walked past the mirror in the dining room, she looked into it and smiled, thinking about how Nate always complimented her. It made her feel a lot better about herself,

knowing that she still had her good looks after
all the hell she'd been through in her life. Even
on rough days like today, when her hair was
everywhere and her house clothes made her look
homeless, she still had a lot of sex appeal.

"Is it safe to come down?" Nate yelled from
upstairs in a joking manner.

"Boy, shut up and come down here," Lisa
yelled back to him.

She had already taken Naomi to school earlier,
so it was cool for Nate to come out of hiding
in Lisa's room. "Well, I gotta get ready to go to
work," he said, walking up behind her while she
wiped down the dining-room table.

He wrapped his arms around her waist and
put his chin on her shoulder, looking at their
reflection in the mirror.

"Are you okay?" he asked.

"Yeah, I'm good, and I'm sorry about this
morning. I didn't want—"

"You don't have to explain. I totally understand," Nate said, cutting Lisa off before she
could justify her actions.

When Naomi got up that morning, she nearly
walked into Lisa's room while she and Nate were
lying in bed naked. Lisa had jumped up and
darted to her door, pushing Naomi back into the

hallway before she could see Nate. It was sort of
an awkward moment for Lisa, but for Nate, it
was well justified.

"We gon' continue to take it slow and be careful until the time is right," he said, kissing her on
the back of her neck.

Lisa smiled and placed her hands over the
top of his while they were still around her waist.
They looked at each other in the mirror.

"We do look good together." Nate smiled, then
kissed Lisa on the neck again.

As bad as she didn't want to admit it, they did
make a cute couple. In moments like this, she
knew Nate was breaking down another portion
of her guard. If he kept it up, there wasn't going
to be anything left to protect her heart with.

"A'ight, now, same rules as before," Fox reminded Falisha after she pulled onto the highway.

The transaction had been a success, and now
all Fox had to do was get the six bricks of cocaine
back home so he could break them down, cut
them, and repackage them for sale. Some of it
was going to be cooked into crack and sold on a
couple of Fox's old corners. Falisha had to be real
with herself; this was the Fox that she had grown
to love. This man was all about his money, and

when he was knee-deep in the streets, everybody had respect for him and everybody ate. She couldn't help but cut her eyes over at him while he was on the phone.

"Yeah, what up, brah?" he greeted one of his boys. "Yeah, ya boy back on deck. I'll shoot through there a li'l later to let you know what's good," he said before hanging up the phone.

Without hesitation, Fox jumped right back on his cell phone. This time he dialed Chris's number.

Falisha paid attention to the road, but she was also listening to the conversation.

"Yo, Cees, wassup, li'l nigga?" he spoke. Chris was on speakerphone, and that's how Fox wanted it to be so Falisha could hear clearly. "I got ya mafuckin' money, homeboy. And make sure that's the last time you roll up on me like you ain't got no sense. Show a fuckin' G some respect next time," Fox based.

Chris didn't feel like getting into an argument with Fox, plus, he knew that Fox was probably fronting for somebody that he was around. So he let him get it off, just as long as he had that bread right.

"A'ight, OG, hit me up when you get down the way," Chris said and hung up the phone.

Falisha smiled, seeing Fox get back on some gangsta shit. However, her smile quickly turned into a frown when she looked into her rearview mirror and saw a state trooper pull onto the highway. She looked at her speedometer to see how fast she was going; then she turned on her signals to change lanes.

"State troopers just got onto the highway," she advised Fox. "What do you want me to do?"

"You good, just keep driving," he answered.

Silence took over the car, and as the trooper closed the gap between them, Falisha got even more nervous. It wasn't until the state trooper got directly behind them that Fox got nervous himself. What made the situation even worse was that it was a K-9 unit.

"Take the next exit, and make sure you use ya signals," Fox instructed.

Before Falisha could follow what he said, the red and blue lights began flashing behind her. "Aww, shit," Falisha screamed, now more scared than ever. The cocaine was sitting right on the backseat. She was starting to freak out.

"A'ight, calm down and be cool," Fox told her, easing the gun from his waist and putting it into the glove compartment.

Fox knew they didn't stand a chance with the K-9 unit. The cold jail cell he knew all too well flashed in his mind. At that point, he knew he couldn't go back to jail. As soon as Falisha brought the car to a complete stop, Fox jumped out and took off through the woods. Falisha's jaw dropped, seeing the way he disappeared into the woods in less than ten seconds. The K-9 dog was barking like hell, so the state trooper made the decision to stay with the car instead of following Fox into the woods.

"Get ya fuckin' hands up," the trooper yelled as he walked up to the car with his gun pointed at Falisha.

Scared to death, she followed every command the officer gave her, and within moments, she was taken into custody. The dog didn't even have to be brought out, because the drugs were in plain view on the backseat. The gun was also quickly recovered. Once backup came, they searched the immediate area where Fox had run off to, but he was nowhere to be found, nor did the dog pick up any scent.

It only took Kim a couple of hours of reading to come up with three issues that could warrant the suppression of several key pieces of evidence in the case. Two of the issues were strong, and they both had something to do with the statement of the witnesses.

"I think I can get at least two of the four statements thrown out," she said, entering her boss's office. "The third statement never identified Mr. Thompson, and as far as the fourth statement, the DA won't dare put a known drug dealer on the stand who had been previously convicted of trying to bribe a police officer," she said, placing the paperwork on his desk.

"And what about the gun?" George asked. That was his main concern.

"Well, the gun was found at the scene of the crime, with no DNA evidence on it. I can file a motion for limited instructions, so the DA won't be allowed to make a connection between our client and the gun," Kim informed him.

This was the reason she was the highest-paid paralegal on the East Coast. She didn't just put words down on a piece of paper and that was it; she also helped the lawyers make sense of it so they could argue it better, which made them better defenders.

"I'll have the final draft of the motion done by the end of the week," Kim said as she left his office.

Falisha sat on the cold steel bench waiting to be seen by the judge so she could get bail. Her charges were extensive, including possession with intent to deliver and possession of a firearm. The thing that was killing her was the amount of drugs she had been caught with. South Carolina didn't play any games when it came to drugs. If convicted, the DA wouldn't seek less than a ten-year sentence, and that was with a plea.

Jingling keys caught Falisha's attention, and when she looked up, an African American man was standing there with a suit and tie on. Without saying anything, he opened the door and stood to the side. Falisha assumed they were about to let her go, thinking that Fox may have turned himself in and took the beef. But that surely wasn't the case.

"Step this way," the man told her, pointing to a small room off to the side. "My name is Detective Carter, and I'm with the narcotics division," he said, pulling out a chair so Falisha could sit down. "You know ya boyfriend is a piece of shit, right?" he said, taking a seat in a chair right in front of her. "He's a coward, if you ask me, taking off and leaving you behind like that."

Falisha sat there listening to the detective go on and on about the charges and also explaining how much time she was facing. He even offered her full immunity if she told him where Fox was.

Falisha wasn't saying a word. If she had learned anything in the streets, it was never to be a rat, especially with somebody like Fox, who could have some of her family members found in a ditch, all shot up. Besides, Falisha already had it in her mind that if anything, Fox was going to bail her out and get her a top-notch lawyer.

"You know, after I leave this room, I'm not gonna be able to help you, right?" the detective said to the silent Falisha, who wasn't even giving him eye contact.

Seeing that she wasn't going to say anything, the detective gave up and walked out of the room, but not before saying something smart. "He should have taught you how to run."

When Fox finally emerged from the woods, he didn't have a clue where he was. It was dark, his clothes were filthy, and his shoes were still wet from running through a creek to mask his scent.

"Where da fuck?" he said, looking up and down the empty road he came upon.

Not one car was driving down this stretch of highway, and for a minute, Fox was about to go back into the woods. The atmosphere resembled the making of a horror movie, and he didn't want to play the role of a hitchhiker who jumped into the wrong car. Looking down the road as far as he could, he could see lights. Hoping that it was a store or a gas station, he began to walk toward it. It might not have been anything, but this was the only option he had.

As Fox walked on the side of the road toward the lights, he couldn't help but to think about Falisha and how fucked up it was that he had to leave her behind like that. That brief moment of guilt was quickly overcome once he came to the realization that he was free and not sitting in a jail cell waiting to be processed.

"Don't be lying here faking like you missed me," Brian joked, looking down at Kim.

She rolled over and straddled him, then reached up and put her long straight weave in a ponytail. "I did miss you a li'l bit," she smiled and leaned over to kiss him.

Brian slid his hands down the center of her back and palmed both of her ass cheeks when he reached them. His muscular touch always did something to her, and before she knew it, her pussy was wet again.

"Don't start nothing you can't finish," Kim said, sitting upright.

Her breasts sat up firm and she looked sexy as hell sitting on top of him. Brian reached up and began to caress both of her breasts, flickering his thumbs lightly across her nipples. Kim bit down on her bottom lip, looking down at Brian with lust-filled eyes. She could feel his erection rising, and once it was at attention, Kim rose up a little, grabbed the base of his dick, and sat down on it.

"Mmmmm," she hummed as his dick pushed through her canal. "Damn boy," she said.

"Shut up and take all of this dick," Brian spoke, grabbing her by the waist and pushing her down farther on his dick. "Dis what you wanted, right? Get it, then."

Kim loved when Brian talked dirty to her, especially when he encouraged her.

"Yeah, let me see you bounce up and down on dis dick like a big girl. Are you a big girl?"

Kim nodded, then braced herself on Brian's stomach. She began bouncing her ass up and down on his dick while looking down at him.

"Yeah, that's right. Damn, I missed this pussy. Come on, give it to me, Kim."

Watching her do her thing on top of him made Brian want to come. He didn't want to, not this early anyway, but if she bounced up and down any further, that's exactly what he was going to do.

"Hold on, baby, let's switch positions," he told her.

Kim wasn't having it. She was already at the point of no return with the first orgasm of this session. She kept bouncing and bouncing away. Her breasts flopped back and forth right in front of his face. As soon as Brian reached up and put his hands around her neck, Kim exploded all over him. Her come splashed on his dick. She wanted to collapse, but Brian sat her back upright.

"It's daddy's turn now," he said, lifting her up and switching her into the doggie-style position.

Kim hardly had time to get herself together before he slammed his dick deep inside her. Within seconds, he was pounding away like a porn star. "Don't run from me," he said as she damn near climbed up the headboard.

Brian had her waist gripped tight. "Oooooh, you killing me," she yelled, feeling another orgasm brewing. At that point, she began to throw it back at him, using the headboard to push off.

"I'm coming, baby!" she yelled.

Brian was at his peak as well. After looking down and seeing Kim's ass clap against his pelvis, he threw his head back and busted off inside her. Feeling his warm, creamy come inside of her did something for Kim as well, and she joined him with yet another orgasm. They both fell onto the bed in a spooning position. His dick was still inside of her, and until they both fell asleep, he kept it there.

After being fingerprinted, photographed, and seen by the magistrate for her bail, Falisha was sent upstairs to a pod. The first night was like hell. She could smell the strong odor of period blood the moment she walked onto the block. There was nothing but dope fiends, prostitutes, and crackheads there, and every one of them walked around like zombies.

"The phone is open," a young girl said as they stood in the line.

Falisha snapped out of her thoughts and walked up to the phone. So far, no one she'd attempted to call was answering the phone. Lisa was off playing house, Kim wasn't even in the city, Tammy was still on her honeymoon, and Fox was nowhere to be found. The last two people she could call were Lamar and her mom, and Falisha really didn't feel like hearing either of their mouths about why she was in jail.

"Let me try this nigga one more time," Falisha mumbled to herself as she dialed Fox's house phone.

She didn't think he was going to be there, but to her surprise, he picked up the phone. The operator stated that the call was coming from the county jail, but Fox didn't respond. Falisha hung up and tried the number again, but this time, the phone just kept ringing. Frustrated and pissed off, she threw the phone against the wall a couple of times before hanging it up. She didn't pay the few females in line any mind when they complained about her almost breaking the only phone they had on the pod.

One female in the line felt Falisha's frustration so much that she got out of line and walked over to the table where Falisha was sitting by herself.

"You mind if I sit here?" the young girl asked, causing Falisha to look up. "My name is Tish," she greeted, holding her hand out for a shake.

Falisha wasn't in the mood to make friends, but at the same time, she didn't want to be rude or disrespectful.

"I'm Falisha," she said, shaking Tish's hand.

Outside of Falisha, Tish was the only other young and attractive person in the place. She was a short, skinny, white girl who had the slang and attitude of a black girl.

"I would cut his balls off when I got home if I was you," she said, referring to Fox.

Falisha had no idea what she was talking about, and the confused expression on her face said as much.

"Oh, ya case was on the news this morning. The cops said that was your boyfriend that took off into the woods," Tish told her. "How much did they set ya bond for?"

"Two hundred and fifty K," Falisha said, still in shock.

In South Carolina, you could pay a bail bondsman ten percent to get you out. Unfortunately, you didn't get any of that money back. Some people even put up property to get out of jail. Falisha didn't know where she was going to get her money from if Fox didn't pay her bail. The last person she was going to ask to put up her house was her mom.

The situation was ugly, and with every minute that Falisha remained in jail, she hated Fox more.

"So, I gotta do a lot of running around tomorrow," Nate said as he walked Lisa out of his apartment complex. "I was wondering if we could have lunch at Max's."

Lisa smiled. "Max's sounds good. I have a job interview at ten o'clock, so I should be out of there by eleven or eleven-thirty. I'll just meet you there," she said, stopping at her car.

When she went to open the door, Nate stopped her. "This ain't ya car anymore," he told her as he grabbed her hand. He spun her around and wrapped his arms around her. "That's your car right there," he said, pointing to an all-white Nissan Altima.

Lisa turned around to look at Nate. "You liar," she said, playfully punching his chest.

Nate wasn't lying at all. He dug into his pocket and grabbed the key. The Altima's alarm beeped when he pushed the button. Ever since the shooting at the dental office, Lisa hadn't been to work, nor had any job, for that matter. With limited funds coming in, she was forced to downgrade her car to a 2001 Grand Prix, which had more than enough mechanical problems for her to handle.

"Damn, Nate, I don't know what to say," she said, looking at the new car.

"You don't have to say anything." He smiled and pulled her close to him. "I just want you to be happy."

Every time Lisa thought that Nate was out of surprises, he came up with another one. If she didn't know any better, she would've thought that Nate was in love with her. She wasn't sure if that was the case, and if it wasn't, she could only imagine how it would be if he did fall in love with her. *Maybe it might not be too bad if that was to happen,* she thought.

Brian lay in bed asleep while Kim sat up on her laptop going over case law so she could start preparing the motion for George. Her phone vibrating on the table motivated her to answer it before it woke him. She couldn't identify the number, but she knew that it was coming from Charlotte. She got up and walked into the other room.

"Hello," she answered, walking over to the window.

"Damn, you just up and leave without saying anything?" Lamar said as he changed baby Jordan.

"I'm sorry," Kim apologized, feeling a little guilty. "I had to come back—"

"You don't have to explain. Just let me know when you're heading back this way. I'm missing you already."

"I'm not sure when I'll be back. I got a court hearing in a couple of days, not to mention I got to get ready for the bar exam."

There was a moment of silence before Lamar started talking again.

"So, I guess this is it for us then," he said, picking up the phone from the bed so he could speak and hear clearly.

"Why would you even say something like that?" she spoke, peeking back into the room to check on Brian. "Now granted, I did leave without telling you, but that doesn't mean that me and you are over."

Kim really didn't sound too convincing, but Lamar didn't want to make a big deal out of it or start any unnecessary arguments. Her actions would soon speak louder than words, and as of right now, that's all Lamar really had to look forward to.

"Whatever the case is, Kim, I want you to know that I will always love you."

Kim could hear the defeat in his voice, and it pained her that she might be hurting him.

"How about you come stay with me for a couple of weeks?" she offered. Immediately, her hand flew to her mouth as if she'd spoken too soon.

The offer actually reassured Lamar that everything was going to be all right. It brought comfort to his feelings, but at the same time, he wasn't really up for the traveling.

"I'm good without the big-city life. You ain't gon' have me rollin' around that crazy-ass place. You know my country ass gon' stick out. I'ma be patient and just wait for you to come back home. I think I can hold out for another couple of weeks," he said.

Kim silently fist pumped, happy he didn't take her up on the offer. As nice as it would have been, she didn't want to risk having Brian and Lamar clash. One thing she knew for sure was that no matter where Lamar was, he would always act like a good ole country boy, ready and willing to get down and dirty with anybody, win, lose, or draw. Kim was also aware that she was in a city where murder stayed on the menu, and although Brian came off as the good guy most of the time, she knew that he was about that murder life for real.

Chapter 15

It had been two days since Falisha's arrest, and today, she finally got in touch with Lisa to let her know what was going on. As expected, her mom was pissed but also very concerned. Surprisingly, Lamar didn't say too much. He wanted to scream "I told you so," but he knew now wasn't the time for it. The main issue was that no one had that kind of money to pay the bail bond so she could get out. Although Lamar was a homeowner and could put up his home, there was no way he would get involved with anything that had Fox and his illegal shit tied to it.

Falisha was up shit's creek without a paddle, and it would be another week or so before she could go before a judge and try to get the bail reduced.

"Don't worry about it," Tish said, patting Falisha's back. "You need to take this as one big learning experience. The good thing is, you're not facing that much time because it's ya first offense."

Falisha looked over at Tish like she was crazy. Just the thought of doing time crushed her. "I can't do no time. I got a son and a mother to go home to. They need me out there," Falisha said with a worried look.

She didn't realize it until she came to jail, but prison was now her worst fear. Now she wished she would have ratted Fox out, so she could have been the one at home.

A knock on the cell door caught both of their attention. A female CO came to the door and told Falisha that the police were calling her name. She and Tish walked out to the officer station where Falisha gave the guard her name and ID number.

"They want you down in R&D," the guard said, giving Falisha a pass.

"R&D? Shit, girl, you done made bond," Tish said, giving Falisha a hug.

Relief washed over Falisha. She was so happy that she refused to go back to her cell and get her things. "I'm ready right now," she said, standing by the door and waiting for the escort to come and get her.

***

"You better not answer that phone," Tammy yelled from the shallow water.

Darious had been lying in a beach chair, watching his new wife strut around the shoreline in her bikini.

"It might be important," he yelled back, looking at the screen. "Yo, what up, cuz?" he answered. "You gon' get me killed."

"Boy, shut up, and why you ain't been answering your phone? I know you on ya li'l honeymoon," Terry, Darious's first cousin, said. "And I'm not tryin' to bust ya little bubble, but a word to the wise; you need to keep ya eyes on that new wife of yours."

"Why you say that, cuzzo?"

"First, I saw her baby daddy at the church—"

"And what that mean, Terry?"

"Damn, if you let a bitch finish, I can tell you what it mean . . . Then I seen his ass snoopin' around the dressing room before the wedding started. You know you my cuz, so I'ma keep it real—"

"Wait, wait, wait. What do you mean you saw him around the dressing room?"

Terry was family, but she was also a gossip queen and knew all the family secrets. She wasn't afraid to expose them either. Darious was used to her trying to tell some shit and knew she always made it more than it really was. But he had also questioned why Chris was there, and the old saying, "where there's smoke, there's fire," rang out in his head.

"Yeah, nigga, you heard me right. I saw the nigga Chris going up to ya wife's dressing room. I don't know what the business was, but all I'm telling you is to keep ya eyes on her. Oh, and you better had signed a prenuptial, even though you ain't got shit."

Upon hearing that, Darious hung up the phone, laughing at how funny his cousin was after all these years. Though his cousin was pretty funny, he started thinking about the last thing she said pertaining to a prenup. They didn't have one, so at this point they pretty much shared everything. Tammy did have a slight advantage if things were to go south.

"Are you going to get in the water?" Tammy yelled, breaking his thoughts.

He stared at her, trying to size her up. She never seemed like she was in it for the money, and for the most part, Darious could feel the love. But at the same time, there were moments when he felt like he didn't have 100 percent of her. He always knew she had some love for Chris, but to what extent, he wasn't completely sure. Terry calling him with the bullshit wasn't helping out any, and though he put a lot of trust in Tammy and loved her dearly, he was going to take his cousin's advice and keep a close eye on her and her kids' father.

On her way down to R&D, Falisha prayed that God gave her enough strength not to kick Fox's ass if he was outside waiting. She knew that he would come through with the bail money, but she hated the fact that she had to sit in jail for the past couple of days, living in the worst conditions ever. He would definitely have to pay her more than ten thousand for all that she'd been through.

"Sign right here and right here," the guard said, passing Falisha the pen. "You can get dressed in that room over there, and when you're done, the bondsman and ya cosigner are on the other side of the door."

Falisha went in the room and got dressed. She'd had more than enough jail experience, and wanted to go home and lie down in her own bed.

When she finally got dressed and walked through the double doors, she was taken aback by who was there to bail her out. She looked around to see if anybody else was with him, but there wasn't anyone. It was only Chris, and, of course, the bondsman.

"You can't be serious," Falisha said, walking over to them.

"That's a hell of a way to say thank you to the person that just bailed yo' ass out of jail," Chris said, giving her a hug.

She never expected this in a million years, and knowing Chris as well as she did, Falisha knew that there was a catch to it.

"A'ight, Falisha, make sure you make every court date, or I will send the bounty hunters after yo' ass," the bondsman threatened while Falisha signed the form. When she was done, he informed her that she was free to go.

It was quiet for the first ten to fifteen minutes of the ride home. Chris wasn't saying too much of anything, but Falisha was sitting there smiling from ear to ear about her freedom.

"What you sitting over there smiling for? You just set me back twenty-five stacks," Chris said.

"Yeah, and about that, I hope you don't think you getting some pussy for this," she said.

"First off, I bailed yo' ass out because nobody else seemed to give a fuck. And despite what you think, I still consider you to be my friend. We practically grew up on the same block. If I learned one thing, it was never to leave a friend behind," he said looking over at her.

She respected that, coming from him.

"Oh, and for the record, I'll never pay that much for a piece of pussy," he chuckled.

Yeah, that's 'cause you never had none of this pussy, Falisha thought to herself.

"Well, thank you for coming to get me," she said in a sincere tone.

"Yeah, well, from here on out, you rollin' wit' the money team," he said, reaching in his center console and grabbing one of the flyers the printing company had sent to him.

"MBM Publishing, the best urban authors in the game," Falisha mumbled to herself as she read the flyer.

"It's about time somebody made good use out of that cute face and sexy body. I want you to run with the money team. You're loyal, dependable, and you go hard. I'm not gonna lie to you or sell you no dreams, but I'm about to do something real big, and I want you to be a part of it."

Falisha sat there looking down at the flyer, thinking about what Chris had said. She appreciated him more than he knew. If it wasn't for him, she'd be sitting in the cell sharing commissary with Tish right now. For that reason alone, whatever Chris had planned for the future, Falisha felt that she at least owed it to him to give it a shot.

"Show me what MBM is all about," Falisha said and sank back in her seat.

Chris had her undivided attention.

Kim had been working round the clock, trying to put together the motion that was sure to get their client off on the double homicide charge. This case was very high profile in the city of Philadelphia. If they were successful in defending their client, it would give Tim and George a lot of exposure, which meant more business. That's just how it was in the city. Criminals from all over were going to hear about the case, and they would all want to be represented by the firm.

"Hey, George, I like the Eagles on Sunday," Kim heard Brian shout.

She poked her head out of the cubicle to see him walking in the office like he owned the place. His friendship with George afforded Brian the opportunity to come and go as he pleased.

Brian had beat a homicide case, several drug-trafficking charges, and a slew of other arrests, all by the time he turned twenty-one. Though it was nearly eight years later, and Brian hadn't been so much as arrested, he stopped by the offices routinely to drop off money, just to have George on deck in case something went down.

"What are you doing here?" Kim asked when Brian walked up and kissed her on the cheek. "You gon' get me in trouble."

Brian grabbed the bobble head doll off her desk and stood it up against the partition. He had a young boyish smile on his face. "You wouldn't believe me if I told you."

"Well, try me, and make it fast because you only got a couple of seconds before George come in here and chew both of our asses out," Kim said.

"I really did miss you while you was gone. I had a lot of time to think, and I came to the conclusion . . ."

He hesitated for a second, not sure if now was a good time to tell Kim how he really felt about her.

"Kim, I'm in love wit' you," he said, looking deep into her eyes.

Kim found it hard to swallow her own spit hearing those words coming from him.

"When you left, it was like my life went on hold. I couldn't focus on anything for more than ten seconds without thinking about you," Brian said in truth.

Kim couldn't stop blushing. As flattering as it was to be loved by someone, she couldn't honestly say that she felt the same way about him. For several months straight, they had been together day after day; whether it was just hanging out or having casual sex, Kim was with him. In fact, Brian was the only man she'd been with since she'd been in Philly. To say that she didn't have strong feelings for him would be a lie. But the question at hand was whether she loved him. Kim wasn't going to say it back to him unless she meant it.

"Brian, I missed you a lot too, and I do—"

"OK, break all this shit up," George said as he came into the room. "Let's go, get back to work." He pointed at Kim, then threw his arm around Brian's shoulder. "Time is money, son," he joked, then led Brian out the door.

Kim took a deep breath. It was like being saved by the bell. She honestly didn't know what she was about to say, But now she was afforded a little more time to think this thing through. And that was exactly what she needed to do.

Chris reached over and tapped Falisha, waking her up to let her know that they were back in the city. The four-hour ride had Chris tired too.

All he could think about was taking a shower, then hitting the sack.

"So where do you want me to drop you off at, ya nut-ass boyfriend's house?" Chris asked, looking out into the road.

All Falisha wanted to do was see her son, but she knew that going over to Lamar's house right now would only cause an argument. Seeing baby Jordan in the morning was a better idea.

"So?" Chris said, seeing the blank look on her face.

Going to Fox's house was out of the question, and Falisha didn't feel like hearing her mother's mouth either. Right now, she just wanted some peace and quiet, and a soft bed to lie on.

"You might have to clean out ya guest room today," she said, looking over at Chris.

Lucky for her, Chris had just moved into a two-bedroom apartment, and had a bed in one of the rooms for Outlaw, whenever he stayed over. Normally, any chick that spent the night at his house would be sleeping with him. But this time, it was a little different. Although Chris had messed up intentions in the beginning of wanting to fuck Falisha to get back at Tammy, now she was only a friend who was in need. At least, that's what Chris had to convince himself of.

***

Lisa sat in the waiting area of a well-known dental office in Durham, going over her résumé before her scheduled interview. Today was a big day for her, since it was her first attempt at getting another job since she'd been shot. This was part of the healing process in the loss of Ralphy.

"Hi, Lisa," the short, thin, white dentist said when she walked out. "I'm Doctor Foster, nice to meet you. Come on back this way," she said after shaking Lisa's hand.

The woman introduced herself as the head dentist of the practice, and from looking around the room at all the plaques and awards, Lisa could see that she was, in fact, the boss. To see a woman in charge was a different twist. It was something that she wasn't used to seeing in this line of business.

"Well, looking over your résumé, you fit all of the qualifications, but I also see that you haven't been employed for the past year. Is there a reason?" Doctor Foster asked.

Lisa didn't know how one question could bring back so many memories of the accident that took place at the dental office, as well as what happened to Ralphy. She sat there in a trance replaying parts of those tragic events in her mind. Doctor Foster's voice is what brought Lisa back down to earth.

"Lisa, are you okay?" the doctor asked.

"Oh yes, I'm sorry. I was out due to the death of my husband," Lisa explained.

"Oh God. I'm sorry for your loss," the doctor sympathized.

Lisa didn't want to go into the whole incident that happened at her job for fear that it might scare the woman away. Sharing Ralphy's death was enough, and it was more than moving for Doctor Foster. She could relate to Lisa in more ways than one, having also lost her husband several years ago. Understanding and wanting to help Lisa's life get back on track, she felt that offering her the job was the right thing to do.

Chapter 16

Falisha caught a cab to Fox's house, but made sure she told the cabdriver to keep the meter running. She had no intention of staying; all she wanted to do was run in and grab some clothes and personal papers, like her and Jordan's birth certificates and Social Security cards. Falisha also wanted to get the few thousand dollars she had stashed in the kitchen.

"I know this fuck nigga ain't changed these damn locks," she yelled when her keys wouldn't fit in the door.

She soon realized that Fox had changed the locks, and it made her even more pissed, something she thought was impossible. Falisha began kicking the door and ringing the doorbell at the same time. She knew that Fox was inside, because both of his cars were sitting in the driveway.

"Fox!" she yelled loud enough for the neighbors to hear. "Fox!" she yelled again.

A few seconds later, he came to the door with his robe on. "Move outta the fucking way," she screamed, pushing past him and entering the house.

"Baby, when did you get out? I was working on coming to get you tomorrow," he lied, following her up the stairs. He definitely wasn't expecting her to come home today or any day soon.

Falisha wasn't trying to entertain his bullshit and only answered the question out of spite.

"I got out yesterday, nigga . . . Oh, and you might wanna add another twenty-five K to what you already owe Chris," she said, opening the bedroom door.

Falisha immediately noticed the female lying in Fox's bed. She turned around and looked at Fox with a scowl; he was so close that they were almost kissing.

Fox was about to grab her arms to keep her from swinging on him, but surprisingly, Falisha showed no signs of wanting to get into a physical brawl with him. In fact, she didn't even look upset.

"She ain't nobody—" Fox tried to explain, but was quickly cut off.

"You know, the sad thing is, I expected this type of shit from a fuck nigga like you. You're just being the dog I know you to be. But I swear,

I never thought you would just bail on me the way that you did. Your trifling ass didn't even have the nerve to come back for me. You left me for dead," Falisha spoke while looking in his eyes.

The young female who was in the bed got up and went to grab her clothes off the floor.

"Baby, I was about to come and pay ya bail tomorrow," he lied, reaching out to grab Falisha's hand.

"Don't fuckin' touch me," she said, smacking his hand down, and then turning and walking toward her dresser.

The young girl was scared to death. Not knowing what Falisha was going to do, she just continued to put her clothes on.

"I'm sorry," she said when Falisha got close to her. "He didn't tell me that he—"

"Girl, I'm not worried about you," Falisha uttered.

Putting her hands on that girl was the last thing on her mind. Falisha just wanted to get all of her shit and get out of there, which she did. She went to the kitchen as well, and got her money from the freezer.

Fox stood in the living room looking stupid, watching her walk out the door.

"Oh, and for the record, it's over, nigga," she told Fox as she walked out and headed to the cab.

Fox couldn't argue with her or justify his actions, and being honest with himself, the only thing he was really concerned about was whether she'd implicated him in the case. If she did, it wouldn't be much longer before the police came knocking on his door, and that's what he feared most.

"I found a job," Lisa said as she got dressed.

Nate sat up in bed so he could hear more about it. Another one of his good qualities was the fact that he was so understanding and supportive in just about everything Lisa did.

"Damn, babe, that's great," he said, scooting up to the edge of the bed where she was.

He grabbed her by the waist from behind, then lifted her shirt up to plant little kisses on her lower back. Lisa was tempted to jump back in bed and get another dose of the good good, but Naomi was about to get out of school, and she didn't want to be late picking her up.

"So, are you ready for our little getaway?" he asked, spinning her around. "Our flight leaves at eight forty-five in the morning," he reminded her.

"Yeah, I'm ready, but I start work on Monday morning, so we gotta come back on Saturday instead of Sunday. I don't want to be tired or late on my first day of work," she said.

Nate looked at her and smiled. He kissed her belly button, then a little bit below it until Lisa grabbed his head and stopped him.

"That's not gonna be a problem at all," he looked up and assured her.

What he had planned for the vacation wasn't going to be affected by shortening it one day.

"I gotta go pick up Naomi," Lisa said, leaning over and giving him a kiss before she left.

As Lisa was sitting in the car, she couldn't help but to feel a little scared. It had been awhile since she was this close to anyone. Nate was beginning to invade her thoughts more than usual. Just the other day, she was talking to Tammy and referred to him as her boyfriend. It was crazy, and although Lisa thought that she was in control, her heart was constantly reminding her that it ran the show. She honestly didn't know where and how this was going to end.

Kim had called Brian over so they could talk. She had a lot on her mind ever since he'd professed his love to her. There were a number of questions that needed to be answered. Some more important than others.

"Where are you?" Kim mumbled to herself, looking down at the clock on her phone.

Seeing that it was rush hour, she assumed it was the cause of his delay. She started to call and see where he was, but before she could pick up the phone, Brian was calling her.

"Yeah, where are you?" she answered, walking over to the window.

"I'm downstairs. It's nice out here, and I thought that we could go for a walk and talk," Brian said as people walked by him to get into the complex.

Kim didn't feel like walking, but she didn't want to be a party pooper.

"Hold on, I'll be right down," she said, walking into her bedroom to put on a pair of sneakers.

"I know you ain't afraid to burn a few calories," Brian joked when she finally came outside.

Kim had to admit, the weather was nice.

"When I was a young boy, I used to come down here to go to the arcade," Brian began as they walked down Chestnut Street. "I remember my mom beat me and my brother's ass when we took like twenty dollars in change from her coin jar. We came down here and spent every dime of it." He chuckled at the thought.

Kim even smiled, picturing him as a kid.

"Can I ask you something?" she said, wanting to get some clarity about what was going on between them.

Brian was one step ahead of her. "You wanna know why I told you that I love you the other day, right?" he asked.

Kim looked over at him and nodded yes.

"Look, we've been seeing each other for how long now? Maybe six or seven months? Probably a little longer if you count those many late-night conversations we used to have when I first met you."

"Yeah, and I specifically remember you telling me that you wasn't looking for anything serious," Kim shot back sarcastically.

"Yeah, but a lot can happen in six months. I told you that I love you, because I do," he said, looking over at her. "You're a hell of a woman, and over the course of time, I've watched you grow as a person. I've never been with someone like you who had their shit together. You have a career that you love, you got ya own money, and you're gorgeous beyond words. How am I not going to fall in love with somebody like you?"

Kim and Brian turned into Rittenhouse Park, two blocks from Kim's apartment. It may have sounded like game, but everything Brian said was the truth. It had Kim blushing.

"But how do you know it's love that you have for me?" she asked.

"Kim, I'm a grown-ass man. You don't think I know what love is?" he playfully shot back.

Kim laughed at him.

"I guess you wanna hear how I think about you until I go to bed at night. Or maybe you wanna hear how sick I was when you went back to Charlotte, and I had nobody to hold on to at night. Maybe you wanna hear how tears came to my eyes at the thought of losing you. If I could spend the rest of my life with someone, it would be you. I swear to God," Brian said, raising his right hand.

Kim knew exactly how he felt because she felt the same . . . for the most part. Brian was a nice guy, and she could honestly say that no man had treated her as well as he had, nor was she as comfortable with anyone as she was with him. Lamar had potential, but he wasn't consistent, and he had already broken her heart once. Over time, her heart had naturally become attached to Brian, and when she went back to Charlotte, she was missing him too.

"Let me ask you something," Brian said, taking a seat next to Kim on the bench. "Can you honestly say that you don't have any love for me?" he sincerely asked.

Kim had been thinking about this all afternoon and going back and forth with herself about it. The conclusion wasn't what she expected it to be, especially after Lamar's proposition back in Charlotte. But she had to be honest with herself, and now it was time for her to keep it real with Brian as well.

"I do love you, Brian. I think I've felt it for a while now," she said leaning her head on his shoulder. "I just don't want to get hurt."

For Brian, nothing else needed to be said. He didn't intend to break her heart or hurt her in any way. He had Kim now, and he was going to make sure he did everything in his power to keep her.

Ran into you yesterday, memories rushed through my brain. It's starting to hit me now you're not with me. I realize I made a mistake. . . .

Lamar lay on the couch listening to John Legend do his thing. His thoughts of Kim were interrupted by the sound of the doorbell. He jumped up from the couch, hoping to catch whoever had rung the bell before they could ring it again. Baby Jordan had just gone to sleep, and Lamar was hoping he could enjoy some quiet time.

When he opened the door and saw Falisha standing there, he knew that was out of the question. "When did they let you out?" he asked, stepping to the side to let her in.

Falisha was getting tired of people asking her that, especially knowing that they didn't really care about her well-being. "I just stopped by to see Jordan," she said, looking around the living room.

"He's upstairs asleep," Lamar told her.

Falisha put down her bag and headed up the stairs. Baby Jordan was fast asleep in his playpen in Lamar's room. He looked so peaceful, she didn't want to wake him like she had first started to. Instead, she simply sat on the edge of Lamar's bed and watched her son sleep. She missed her little man and had thought about him every second that she was in jail.

Lamar made his way upstairs and stood by the bedroom door, watching Falisha.

"When he gets fussy, I show him a picture of you, and he stops crying," Lamar said.

It made Falisha smile to think about him trying to eat the picture.

"I know you might not wanna hear this, but you gotta make better choices in ya life. You're no good to our son if you're stuck in jail or dead in a ditch. He needs you more than anybody in this world, including me," Lamar spoke genuinely.

Those couple of days in jail had given Falisha plenty of time to think about what Lamar was talking about. She even thought about how nasty she had been to him over the past few months.

"I'm sorry I was acting like a bitch. I know by now you probably hate me, and I need you to know that I never once regretted having your son. He means everything to me," she said, looking down on baby Jordan.

Tears sprang to her eyes at the thought of being taken away from him, or not being able to be there for him when he needed her.

"It's okay if you wanna take him for a while. Just call me when you wanna bring him back."

"I'm not gonna take him right now. In fact, I need him to stay here with you until I find my own place. I'll come by and see him every day, and if you need me to watch him while you go to work, I can do that for you also," she said as she continued looking down at her son.

Lamar could see that being in jail for those couple of days had really humbled Falisha. She wasn't loud and obnoxious like she used to be, and for the first time in a long time, he saw submission in her eyes. He didn't know how long it would last, but he sure hoped that she would stay like this. It was a good look on her, and Lamar could see himself getting to like this side of her again.

Chapter 17

Lisa, Nate, and Naomi landed in Orlando, Florida, and were at Disney's Grand Floridian Resort and Spa by noon. After checking into the hotel, they wasted no time hopping on the monorail and heading to The Magic Kingdom. Naomi had a field day running into all of her favorite characters and took picture after picture with each princess she encountered.

"A'ight, so according to this map, Crystal Palace should be right up ahead on the left," Nate said, lifting his head up to see where they were.

He looked over and saw that Lisa was zoned out in another world as they walked along. "Are you okay?" he asked as he folded the map.

Lisa couldn't believe how much she had been thinking about Ralphy. This family vacation wasn't making it any better, especially since Disney World was one of the places Ralphy had wanted to take her when he was alive. She wasn't sure why she was feeling guilty about being there with Nate. No matter how much she wanted to move on, her heart maintained that this family belonged to Ralphy.

"I really gotta use the bathroom," she said, scrunching up her nose into the poo-poo face.

Nate found it a little funny that she had to take a dump while they were in the middle of the park.

"I'ma run back to the room real quick. I'll meet y'all at the restaurant," she said, digging into her bag for the room key.

She didn't really have to use the bathroom. Lisa just needed a moment to get herself together so she wouldn't break down in front of Nate. She didn't want to be the one who messed up a perfect day with all her feelings and emotions. Taking a few minutes for herself was the best thing to do in this situation, or this vacation could easily turn into a disaster, which was something she did not want.

Falisha walked up to Chris's bedroom door and knocked. She knew he was in there but didn't know if he had company. Since he let her stay there until she got her own place, a set of rules and boundaries had been put into place.

"Wassup?" Chris greeted when he opened the door. He had just woken up, so he still had cold in his eyes and drool in the corner of his mouth.

"Boy, get ya'self together," she said, peeking in to make sure he didn't have anyone in there with him.

Falisha couldn't help but notice how tatted up Chris was. All he had on was a pair of gym shorts, so she could see every tattoo on his ripped body.

"Here," Falisha said, coming out of her pocket with a wad of money. "It's not twenty-five K, but I promise you that I will get the rest of it to you as soon as I can."

Chris turned around without taking the money. "Don't nobody need no money, Falisha," he said, crawling back into his bed. "I bailed you out because I fuck wit' you like that."

Falisha walked over and took a seat on the side of his bed, while placing the money back in her pocket. Not too many men did things for her without wanting something in return. Not once had Chris made any sexual advances toward her or indicated that he wanted something in return for the good deed of getting her out of jail.

"I know I said this before, but I'ma say it again. Thank you, Chris, for coming to get me out of jail."

"That shit was nothing. Just be careful of the type of nigga you associate yourself with. Never let a nigga talk you into doing something that you know in ya heart is wrong. You got people out here that need you, and believe me, you're no good to them sitting in a fucking jail cell."

Falisha took it all in, agreeing with every word he spoke. It had really been awhile since somebody gave her some game that she could truly use. The knowledge Chris kicked was actually turning her on, and if he would have made a move, there was no way she wouldn't have given him a shot of pussy.

"Now get out of my room so I can go back to sleep," he said, playfully kicking Falisha from under the blanket.

She thought about hitting him back, but she didn't want to risk being turned on even more. Instead, she just got up and left the room with a smile on her face.

Kim and George sat in the back of the courtroom going over the motions she had put together for the Thompson case. It was an airtight win, as long as George argued all of the issues correctly. In any event, the quicker it went, the faster Kim was going to be able to get back to her vacation.

"Let me step out of here for a minute." She excused herself when she looked down at her phone and saw that Lisa was calling. "How's Disney World?" Kim asked when she stepped out into the hallway for a little privacy.

Lisa started freaking out on the phone, talking a mile a minute, to the point where Kim could hardly understand what she was saying. It had to be something pertaining to Ralphy, because that was the only name that Lisa kept repeating.

"Calm down, Lisa. Take a deep breath and just calm down," Kim instructed.

Lisa inhaled intensely a few times, then began to explain how much she missed Ralphy, and how guilty she felt being in Disney World with Nate, like they were this happy family. Kim listened, but she didn't have much time to respond because the hearing was about to start. She tried to give Lisa the best advice she could think of quickly.

"Lisa, you know Ralphy better than anybody. So ask yourself this question . . . Do you think that he would have wanted you to move on and be happy? I didn't know him as well as you did, but I think that he would approve of you and Nate doing y'all thing. I don't think he would have wanted you to be miserable for the rest of your life."

Lisa sat on the edge of the hotel bed thinking about what Kim had said. Lisa did know Ralphy better than anyone else, and it was true that he would have wanted her to move on. She just thought that it may have been a little bit too early. But this was the confirmation that she needed, and it was a blessing that Kim was there to deliver the reminder of not only how great a man Ralphy was, but also how understanding and loving he was as well. Now, she could go back to enjoying her vacation with Naomi and Nate.

Chris took a piss and a shit when he woke up, then hit the shower in order to get the day started. Today, he had a meeting with a major publishing company who wanted to publish one of the books he had sent to them awhile back. Though he was in the process of starting his own company, he was interested in seeing what they had to offer. If the money was right, he would really consider working out a deal with them.

In the middle of his thoughts, he heard the bathroom door open.

"I'm in here," he yelled.

Hearing the door close, he went back to doing his thing. But instantly he felt like someone was in the bathroom. He pulled the curtain back to see Falisha standing there. She got a good look at him from head to toe, then reached out and put her hand on his chiseled abs.

"What are you doin'?" he asked as he wrung out his washcloth.

Falisha pulled her tee shirt over her head while looking at him in a seductive manner. Her bra was next, and then her pajama pants, which she had on with no panties underneath. Her body was thick and curvy, and undeniably the sexiest body Chris had seen in a long time. He stepped to the side to allow her to get into the shower with him.

"Are you sure about this?" he asked in a low voice.

Falisha leaned in and kissed him on his chin, and then again on his bottom lip.

Chris returned her kisses, wrapping his arms around her. Passion was in the air, along with heavy breathing and lip smacking. Under the shower, Chris licked and sucked on Falisha's breasts; then he went farther down south until his mouth landed on the lips of her pussy. She raised one leg up on the edge of the tub, giving him full access to her juice box. Warm water streaming down her body, along with Chris's warm tongue, had Falisha climbing up the wall. It didn't take long before her first orgasm reached its peak. With her hand on the back of his head and the other one pinching down on her nipple, Falisha came in Chris's mouth.

"Oh, oh, oooooh," she yelled as she shivered and shook from the sensation.

Chris stood back up and grabbed her breast while sticking his tongue back into her mouth. He lifted both of her legs onto the edge of the tub and pushed her back up against the wall. Then he turned the showerhead to the side so that the only wetness he felt would come from her. He rubbed his dick up and down the center of her pussy, making a circular motion around her clit. Then Chris pushed his stiff member inside her.

Falisha moaned as he filled her canal with his pipe. She bit down on her bottom lip, while her arms draped over his shoulder. She sucked on his tongue as he stroked. He went full throttle with his strokes, making sure the head tapped against her back wall.

"Fuck me from behind," she pleaded after about ten minutes of him dicking her down.

Chris complied, and before she knew it, Falisha was in doggie-style, holding on to the back of the tub with both of her hands. Her ass was fat to death, and she had no problem throwing it back at him. The sounds of her ass clapping echoed throughout the bathroom, along with her cries for Chris to go harder. When he gave her what she asked for, it was too much, because two minutes into him beating it up, Falisha was coming again.

"Oh shit," she yelled, trying to pull away from him.

He gripped her by her waist and continued his thrashing.

"This what you want, right?" he said, deep stroking the hell out of her.

Chris could feel his nut rising, and right at the moment he was about to come, he pulled out, squeezing his dick tight, then waited for Falisha to assume the position. When she did, his dick was right in her face, and as she looked up at him, she took the length of his come-filled dick into her mouth.

He grabbed the back of her head and released his thick creamy come into the back of her throat.

Falisha sucked him off until his knees started to buckle.

He looked down at her, and the only two words that came out of his mouth were, "Damn, girl."

***

After the two o'clock court hearing, George gave Kim the rest of the day off. The judge was impressed with the motion and the way George argued it, but he wasn't going to make a decision on it until he had a chance to analyze the case a little more.

After parking her car, then walking around to the front of the building, Kim decided to call Brian to let him know how things went in court.

"I'm sure you did good. It's gonna be a couple of weeks before the judge makes his final ruling," Brian spoke into the phone.

"I know, I just wish he could do it sooner," Kim said, watching as some of the residents walked past her.

"So how much longer do I have until you go shooting back down to North Carolina?" he asked, not really wanting her to leave.

Kim wasn't even sure if she wanted to go back, at least not right now anyway. She had a lot going on as far as the case and the upcoming bar exam, which she had to study for. Traveling back and forth now would probably cause more harm than good, she told herself.

"I really don't know if I want to leave right now." Kim smiled, thinking about how she wanted to spend more time with Brian. "If I stay, will you help me study for the bar?"

Kim picked her head up and didn't even hear Brian's answer when she almost dropped the phone from her ear. The cab that had just pulled up in front of the building had her attention. As Lamar got out of the back, Kim's jaw dropped to the ground.

Brian's voice snapped Kim out of her stare.

"Baby, I'm sorry. I'm trying to do too many things at one time. Let me call you back when I get in the house," she said, watching as Lamar paid the cabdriver.

"As a matter of fact, call me tonight. I got a lot of running around to do," Brian corrected.

Kim agreed, and then quickly hung up the phone.

When she turned around, Lamar had walked up to her with a huge smile on his face. "Lamar, what are you doing here?" she asked, giving him a hug. "And where's Jordan?"

"Aww, I thought you could use some Southern hospitality. Oh, and Jordan is at his grandmom's house for the rest of the week. His mom just got out of jail, so she's gonna be spending some time with him."

"Wait—jail?" Kim asked, not aware of the drug case. "Oh shit."

"Yeah, we can talk about that a li'l later, though. Now, are you gonna invite me in, or are we gonna stand out here and mess around?" Lamar joked.

Kim wasn't sure what to do. With her and Brian just now coming around to establishing the love they had for one another, she didn't want to disrespect him by having another man in her house when he wasn't there. That could cause all kinds of problems, which could lead to somebody getting hurt, both mentally and physically.

On the other hand, Lamar wasn't just some random guy she had met in the streets. This was a man who she was once in love with, and still had a nice amount of feelings for. He was somebody who she recently had plans to run away and spend the rest of her life with. No way would she ever front on him, not now, and maybe not ever. The situation was ugly, but Kim had to do what was best for her, and right now, that was getting Lamar off the sidewalk and into her apartment.

Chris was in his room getting dressed when Falisha knocked on the door. She had just got out of the shower, and the only thing she had wrapped around her body was a towel. She looked sexy as hell standing there with her hair wet and slicked back. This was the first time Chris had seen her in this light. He didn't want to say anything, but he was really feeling it.

"So now what?" she asked, walking over to the vanity mirror by the dresser. "You know we dead wrong."

"Shit, we grown," Chris shot back, looking into the mirror to check himself out. "What do you want to happen now?" he said playfully, moving her over so he could get a better look at himself.

Falisha shrugged. She was so confused right now and didn't know if she'd just gotten caught up in the moment, or if Chris was really somebody she could kick it with on another level. She couldn't believe she was even considering the possibilities. Chris, on the other hand, didn't care how this whole situation played out.

"Tammy gon' kill both of us," Falisha said, putting her head down.

Chris got serious for a moment. "Fuck Tammy. What, did you forget that she's married? She ain't got a damn thing to say about who I mess around with. I hope you not gon' let her dictate what's going on in ya life either," he vented.

It was obvious that he was still hurt about Tammy getting married, and Falisha hoped that Chris wasn't just running game to get back at Tammy by sleeping with her. What he said

230

was one thing, but the way that he acted was something different. Chris grabbed her by the arm so that he stood behind her in the mirror. He wrapped his arms around her waist, then spoke softly.

"To be honest wit' you, I don't know where this thing is going. What I do know is that we got a hell of a chemistry, and I'm feeling you," he told her.

Falisha looked at him through the mirror with her innocent eyes. She didn't know what it was, but she too could feel the connection between them.

"And trust me, you don't have to worry about my baby mom. The things I know about her, she would never even fix her face to say anything to either one of us."

Chris was referring to the fact that he had fucked Tammy just moments before she walked down the aisle. He definitely was going to use that to his advantage, and once he gave Falisha the spill about what happened, she too was going to be immune from any negative comments Tammy might have.

Darious hadn't been back from his honeymoon for more than two hours, and he was already getting an earful from Terry and his mom about his new wife's ex being at the wedding. It was a good thing he dropped Tammy off at home before he went to his mom's house.

"I don't care how many kids they have together, there's no reason why that boy should have been at the wedding uninvited, let alone up in that girl's dressing room," his mother chastised him.

Darious sat on the couch with his head in his hand. "It's not that deep, Mom," he shot back.

Terry let him have it though. "Don't be a fool, cuzzo. I got a baby daddy, and even though we ain't together, he can double back and hit this whenever he want to," she said. "Let me give you some game about the baby daddy. In most cases, they fuck so good, that's the reason why we get pregnant in the first place. And after you have the baby, no matter if you stay together or break up, the parents always have that special bond. If the nigga played his cards right, he can get the pussy on command. Hell, I got a boyfriend, but me and my baby daddy is still fuckin'. Trust me, cuz, they still fuckin', and if they're not now, they will be eventually. Sometimes we like to dib and dab in what we know is a sure nut," Terry said with a squeaky laugh.

"You better listen to yo' cousin," his mom cut in.

Darious really didn't feel like hearing any more. What Terry had said was starting to make too much sense, which was only making him more upset. He loved Tammy and trusted her beyond words, and for her to break that trust would be a devastating blow—one that he wasn't sure he could recover from, especially if he found out that Tammy was just like the rest of the women out there who lied and cheated.

Enough was enough, and instead of listening to his family and the horrible advice they were giving, Darious was about to go home and get a full understanding about what was going on. It seemed foolish, but it was necessary.

Chapter 18

Kim hated going into the hood section of Philly, mainly because it was way too dangerous. North Philly was the worst too. Almost every corner was a drug corner, and just about every man, woman, and child had a gun. Down South, it was violent, but not nearly as violent as it was in the city.

When she pulled onto Brian's street, there were guys standing out on the corner and a heavy flow of crackhead traffic going up and down the block. Kim could have sworn she saw somebody on the roof.

"I'm about to take my ass home," she mumbled to herself, feeling very uncomfortable. When her phone began to ring in her pocket, she almost jumped out of her skin. "Where are you?" Kim spoke into the phone when she saw that it was Brian.

He laughed for a second, and then answered, "Park the car wit' ya scary ass."

"Boy, don't be laughing at me. Y'all niggas are crazy out here," Kim said as she parked her car. "Come outside."

A knock at her window startled her yet again, but this time it was Brian standing there with a smile on his face. His presence actually made her feel a little safer.

"Now what's so important that you couldn't wait until I came over later?" he asked looking up and down the street at the flow of traffic.

Kim put her head down, then leaned against the car. She didn't even know where to begin.

"Lamar flew into the city earlier today," she answered, then paused and waited for a response.

"Oh yeah? So he just poppin' up, now?" Brian asked with an attitude. "So where he at now? And please don't tell me your place."

Kim remained quiet, indicating that Lamar was, in fact, at her apartment.

"Are you serious, Kim?"

"I'm sorry. I just didn't want to leave him on the sidewalk—"

"Find that nigga a hotel, and why da fuck is he up here anyway?" Brian snapped, getting madder.

"Come on, Brian. It ain't like I didn't tell you about him. You know the situation already."

From the beginning of their relationship, Kim had told Brian about Lamar, and how complicated their relationship was. Even when she came back to Philly from her vacation, she'd told him about her run-ins with Lamar. She just failed to inform him that Lamar was still in love with her and wanted to work things out. Until now, Brian hadn't cared too much about what she was saying concerning him.

"So what is this that we got?" he asked with a confused expression. "I would like to know, so I won't play myself any further."

Kim leaned back against the car and didn't say anything at first. "I don't know," she answered, putting her head down.

Brian gritted his teeth but restrained himself from showing how angry he was. "And you say you love me, huh?"

"Brian, I do love you. I'm just confused right now. I don't know—"

Brian was done talking. He didn't have anything else to say. He looked into Kim's eyes for a brief moment, and then just walked off. Kim called out his name several times, but it fell on deaf ears as Brian walked across the street, up the steps, and into the house, slamming the door behind him.

***

The Apex bar was poppin', and some of the neighborhood's finest were there. It was turned up too because Chris had thrown a last-minute party to celebrate signing a three-book deal with Dynasty Publications for over $75,000.

The meeting had gone great, and they were feeling his manuscripts along with his ideas to sell the books. It was a no-brainer that somebody was going to pick him up, and Dynasty wanted to be the one who did it.

"Everybody, the bar is officially open," the bartender announced at Chris's request.

Yo Gotti blasted through the speakers, females were dancing in the aisles, and everyone was taking pictures on their camera phones from all angles. The nice-size bar had been easily turned into a small club, and with all the females that showed up, a bunch of niggas had followed.

"Yo, heads-up, ya boy Fox just stepped into the place," Outlaw said, seeing Fox walk through the door.

Outlaw stayed strapped, so Chris wasn't worried about Fox doing anything stupid.

"Damn, playboy, I'm hearing good things about you," Fox said when he walked up to Chris.

When Fox reached into his pocket, Outlaw instinctively reached for the gun on his hip.

"Whoa, whoa, whoa," Fox said, taking the money out and passing it to Chris. "That's half of what I owe you. Give me a couple of days to come up with the rest."

Chris was having a good night, and he didn't feel like ruining it with Fox's mess. He gave him a pass, reaching out and giving him a dap of approval. As Fox was heading for the other side of the bar, the music shut off completely. The DJ jumped on the mic when he saw who had just walked in.

"Aww, man, Falisha just stepped into the building," he announced.

Every time Falisha blessed the Apex with her presence, she shut the place down. She was the hood's supermodel, and tonight wasn't any different. She had on a white minidress, showing off her curvy body, a pair of pink Christian Louboutin heels, and in her hand was a Brahmin carry bag. Her hair was long and curly, and her accessory game along with her makeup game was on fleek. All eyes were on her, even Fox's.

"Damn, can I holla at you for a minute?" Fox asked, trying to stop her as she walked past him.

Falisha pulled away and gave Fox the ill face before walking off. Fox stood there staring at her ass as she walked away. Her body was crazy, and he couldn't help but to watch her fat ass swing side to side with every step she took. All the fellas in the place were looking to see where she was going to be sitting tonight. To Fox's surprise, she walked right up to Chris, wrapped her arms around his neck, and kissed him on the cheek.

Chris was on some playa shit too. He quickly pushed his chair back so Falisha could sit between his legs. She was all giggles and laughs as she pulled out her phone and took a selfie with him.

Fox couldn't take it, but as bad as he wanted to go over there and say something, he opted against it. Instead, he tossed back his drink and hightailed it out of there. Tonight, Chris and Falisha were making a statement. She was officially taking her place on the money team, and it was crazy because she and Chris actually looked good together.

Darious got home and could smell that Tammy had been cooking. She was nowhere in sight, but he knew that his food was either in the oven or in the microwave.

"Here we go," he mumbled to himself after finding his food in the oven. He was hungry, but had a lot on his mind also.

He placed the food back into the oven and headed upstairs to talk to Tammy about what was going on with her and her baby daddy.

When he got to the bedroom, Tammy and Sinniyyah were in bed asleep. They looked so peaceful; he didn't want to wake her, especially for something so foolish. His mom and cousin really had him on some nut stuff, and it was high time he started putting some faith in his wife, instead of listening to what people were saying about her. The bottom line was, he loved her, and as he looked down on his beautiful wife, Darious came to the conclusion that he wasn't going to ask her about the matter, not now or ever.

Brian woke up from his little catnap, and looked over at the clock to see that it was a little bit after midnight. He was ready to check up on his money, and then head back home for the night. When he opened the door, he automatically reached for his gun, seeing someone on the steps. Further examination revealed that it was Kim. She had been sitting out there for hours, waiting for him to either come out or answer his phone.

"Kim, what's going on?" Brian asked as he walked down the steps. "How long have you been out here?"

Kim shrugged. "I don't know. I been trying to call you, but you turned ya phone off."

Brian pulled out his phone to check it. The battery was dead. Looking at her face, he could tell that she had been crying. He took a seat on the edge of the step and put his arm around her.

"I'm not going home tonight," she said, blowing her nose. "The difference between the two of you is that I got love for Lamar, but I'm in love with you." Kim's voice broke as her eyes began to water again. "I don't want to lose you, Brian, and I never want you to think that my love for you is fake."

The whole time Kim had been sitting out on the steps by herself, she had time to consider all the possibilities of being with either Brian or Lamar. After careful thought, her choice was made. Brian now had her heart, despite all the time she had in with Lamar. Being honest with herself, she knew she still had love for Lamar, but it was time for a change. It was time to see what love was like with someone else. Someone who constantly made her happy. Someone she never had an argument or a fight with. Someone Kim felt safe with and could depend on when or if she ever fell. When it came down to it, that person was Brian, and Kim couldn't afford to pass that up. This was what she wanted. This was what she needed, and as soon as she got up enough courage, that was what she was going to tell Lamar.

Chapter 19

Tammy's phone vibrated on the nightstand. It was seven o'clock in the morning. Darious had already left for work, and the kids were still asleep. The phone continued buzzing, and in the nick of time, she grabbed it right before it hit the ground. Her eyes were still hazy, so she didn't bother looking at the screen.

"Hello," she answered in a groggy voice.

"Hey, bitch," Ernie yelled into the phone, apparently wide awake and bushy tailed. "You could have at least called me when you got back from ya li'l honeymoon."

"Child, please," Tammy shot back. "But wassup, tho, and why the hell is you calling my phone this early?" she asked in a humorous way.

As much as Ernie always liked to gossip, he really couldn't wait to give Tammy this bit of information. "When ya ass wake up from that beauty sleep of yours, go on Falisha's Instagram and see how ugly shit got last night. You gon' blow a fuse when you see this shit."

"What in the world is you talking about?" Tammy asked, hating when Ernie talked in riddles.

"All I'ma say is yo' baby daddy ain't shit," he said, then hung up the phone.

Tammy looked at her phone, then put it back on the nightstand, thinking that Ernie was tripping. She lay in the bed for every bit of two minutes before what he had said about Chris registered. She sat up in the bed and began to scroll. Tammy thought that she was seeing things when she saw pictures of Falisha and Chris hugged up somewhere. She put the phone down to clear the cold from her eyes, and clear as day, Falisha was sitting between Chris's legs taking a selfie. The caption below the picture had Tammy in her feelings. A new power couple, #MBM, it read.

"A new power couple?" Tammy mumbled to herself, analyzing every inch of the picture.

Another selfie of Falisha kissing Chris on the cheek read Bonnie and Clyde. That picture too was analyzed closely by Tammy.

On the first picture, he had his hand around her waist, and in the second one, he had his hands on her ass. Tammy wanted to cry. She was mad but also confused about what they were on. Both of them were way out of pocket and disrespectful beyond measure. Tammy wasn't sure how and when, but she definitely had an ass whooping on her mind, and the first person she had in her crosshairs was her supposed good friend, Falisha.

The scent of sausage and eggs awakened Kim. She looked around, confused about where she was. A king-size bed with a mahogany head-board and trimming, along with mahogany dresser drawers to match came into view. On the wall right in front of her rested a 60-inch flat screen, and off to the side of the room was a glass door that led to a small balcony. Kim was in awe.

"Brian!" she yelled as she walked down the short hallway toward the stairs. The rest of the house looked just as good as the bedroom. She called out to him again and was finally answered.

"I'm in here," he yelled from the kitchen.

"Baby, where are we?" Kim asked when she walked into the kitchen.

The kitchen had an island with a pot rack hanging from the ceiling, a six-burner stove with all the little appliances to match, and in the corner was a huge double door stainless steel refrigerator that looked like it could fit a small grocery store inside of it.

Brian walked over to the island where Kim was sitting and put a plate of food in front of her.

"Baby, we are home," he said with a smile on his face as he walked back over to the stove to prepare his plate.

"Home? What do you mean, home?"

Brian took his plate and sat right next to her on the island. Kim was really starting to regret falling asleep in the car last night. She was so tired, Brian had to carry her from the car, into the house, and put her in bed. She'd missed the whole outside view of the home. This was the first time she had actually seen the house, and Brian was loving the effect.

"When two people love each other, they move in together," he said sarcastically.

Kim playfully punched him in his arm.

"I know that," she said, getting up and walking over to the French-style glass doors that led to the backyard.

Brian got up and followed her.

"I bought this house about a year ago with my mother's life insurance, or at least I used it as a down payment," he said, walking up behind Kim and wrapping his arms around her. "The mortgage is low, and the upkeep is cheap. It's in a good neighborhood, and it's an easy commute for you to get to work," he explained.

It seemed too good to be true, and though Kim would have loved to live this good life with this great man, she had a major concern that could ruin everything in a heartbeat. She turned around to face Brian, looking directly in his eyes.

"For me to even consider moving in, you have to leave the streets alone. I don't want to get any phone calls in the middle of the night telling me to come and identify ya body, and I damn sure don't do the prison life. Never have and I never will."

Brian smiled and placed his hands on the side of Kim's face. She didn't know it, but he was already in the process of ending his role in the North Philly drug game. The streets were drying up anyway, and the only thing left out there was the stickup kids. Transitioning from the streets to the legal life wasn't going to be hard at all.

Brian smiled, knowing that he had a stipulation of his own. "I'm off the streets from this day forth, but now . . ." he said, descending to the floor on one knee.

Kim covered her mouth with both of her hands as he reached into his sweatpants and pulled out a little red box. "It don't have to be today, it don't have to be tomorrow, or a week, month, or a year from now. But one day, when you feel that you are ready, can you please be my wife?" Brian asked, pulling the diamond ring from the box.

He looked up at Kim who was shedding tears of joy, and it wasn't until she finally said the word yes that he slid the ring on her finger. It was a perfect fit, the same as he felt Kim was in his life.

Nate and Naomi both began jumping up and down on the bed at the same time, waking Lisa from her sleep. Grumpy for only a few seconds, she sat up fast and snatched Naomi out of the air. She tickled her until she almost peed her pants, and just when Lisa thought it was over, Nate jumped down and started tickling her. Naomi joined in, and for a second, Lisa thought she did pee on herself.

"Watch out, I gotta pee," Lisa said, jumping up and darting to the bathroom.

Naomi and Nate sat on the bed cracking up laughing, giving each other high fives.

"I got a big day planned for us," Nate yelled toward the bathroom.

"Yeah, Mommy, a big day," Naomi chimed in.

"Is that right?" Lisa asked, coming out of the bathroom. "I hope it don't include any rides, 'cause I'm not getting on any," she said, walking over and kissing Naomi on her head. She gave Nate a kiss too, then walked over and grabbed her shower stuff.

Lisa had to admit, this was the happiest and most open she'd been in a long time, and like many people tried to tell her, this was the exact thing she needed in her life. Not only was she happy, but so was Naomi. She couldn't get enough of Nate. For some reason, he reminded her of her daddy in so many ways.

By no means was Nate trying to replace Ralphy, but he wanted to provide somewhat of a father figure to a little girl who'd captured his heart from the first day he met her. If he planned to be with Lisa the way he wanted, it was going to become his responsibility anyway.

For the first time ever, Falisha woke up in a bed next to Chris, who lay there completely naked. Falisha was naked also. After multiple rounds of sex the night before, both were too exhausted and lazy to move. She watched as Chris slept and was intrigued by how peaceful he looked lying there breathing lightly and looking as innocent as a baby. Falisha couldn't help but to lean over and kiss him on the side of his lips.

He jumped, but didn't wake up.

"You are out of pocket, Falisha," she mumbled to herself. *It's Chris, for crying out loud,* she thought. *Tammy is your friend, but damn, this nigga look good, and he fuck like a porn star. I know I'ma burn in hell for this, but his ass is gonna burn wit' me. I guess we'll be fuckin' up a storm in hell then.*

Falisha almost burst out laughing at her crazy thoughts and had to roll over for fear that Chris would catch her and think that she was a weirdo.

"You mine now," Chris blurted out, getting her attention.

Falisha rolled back over, thinking that he might've been talking in his sleep. She waited to see if he was going to say anything else. He remained still for a second before he spoke again.

"I'm not playing with you, either," he said, opening his eyes.

"Oh, is that how you feel?" she shot back, inching a little closer.

"I don't see it happening no other way."

Whatever Falisha and Chris had was clicking on all cylinders, and it didn't look like either of them was willing to call what they had just a simple fling. There was more to it than that. It wasn't love yet, but it was something strong enough to make them content with being together.

"You know we gon' get a lot of backlash behind this," Falisha said, making sure Chris understood.

"Yeah, I know, so we gotta make the best out of it and do the damn thing big so it be worth it," he replied, putting his arm around her. "Don't get scared now."

"Boy, ain't nobody scared. You know me better than that," she said, rolling over on top of him.

Falisha looked down into Chris's eyes and saw something that she'd never seen in any man that she'd ever been with. She saw devotion and the highest level of sincerity one could have. It was enough to convince her that what they were doing was okay, and if all else failed, at least she knew he had her back.

"Let me show you how I wanna wake you up every morning," she said before leaning over and kissing his chest.

Falisha kept moving down the center of his stomach until she reached his dick, and then she took all of it into her mouth.

Since the judge had not ruled on the motion yet, there was no need for Kim to go to work. It gave her a little more time to think about how she was going to tell Lamar that she wasn't going to be able to run off with him like he'd hoped.

The whole ride back to her apartment, she went over her lines a thousand times, and no matter how many times she said it or what tone she used, it still sounded fucked up. It was going to crush Lamar, and Kim knew it, but this was something that needed to be done. She didn't want to drag him along any further, knowing that her heart had chosen who it wanted to love.

"He'll understand," she mumbled to herself as she parked the car.

What was usually a two-minute walk from the garage to the apartment turned into a fifteen-minute walk, including a five-minute talk with the doorman and another five-minute conversation with one of her neighbors.

Twenty minutes after parking, she was finally opening up her apartment door.

"Lamar, I'm back. Sorry, I got caught up with work," Kim called out when she walked into the apartment.

It was so quiet, she thought that Lamar might have been asleep, but a quick sweep of the apartment revealed that he wasn't there, and neither was his luggage. She walked back into the living room and was about to call his phone, but an envelope on the coffee table in the living room caught her eye. She picked it up and opened it, taking a seat on the couch. A white gold diamond ring fell out of it when she pulled the piece of paper from the envelope.

Her heart started to beat fast, thinking that Lamar was trying to propose to her. She looked around the room, waiting for him to pop up out of nowhere, but he didn't. Kim put the ring on the table, then started to read the letter.

Dear Kim,

Truthfully, I really don't know where to begin, or even if my words matter to you at this point. Before I get into the reason why I left, let me first start off by saying that I love you. I know that somewhere in your heart you know this. I know that in the past, I fucked up big time, but when you came back to Charlotte, I thought that I had another chance to make things right. Believe me, I was going to do everything in my power to fix my wrong. I wanted to make sure that every day, for the rest of your life, I would make you happy. I swear on my son's life I was going to do right by you. I'm not going to lie, I noticed something about you the last time I looked into your eyes. I could see that somebody else had ya attention, and it was more serious than what you told me. To a certain extent, I can see why you didn't want to tell me the truth, but I really wish you would have, so I wouldn't have gotten my hopes high, thinking that we could make it work. It took me traveling all the way to Philadelphia to realize that it wasn't me who you was in love with.

It was evident that you wasn't expecting me to show up, and you rushed out of here before you got a chance to clean up. His clothes are still here. You got pictures of you and him hanging up everywhere, and he even has an X-Box One here with Call of Duty *at the ready . . . lol. Leaving his X-Box here was like a dog that pissed on a tree to mark his territory. You might not understand because it's a guy thing. In any event, this is his territory, so I left. I want you to know that I'm not mad at you. A little disappointed and hurt, but not mad at all. I still got love for you, and I wish the best for you and your new relationship. As far as the ring, you can keep it or throw it away. Either one is fine by me. If you didn't do anything else, you sure did earn that much from me. Well, look, I think I said enough. I'm taking my country black ass home. Take care of yourself, and don't be afraid to come to the city every now and again.*

Much love,
Lamar

Kim sat back on the couch reading bits and parts of the letter over again. It sounded like Lamar was letting go for good this time, which touched Kim in a way that she didn't expect. It sort of felt like she was losing Lamar, not only as a lover, but also as a friend. She felt like she had betrayed him in more than one way, and that was the last thing she wanted to do. It was officially over, but Kim didn't want it to end like this. On the flip side of the coin, she was also a little relieved. She didn't have to juggle two relationships in separate states, and she didn't have to worry about two men playing tug-of-war with her heart. Kim was free to try something new, and this time, she was more confident than ever that Brian was the one for her. The risk was worth it.

As mean as it seems, losing Lamar may have been the best thing to happen to her. The heart was only made to be in love with one person, and anything more than that could prove to be a chaotic situation.

After a fun-filled day at Disney's Hollywood Studios, the sun had finally set and the night had taken over the sky. The day was not nearly over, but Naomi and Lisa wanted it to be, considering that they had been on their feet all day.

"So, where are we now?" Lisa asked, looking around at the large crowd of people in the outdoor arena that seemed to be set up for a show.

"Mommy, I'm sleepy," Naomi said, wiping her eyes.

Lisa lifted Naomi onto her lap and looked over at Nate. "We should be getting back to the hotel. I'm tired too," she said.

"A'ight, just give me one minute," he said, knowing that the show, *Fantasmic*, was about to start.

As soon as the music began and Mickey Mouse emerged on the stage in a cloud of smoke, Naomi woke right up and watched the dazzling light and water display. People *ooooohed* and *ahhhhed* in astonishment as Mickey directed the pyrotechnics in his famous wizard hat and robe. Naomi's eyes were glued to the show, and it was a perfect time for Nate to do his thing.

Nate wrapped his arm around Lisa as she held Naomi on her lap. He nudged Lisa, causing her to look down. She couldn't believe her eyes. Nate had a ring in the center of his hand. Lisa looked up at him in confusion. The music changed, and Belle and the Beast danced across the stage. It was the perfect backdrop for such a romantic gesture.

"What are you doing?" Lisa asked, almost in a panic.

"I'm doing what any man in his right mind would do if he was in my situation," Nate said, grabbing Lisa's left hand.

Her heart raced, and at one point, she even found it hard to breathe. Her thoughts were everywhere. *Why is he doing this? What's he thinking? Does he not see Naomi on my lap? It's too soon!*

"I can't marry you, Nate," she said before he could get the ring on her finger.

Nate's heart dropped to the bottom of his stomach, and he felt like he wanted to shed a tear or two. He immediately put the ring back into his pocket in an attempt to save face.

Lisa couldn't believe him. It was way too early in their relationship for him to pull a stunt like this. Moments like these made her reconsider being in a serious relationship with anyone.

"I apologize. Let's just pretend that none of this ever happened," he suggested.

Things were already awkward, and neither Lisa nor Nate felt that the rest of this vacation was going to be much fun with this hanging over their heads. The only thing Lisa wanted to do at that point was take Naomi home. Embarrassed and feeling like a fool, Nate also felt the need

to get out of there. After tonight, the Disney
vacation was officially over, and it was back to
Charlotte for everyone.

Falisha's initial appearance in court was only
a couple of days away, and though it was only
the beginning of the process, things weren't
looking too good. The public defender she had
in South Carolina was bogus and didn't know
jack squat about being a lawyer. Today was the
first time he had read the police report. If he
stayed on the case, Falisha was going away for
sure. The only person that could help her was
Kim. She hated to have to call on her after all the
beefing they had been doing, but Falisha really
didn't have any other choice. Kim was the only
person she could trust with her freedom.

Putting her pride and ego to the side, she
pulled out her phone and dialed Kim's number,
hoping that her once best friend would help her.

Tammy damn near ran Chris's car off the
road when she saw him on Hudson Street. He
swerved right in the nick of time, avoiding driver-side impact. Traffic was almost at a standstill
except for a few cars that had enough sense to go
around the two stopped cars.

"Roll ya fuckin' window down!" Tammy screamed while banging on the window with her fist.

"What do you want, Tammy?" Chris asked in a calm voice as he slowly rolled down the window.

Tammy started swinging and cussing him out at the same time.

"You fuckin' my girl? Really, nigga, you fucking Falisha?" she snapped, trying her best to connect one of her punches to his face.

Chris slipped every attempt and began to roll his window back up.

"My arm!" Tammy screamed when she couldn't get it out in time.

Before she broke the glass, Chris let the window down slightly to release her arm.

"Get outta the fuckin' car," she yelled as she kicked his door.

Chris wasn't trying to entertain Tammy; he had already had enough of her foolishness. But he knew this was going to have to go down at some point, so today seemed like it was going to be it. He jumped out of the car, slipped the two punches Tammy threw, then gripped her up by the neck and slammed her against the vehicle. She squeezed her cheeks together like she was about to spit on him, but he squeezed her neck even tighter, almost making her choke on her own spit.

"I swear on my kids, I will break ya fuckin' jaw if you spit on me," Chris threatened in a serious tone.

Confident that she knew for sure that he wasn't playing, he let her neck go.

"Fuck is yo' problem?"

"I saw you and Falisha on Instagram, nigga. Are you fucking her? And don't lie to me either."

Chris took a step back, glancing over at the traffic going around his car.

"You know you got some fuckin' nerve questioning me about who I'm fucking. Bitch, you left me while I was in jail, then you go and get married when I came home. Who da fuck do you think you are? I can fuck whoever I want."

"My fuckin' girlfriend, tho?" Tammy shot back.

"You got me fucked up, Tammy. You lost yo' rights the minute ya nut ass walked down the aisle. I'm doing me now."

"Oh yeah? By fuckin' wit' my friend?"

"Yeah, and I'm not just fuckin' Falisha. That's my bitch now."

Tammy couldn't believe what she'd just heard. She looked around, and right when she was about to tee off on Chris again, Darious's car came to a stop behind both of their cars.

He jumped out, pissed, wondering what his wife was doing out in the middle of the street arguing with Chris.

"What's the problem?" Darious asked, walking up on them.

Chris gave him a stern look, then turned to Tammy.

"Yeah, what's the problem?" he asked Tammy, trying to put her on the spot.

Darious looked at her, searching her eyes for an answer, but Tammy stood there with the mean mug on. She wasn't about to expose her hand the way Chris wanted her to, but she definitely wasn't going to leave without saying something.

"Fuck you, Chris," she said, then walked off toward her car.

"Yeah, that part of our relationship is over," Chris said and laughed. "Oh, and a news flash . . . Falisha ain't yo' friend anymore," Chris concluded before jumping back into his car and pulling off in traffic.

Darious stood there confused as shit, unsure of how he was supposed to take what little he'd just heard. He wasn't going to cause a scene, but when he got home, he was going to get an understanding about what was going on. All that trust shit was now out the door.

"I have to go back to Charlotte for a few days," Kim told Brian as they lay in bed.

Brian acted like he didn't even hear what she said.

"I know you heard me and don't lie there and act like you didn't," she said, biting down on his side.

"Ah shit," he yelled, pulling away from her hold. "I heard you."

She went on and explained the whole situation with Falisha and the case that she caught. They weren't on the best of terms right now, but that was still Kim's friend, and she wasn't going to leave her hanging out to dry.

"You should come with me," Kim suggested. "You can meet all of my people, and I can show you some of that Southern hospitality." She smiled and rubbed the bite mark with her thumb.

"Even if I wanted to go, my parole officer wouldn't let me, especially on this short of a notice. Go ahead down there and take care of ya business. I'm not trippin', tho," Brian told her.

Initially his heart was against it, knowing that she would more than likely be around Lamar, but then Brian came to his senses and realized that he had nothing to worry about. Not only was he confident that Kim wouldn't do anything to jeopardize their relationship, he trusted her to be loyal and faithful during her trip. He had put too much work in with her for it to go any other way. There was nothing for him to be insecure about.

"You know I love you, right?" Kim said, seeing the concern leaving his face.

Brian looked over at her and smiled. "Yeah, I know," he said, then went right back to looking at the TV with no worries at all.

Little things like this made Kim love Brian even more. She couldn't conceive of the thought of doing something stupid. Nothing or nobody was worth it.

"Ms. D, I don't think Sunday dinner will be possible," Lisa said into the phone.

Ms. D wasn't trying to hear it. This was a dinner she'd insisted on having, especially since she was about to check into the Cancer Treatment Centers of America in Arizona. Not knowing how long she would be gone or whether she would be coming back at all, Ms. D wanted to have dinner with everyone she loved before she went away. After explaining all of this, Lisa assured her that she would do everything in her power to get everybody to come. It was a task, because the crew was scattered about doing their own thing, but just as she promised, Lisa was going to make something happen.

***

"Damn, bitch, you been MIA," Carol yelled from across the street when Falisha came out of her mom's house with Jordan in her arms.

"And I heard about you and Chris all hugged up on Instagram," Ernie chimed in when Falisha made it across the street. "You bold as shit. You know Tammy gon' kill both of y'all asses," he continued as he put the weed out because of the baby.

"Hating never looked good on you, Ernie," Falisha shot back.

"Hating? I know you didn't just say that I was hating. We all supposed to be friends, Falisha, and friends don't sleep with other friends' baby daddies."

Carol looked off, thinking about the encounter she and Lamar had when he was trying to get information out of her.

Falisha looked at Ernie like he was crazy.

"Friends, Ernie?" she said, shifting Jordan into her other arm. "I sure as hell didn't see you coming to my aid when I was sitting in a jail cell. Don't talk no shit about friendship, and don't think that I don't know about you fuckin' with my baby daddy," Falisha said, rolling her eyes over at Carol.

Falisha was just getting started, but before she could burn Ernie's ass up with a vicious tongue-lashing, Fox's F-Type Jaguar turned down the block, making Falisha even more frustrated than she already was.

"I'll deal wit' y'all in a second," she told them, then turned around to see what Fox wanted.

He stopped and slowly exited the car. The nigga even had the nerve to look like he was mad.

"What do you want, Fox?"

"I just came to check up on you. I know you got a court date in a couple of days," he said, leaning against the car.

Falisha knew Fox all too well and knew that this wasn't a regular checkup.

"Why don't you just ask me what you wanna ask me?" she shot back.

Fox took her up on the offer. "Did you tell them anything about me?" he asked, analyzing her body language.

"I'm not no fuckin' rat. Next," she said, popping her neck.

"Are you sure about that? 'Cause I wouldn't want anything to happen to you," he casually threatened.

He didn't scare Falisha one bit. She knew too much about him.

"You might wanna consider the fact that I know *everything* about you. I know where you live, security passcodes to your house, what times you go out, and when you come home. Hell, I even know what side of the bed you like to sleep on. You know, little important shit like that can go a long way. And let's not forget who I'm in bed with right now. I can text him and have you dead before you get home," Falisha promised. "Now carry ya tired ass on. I'm done wit' you."

Fox looked at Falisha and cracked a crooked smile before getting back into his car. He had underestimated her and what she was truly capable of doing to him. Having Chris and his crazy-ass brother on her team was a deterrent to any violence. The best thing he could have done when he pulled off was forget about it altogether and keep it moving.

The scent of Ed Hardy rushed Lisa's nose, causing her to wake up from her sleep. This particular fragrance was significant to her because it was Ralphy's favorite cologne. She opened her eyes—and froze when she saw Ralphy sitting in a chair by the foot of the bed.

"Hey, sleepyhead," he said, causing Lisa to cry. She knew this had to be a dream, but she sat up in the bed and cleared her eyes anyway.

"It's time for you to move on. I know that you wanna hold on, but you can't. You gotta live ya life . . ."

"I miss you so much," Lisa cried. "I don't wanna move on. It's too hard," she continued, letting the tears fall freely.

"You can't be that way, baby. You can't do this to yourself. You can't do this to Naomi. Just trust me, Lisa, you gon' be all right. I love you and our daughter," Ralphy said before getting out of the chair.

As he walked away, Lisa tried to get up and follow him. When she got off the bed, it was as if she had stepped off a cliff and was falling through the sky. Right when she was about to smack into the ground, she woke up.

"What da fuck was all that about?" Darious snapped when he walked into the house. "Oh, you quiet now?" he asked, walking over to Tammy as she sat on the couch.

Darious had caught the tail end of the confrontation, but when he pulled up, things looked real heated.

"I'ma ask you one more time. What da fuck is going on?" he said again.

Tammy threw back the shot of Patrón she had in her glass, then set it on the coffee table.

"I just found out that my kids' father is messing around with one of my best friends. I saw him in traffic, confronted him about it, and that was it," Tammy responded like it was no big deal.

After sitting there with a confused look on his face, trying to let her words register, Darious spoke on it. "Why does him messing around with one of your friends bother you so much? Are you still fucking that nigga?"

"No," Tammy answered quickly.

"Do you still love him?" he asked, lifting her chin up so he could look into her eyes when she answered the question.

Tammy didn't hesitate to respond with a "No."

"Well, it shouldn't fuckin' matter to you who he's sleeping with," Darious shot back.

His cousin's words about the relationship between women and their baby daddies flooded his thoughts. It made him want to probe a little deeper.

"Let me ask you something, Tammy, and if you love me the way you say you do, then tell me the truth," Darious said, taking a seat next to her on the couch.

"What happened when ya baby daddy came up to your dressing room on the day of our wedding?"

Tammy's face had *busted* written all over it, but there was no way in hell she was about to tell him the truth about what happened. That was something Tammy vowed that she would take to the grave with her, and she hoped that Chris and Lisa would do the same. She quickly got her lie together and made sure her facial expression displayed nothing but the look of truthfulness.

"When Chris came to my dressing room, he asked me if I was sure about marrying you. He told me that there will never be a chance for me and him to get back together if I went through with it," she lied with a straight face.

Darious couldn't tell if she was lying or telling the truth. "And what did you tell him?" he asked.

"Nothing. I walked down the aisle and married the man that I was supposed to be with," she said, even mustering up a couple of pitiful tears.

Darious was still a little confused, and even if it was the truth, he still felt betrayed because she never told him about it. He sank his head into his hands, trying to figure out a solution for all of this. Only one thing came to mind, and it was probably the best thing that Tammy could do.

"I want you to listen to me, Tammy, and this is not up for negotiation. Leave ya baby daddy alone. If it ain't about the kids, you shouldn't have nothing else to say to him. I don't give a fuck about who he's screwing or what he's doing, and neither should you. If you care anything about this marriage, you'll do what I tell you to do," he said, looking over at her. "Are we clear?"

Tammy nodded, but that wasn't enough for him. "I wanna hear you say it."

Tammy wiped the tears from her face and cleared her throat. "If it ain't about the kids, I'm not worried about what Chris got going on."

All Tammy had was her word, and Darious was going to hold her to every letter of it. At the same time, he was going to be more on point from now on, knowing that Tammy wasn't as truthful as he thought.

Chapter 20

Kim paced back and forth in her hotel room talking to Falisha's lawyer and going over the motion she had prepared. It challenged the traffic stop that started everything. No violations occurred to stop the car in the first place, and though this was the only thing that Kim could come up with, her chances of winning this in a suppression hearing was high. But she knew that it would all come down to how well the motion was argued.

"A'ight, make sure you get up early, because your hearing is at nine o'clock sharp. I'm going to go with you, so your lawyer don't fuck this up," she told Falisha as she walked over to the window.

"Thanks, Kim, you're a lifesaver," Falisha said. "And I been meaning to talk to you about something. The whole—"

"Falisha, you don't have to explain yourself. That shit is water under the bridge. At the end of the day, I still love you like a sister." Kim spoke genuinely, and Falisha knew that it was coming from the heart.

They had been through so much, and not just the whole Lamar experience. They'd known each other from as far back as they could remember, and growing up together from toddlers had only strengthened their bond. Elementary school, middle school, and high school were some trying times as youth, but they always stuck together. All of them stuck together, Kim, Tammy, Falisha, and Lisa, so it was going to take a lot to break that structure down.

Little did they know, today was going to be the day that all the love they had for each other would be tested. Today might even be the day when all the walls of friendship collapsed. It was a sure thing that if they could make it through today, they would be able to make it through anything.

"Let's go. Push it out," Nate's weightlifting coach yelled as he bench-pressed 275 pounds for the tenth rep.

Nate and Lisa hadn't really spoken much since they had come home from Disney World two days ago. The lack of communication fell on both of them since both needed some time to think and reevaluate their respective situations. For Nate, the whole ordeal was stressful, loving somebody who he felt really didn't fully love him back. The gym was the only place where he found comfort, and it was also a good way for him to relieve his tension.

"Good workout today," the trainer concluded, giving Nate a fist bump.

As Nate began to gather his things and put them into his gym bag, a shadow appeared in his peripheral, causing him to look over. Lisa was standing there looking down on him with a smile on her face. She looked good too, rocking a pair of blue jeans, a white tee, and some cute sandals. Her hair looked like she'd just come from the stylist, and she seemed to have a nice glow to her.

"Hey," they spoke at the same time.

"What's going on? Is everything all right?" Nate asked with a hint of concern on his face.

"Yeah, everything's good. I guess I just wanted to see you."

There was no doubt that Lisa had missed him, but it was obvious that things had changed since she turned down his proposal. Over the past couple of days, she fought with herself about how she had let her love for Ralphy take over her life. He was a great husband, and Lisa's infidelities were the ultimate reason why he was now dead. Coming to terms with that had been the hardest thing she had to do, but it was necessary if she wanted to move on.

"I think I'm . . ." Lisa paused, then corrected herself. "I know I'm ready," she said, walking over to where he was sitting on the bench. "Whether or not you believe me, I really do wanna marry you," she spoke.

"You don't have to do this, Lisa. I understand—"

"See, that's one of the many reasons why I love you so much," she said, cutting him off.

Lisa didn't care who was in the gym or if they were watching her.

She reached into her back pocket and pulled out a male diamond wedding band. "I know this isn't the traditional way of doing things," she said, getting down on both of her knees between his legs. "Will you be my husband?" she asked, wiping the single tear that fell down her cheek.

A few people in the gym turned their attention to Nate and Lisa.

Nate was speechless, and if it wasn't for the fact that he had to maintain his manly image in front of his peers, he would have shed a tear himself. Marrying Lisa was the only thing he wanted to do. The only thing he'd thought about from the first day he laid eyes on her.

"Yeah, I would love to be your husband," Nate said with a big smile on his face as he leaned in to kiss her.

The people looking on began to clap and congratulate them. Nate never thought in a million years that Lisa would do something like this, but he was glad that she did. It was a long, hard road ahead for them, and it would be full of obstacles, but in their minds, it was well worth the travel. This was only the beginning.

Chris was the first person to pull up to Ms. D's house. As he was parking, Lamar came out of his front door. Lamar was still unaware of the fact that Chris and Falisha were messing around. Shockingly, the word hadn't gotten to him via the gossip lines. Being the man that he was, Chris was going to speak to Lamar personally to let him know what was going on. He didn't know how Lamar was going to act, but just in case it got out of hand, he was ready for a little scuffle.

"Aye, yo, L, I need to holla at you about something, brah," Chris yelled when he got out of his car.

"Damn, homie, I didn't even know that was you," Lamar said, walking over and giving Chris a fist bump while he checked out the Impala.

"Yo, so check this out," Chris said, inconspicuously sizing Lamar up.

A car coming down the block caught both of their attention, and to Lamar's surprise, it was Kim. She had Falisha in the car with her, and he wondered what they could be up to together.

"Damn, can we holla about that a li'l later?" Lamar asked Chris as he watched Kim get out of the car.

Chris didn't want to press the issue, so for now, he was going to leave it alone.

"A'ight, homie, we can hit the bar later," he responded.

Lamar didn't even speak to Falisha when she and Kim got out of the car. He was fixed on Kim looking sexy as ever, wearing a pair of hip-hugger capris, a belly shirt, and some sandals.

"Did you say anything to him?" Falisha asked Chris when she walked up to him.

Lamar had stopped Kim a nice distance away, so he wasn't able to hear the conversation between Chris and Falisha.

"Nah, I didn't tell him yet. We gon' hit the bar later on. I'll explain it to him then."

Falisha so desperately wanted to kiss Chris as he stood there looking handsome. But she refrained from doing it. Instead, she turned and started walking toward Ms. D's house.

Chris walked behind her, thinking about how much he wanted to do the same. Them not coming out yet to the crew was really putting a damper on Chris being able to show public affection to his girl.

"So, is that official?" Lamar asked, looking down at the engagement ring on Kim's finger. "It's really that deep?"

Before Kim came back to Charlotte, she debated with herself about wearing the ring. She didn't want to seem like she was throwing it in Lamar's face. But she decided that if she was serious about marrying Brian, she needed to embrace it.

"Yeah, he's a good guy," she said, looking down at the ring with a smile on her face. "I'm sorry I didn't tell you . . ."

Kim couldn't get out the rest of what she wanted to say before Lamar walked off on her. He was in his feelings and really had nothing else to say. She inhaled, then exhaled deeply as she looked into the sky. By the time she looked down the street, he had disappeared into Ms. D's house. Kim shook her head, knowing that it was going to be a long day.

***

Lisa and Nate arrived at the house, and not too far behind them was Tammy and Darious, who was skeptical about coming to the dinner. If it wasn't for the extreme circumstances concerning Ms. D's health, they wouldn't have come. It seemed that as soon as they walked through the door, everyone became silent. Lisa was the first person to get up from the couch to hug and greet Tammy and Darious.

Tammy's coat wasn't off for two seconds before Ms. D yelled out from the kitchen, telling the girls to come and help her with the food. They all did, leaving the men in the living room. Lamar and Nate spoke to Darious, but Chris just gave him a nod of the head. After that, things got awkward. No one was interested in talking, as they were only there for Ms. D.

"A'ight, y'all, the table is ready," Lisa announced.

Within a few minutes, the many pans of food, along with a bottle of Grey Goose, sat in the middle of the table.

Standing around the table was Ms. D at the head, Kim, Chris, Falisha, Lisa with Nate standing behind her, Tammy with Darious standing behind her, and then Lamar, who was on the other side of Ms. D, right across from Kim.

Ms. D looked around the room at all the somber faces. Most of them were like her children, and she could tell that something was wrong. It was so quiet, you could hear a mouse piss on cotton.

"Yeah, it's nice and thick up in here. You can cut it with a butter knife," she said, referring to the tension in the air. "Yeah, I think we need to say grace. Lord knows we're gonna need it," she said interlocking her hands and bowing her head.

Chris was Muslim, so he got up and excused himself, then came back at the conclusion of the prayer.

Usually people couldn't wait to dig into Ms. D's cooking, but for obvious reasons, no one wanted to eat right away, except, of course, Lisa, who was currently drama free and probably the only person with good news.

"I'm engaged!" she yelled, stopping in the middle of fixing her plate to show off her ring.

"Me too!" Kim chimed in, flashing her ring as well.

Everyone congratulated them. Ms. D, Tammy, and Falisha all said how happy they were for both of them. This was a huge step for Lisa, one that nobody thought was possible, and for Kim to go off and want to marry somebody from Philly was also a shock to most. The joy of those two announcements lasted every bit of five minutes before the room went right back to dead silence. The tension was back and in high gear this time.

Ms. D had enough. She felt like her dinner was already ruined, so now it was time to find out what the hell was going on. She tossed her fork onto her plate, wiped her mouth, then sat back in her chair.

"All right, so what in the hell is going on?" she asked, looking around the room.

No one was in a rush to answer her, so she called on the person who she knew wouldn't have a problem with getting the party started.

"Falisha, what in the hell did yo' ass do now?" Ms. D asked, knowing that she had something to do with it.

"Ms. D, I didn't do anything," Falisha chuckled. "Why every time something happens you think I'm involved?"

"'Cause it's you who always doin' something," Tammy mumbled under her breath, but not low enough for Falisha not to hear her.

Falisha stopped laughing. "You got something you wanna say?" she asked, putting Tammy on the spot.

The more Tammy looked over at her and Chris sitting next to each other like nothing was going on, the more upset she became. She knew that Darious was going to be mad at her, but she just had to speak her mind.

"So how long have y'all two been fucking?" Tammy asked, shocking everyone at the table.

Lamar had a puzzled look on his face as he cut his eyes over at Falisha and Chris. Darious tried to put out the flames, telling Tammy that they were leaving, but it was too late. The fire was lit, and there was no turning back.

"You sure you wanna do this, Tammy?" Chris asked, trying to give her a way out.

Tammy wasn't thinking straight. She let her feelings and emotions get the best of her. "Dumb bitch. You heard what I said," Tammy shot back.

Falisha didn't like to be talked down to, nor was she fond of being called out of her name. She looked over at Chris for his approval, to which he simply shrugged as if he didn't care anymore.

"I started fucking Chris about a week after the last time he fucked you," Falisha said, getting everyone's attention.

Even Chris was a little shocked that she went that far, but again, he really didn't care.

"And when was that?" Darious interrupted.

"Yeah, when da fuck was that?" Lamar also cut in.

Falisha looked over at Chris for his approval again. He gave her the nod to go ahead.

"Falisha, don't do this," Lisa pleaded, seeing that things had gone too far.

Falisha wanted to take it to the max, however. "The last time Chris fucked Tammy was on the day of your wedding," Falisha said, looking into Darious's eyes.

"Oh shit," Kim mumbled.

"Damn," Lisa said, putting her head down.

Darious looked down at Tammy for an answer. He was expecting her to put up some type of protest, but she didn't. His heart sank into his stomach.

"Is that true?" Darious kneeled down and asked Tammy, trying to get her to look him in his eyes.

When she turned to face him, she finally understood what she had done. Tears flowed down her cheeks, which was confirmation to Darious. Everyone sat there in shock. As Darious rose back up, rage, hurt, and anger caused him to backhand the shit out of her.

Tammy and the chair flipped over on to the ground.

Chris immediately jumped up from the table. "I'll give you that one," Chris warned Darious.

Tammy was still the mother of his kids, so a beat down was out of the question. Chris went over to help her up, but before he could grab her hand, Darious rushed him, throwing a two-piece combination.

Chris slipped it, then scooped Darious off his feet and took him to the ground. He mounted Darious, then hit him with multiple blows to the face like he was a UFC fighter.

Kim, Lisa, and Falisha yelled for Chris to stop.

Tammy was knocked out cold on the ground, counting sheep, and Nate sat there and enjoyed the fight, all the while holding Lisa back.

Ms. D didn't move from her seat. She just watched as the drama unfolded. Lamar, who was hot under the collar about Chris fucking Falisha, thought that he would sneak Chris while he was occupied beating Darious's face in. Lamar got in a couple of punches before Chris rolled off of Darious. He whipped out a compact .45 automatic from his pocket and pointed it at Lamar's face, silencing the entire room. Everyone thought that he was about to shoot Lamar, including Lamar himself.

Ms. D slammed her hand down on the table, getting everyone's attention. "That's enough, Chris. It's over," she spoke in a stern voice. "What did I just say?" she yelled when he didn't lower the gun.

Chris gave Lamar the evil eye before lowering the gun and putting it into his back pocket. He looked down at Tammy, who was just waking up, and then at Darious, who had managed to get to his feet.

"Do anybody else got a problem wit' Falisha being my girl?" Chris yelled, looking around the room. "Speak!" he yelled again, holding his hands up.

Nobody in the room said a word, and even if they wanted to, they still wouldn't have said anything to Chris's crazy ass.

"You can keep dat bitch," Lamar said, walking past Chris and leaving the house.

Darious swallowed the blood in his mouth, fixed his clothes, and then he too left the house. Despite Tammy calling out his name several times, he never stopped, causing her to get up and run out the door behind him.

"*Wheeeww*, I'm taking my ass back to Philly today," Kim said, gathering her things to go.

"Come on, let's get out of here," Nate told Lisa, putting his arm around her and leading her toward the front door.

Chris looked over at Falisha, who sat down at the table. No words needed to be said. If it wasn't clear before about them two being official, everybody now knew it. At that moment,

Falisha knew that she had fallen in love with Chris. She knew now that he just didn't talk about it, but he was a man of action, and his actions said that he wanted this to last. Falisha wouldn't have it any other way.

"I gotta get some air," Chris said before turning around and walking out of the house.

Falisha was about to get up, but Ms. D stopped her. "Sit yo' ass down, girl," she said, sticking her hand out.

Falisha did exactly as she was told. She did reach over, grabbed the bottle of Grey Goose, and poured herself a shot.

Ms. D just sat there staring at her. Falisha was like a daughter to her, and she loved her to death, but every time Ms. D turned around, she was in the middle of something.

"Girl, you are the devil in Louis Vuitton," Ms. D said, grabbing the bottle of Grey Goose to pour herself a shot too. "Pure evil." She chuckled, amazed at how Falisha's good looks could cause a storm at any given time. The thing is, Ms. D knew that what she did wasn't intentional.

"Ms. D, I'm not evil. You know I don't do well when I'm backed into a corner. After that, I'll say whatever."

"I know, baby. That's why I'm going to miss you the most. I'm gonna miss all of you and all the drama y'all be having." Ms. D laughed and threw back the Grey Goose. "But let me leave you with this," she said, getting out of her chair. "Just make sure you can stand on the things you do in life. And I think even you know now, you can't trust nobody . . ."

Chapter 21

Lamar sat in the courtroom talking to his lawyer, going over the procedures for the day. The task of trying to get full custody of his son Jordan was proving to be more difficult than anything in his life. Over the past five months, he had been to four hearings, two meetings, and with all that, had still only managed to see Jordan once, and that was merely for an hour.

"Don't look so down," Anne, Lamar's attorney, said, nudging his side. "I really think you're going to make out today. Everything is in order," she assured him.

Unlike many men who try to gain custody of their children, Lamar had a number of good things going for him. A nice job, good credit, his own house, car, blocks away from a good day care, health insurance, and plenty of help from family.

"Oh God, I was hoping she wouldn't make it," Anne said, looking over and seeing Falisha coming into the courtroom.

Lamar begged to differ, seeing that she had Jordan with her. It had been almost three weeks since he saw him last, and at the sight of his son, it was impossible for Lamar to resist. He got up from his seat and walked over to Falisha. "Hey, li'l man," Lamar smiled, reaching out for Jordan. Falisha quickly spun Jordan away, not allowing Lamar to touch him.

"Don't touch my son," she snapped.

It took everything in Lamar for him not to grab Falisha around her neck and make her choke on those words. Good thing he didn't because as he stood there giving Falisha the evil eye, the judge walked into the courtroom. Anne grabbed Lamar by the arm and pulled him back over to the table.

"Let me do my job," she told him, then went into attack mode. "Your Honor, my client has complied with everything the court has asked of him, and he stands before you seeking full or joint custody of his son."

Falisha's lawyer wasn't a pushover and attacked as well, sitting and quoting laws pertaining to parental rights, specifically the ones of a mother to her child. Today was a battle without a doubt and definitely the most intense one yet. Lamar just knew that he was going to walk out of the courtroom with his son, or at least in a better position than the one he was currently in. The hearing lasted every bit of two hours, and after taking a ten-minute recess, the judge walked back into the courtroom, sat in his chair, and prepared to give his ruling.

Brian sat on the hood of his car outside in the parking lot, waiting for Kim to emerge from the legal building. He smiled when she walked out of the glass double doors. "So, how did you do?" he asked, passing her a bottle of water.

Kim paused for a moment, trying to make it a little suspenseful. "I got a perfect score," she busted out in joy, a little surprised that she did that good. The bar was tough, but for Kim, it was a walk in the park. Being a paralegal for so long and studying the law helped out in a major way. Aside from being confident, she really did know the law and every intricate detail about the United States Constitution. It was a wonder it took her this long to give the exam a crack.

"You know Tim is gonna end up making you a partner," Brian joked. "One thing I know about him is that he loves money, and you're making him plenty."

Kim smiled at the thought but didn't think that it would be realistic at this time, especially since Tim already had a partner. "What about you, did you take care of that situation?" Kim quizzed, looking to get some eye contact from Brian.

She was referring to a number of illegal items he had at his and her house, which he promised to get rid of. Assault rifles, drugs, and body armor were just a few of the things he possessed. Not even Kim could help him if the feds decided to run up in his house.

"Nah, I didn't do it yet, but I will," he said, grabbing her waist and pulling her closer to him. That wasn't enough for Kim, though. The promise was a little bigger than just getting the items out of their house. Brian was supposed to be getting out of the game, which he was knee-deep in. That was the real promise and was supposed to be carried out before Kim walked down the aisle.

Tammy looked down at the large pile of laundry sitting on the couch, dreading the fact that she had to fold every piece of clothing without any help. Having already cleaned the entire house, this was the last of the chores that needed to be done before a little relaxation could take place. As she stood there and was about to reach for the first article of clothing to fold, the locks on the front door could be heard clicking. This was out of the ordinary, since Mr. Jimmy changed all the locks before she moved back in. She grabbed Anthony's trophy off the coffee table and was about to let whoever walk through that door have it.

"Boy, you lost ya damn mind?" Tammy yelled at Chris with the trophy raised in the air.

Chris was lucky to have grabbed Tammy's wrist before she could administer the blow.

"Whoa, girl," he grinned, amused at her being in attack mode.

Tammy snatched her wrist away, then put out her hand, insisting that Chris give up the key.

"I don't know what you said to Mr. Jimmy for you to get a set of keys, but you need to turn them the hell over. This is my house, not yours," she barked. Not wanting to get into an argument about it, Chris reluctantly handed over the keys.

"Now, the kids are not here so what do you want?" she asked, walking back over to the couch.

Chris didn't expect for Tammy to be home, and the only reason why he came there today was to retrieve some money he had stashed in the basement. He wasn't about to let her know that, though. "I came by to check up on you," he said, walking up behind Tammy and attempting to wrap his arms around her waist. His touch sent chills down her spine. She pushed off and turned around with her face turned up. Chris gave her a seductive grin, licking his bottom lip as he took a couple of steps toward her.

"Come here. I know you miss daddy dick," he said, reaching out for her hand. He was arrogant, thinking that Tammy would always want him, and though he may have been partially right, it wasn't the way he thought. She couldn't believe he was coming on to her yet again, and more so on the touchy-feely level now. In any event, Tammy wasn't going to entertain him. This was the reason she was by herself now, after the big fight at Ms. Dee's house. She and the kids had moved back into their old apartment.

"Chris, let me be straight-up wit' you so there won't be any confusion. You will never, ever, ever, ever, taste this pussy again. I put that on the lives of our children," she said with sincerity in her eyes. "So please stop trying and let's just call it what it is."

"I don't believe you. You mean to tell me that I'll never be able to suck on dat pussy again? You telling me that ya kitty don't purr for this pipe?" Chris smiled, grabbing a handful of his crotch. He had seduction in his eyes, but Tammy had nothing but hatred in hers. In the past, she probably would have been weak and fell for his game, but now, her heart took a turn for the worst, and Chris no longer had any influence on her life.

"It's time for you to leave," she concluded, walking over to the front door and opening it.

Chris could see that she wasn't impressed by his charm, so he figured now wouldn't be the time to try to make his way to the basement to retrieve his bread. Instead, he turned to walk out the door, but not without having a serious attitude. And mumbling the word.

"Bitch!"

Lamar watched as Falisha and Jordan got onto the elevator. His lawyer could see the pain in his eyes. It was actually a turn-on to her. She had never seen a responsible man as passionate as he was and willing to go through everything he'd been through in order to be with his son. She was his lawyer, but as a woman, she was feeling him.

"I give you my word, I'm going to do everything I'm able to get you back in ya son's life," Anne said, placing her hand on Lamar's back in an attempt to comfort him.

There was nothing she could say to make him feel any better at this point. All he wanted was his son, and thoughts of doing something vicious to Falisha in order to get him back kept entering his mind. The games Falisha was playing were unnecessary and out of pocket, but since this was the game she wanted to play, he was going to make sure it cost her in the near future.

When Falisha exited from the courthouse, she immediately pulled out her cell phone to cut it back on. It had been killing her sitting inside the courtroom and not able to check her Instagram and Facebook. Before she could click on the app icon, her phone began to ring flashing the word Unknown. Falisha knew exactly who it was calling her from a private or blocked number. Fox had been trying to reach back out to her ever since word got out that she had beat the drug case. Fox just assumed that there was no way for Falisha to get out of a case like that without ratting him out. He knew she didn't have the financial means to hire the type of lawyer that could beat a potential federal case. He wanted her to agree to meet with him so he could check her temperature and see just how much she told the cops. If it was as much as he assumed, they would have wanted to dismiss her case. Fox had already made up his mind that he would have to do the unthinkable. Although he had some feelings for Falisha, they were nowhere near the amount he would need to risk his freedom for. He also didn't want the beef that he knew would come from Chris. But again, he wasn't going to end up in prison for trying to avoid it.

"Damn, babe, I'm proud of you," Brian yelled out from the bedroom to Kim who was in the bathroom sitting on the toilet. She looked down at the box which contained the First Response pregnancy test and ripped it open. She could vividly remember the time when she was in this position before, messing around with Lamar. With some of the signs her body gave, she was almost certain that she was pregnant. Within about a minute of pissing on the little stick, her suspicion was confirmed. "Oh God!" she exhaled, gliding her fingers through her hair. Weighing the options of whether to tell Brian began to creep into her thoughts. She was leaning toward giving him the news being as though they were about to get married, but then Brian's lifestyle choices prevented her from wanting to do so.

"What are you doing in there?" he yelled, knocking on the bathroom door.

Kim quickly got up and hid the test in-be-tween some towels in the cabinet. She made up her mind for now that she wasn't going to tell him. She had to be sure that she was going to keep it first. That decision was going to be entirely up to the choices Brian made in the near future. The wrong ones could mean the end of fatherhood for sure.

"Okay, Mom, just give me like ten minutes," Falisha said into the phone. "I know, I know, just give me ten minutes."

Chris sat on the edge of the bed, tapping away at the keys on the laptop. He was all over Facebook and Instagram, seeing the latest flicks Tammy had posted. He didn't want to admit it, but the lack of interest Tammy had in him made him kind of want her even more. It was as if she wasn't feeling him at all.

"Can you watch him real quick so I can go help my mom with something?" Falisha asked as she was fixing her hair in the mirror.

Chris looked up at her like she was crazy. "You know I'm not a babysitter," he shot back. "Take him wit' you."

Jordan was asleep in their bed and had been for the past thirty minutes.

"Babe, I'm gonna be a half hour. Besides, he's asleep."

"I don't care if he's asleep or not. I'm not watching him," Chris snapped back, making Falisha cut her eyes over at him.

It wasn't what he said, it was how he said it. This was the first time he'd gotten nasty like this about watching Jordan. It was rare Falisha ever asked him to, but when she did, he never had a problem with it.

"What da hell is ya problem?" she asked, walking over to Chris who was still looking in the screen of the laptop. "Hello! I know you hear me."

He looked up, then rolled his eyes back to the screen with an attitude. This only made her madder. She snatched the laptop out of his hands and was about to slam it shut, but before she did, she got a glance at what was on the screen. Now she was *really* pissed. Tammy's Facebook page was on the screen with a couple of cute pictures of her and the kids she had just posted.

"Gimme my shit," he yelled, snatching the laptop back from her. "Go ahead and go where you're going."

"No, I'm not going anywhere. Why da fuck is you on her page? What, you miss that dumb bitch? You want that bitch back?"

"Yo, watch how you talk about the mother of my kids," Chris checked. He was already upset about what happened with Tammy earlier, and now Falisha was getting the bad end of the stick, and she didn't even know it. At this point, he really didn't care what came out of his mouth.

"I barely watch my own kids, so what makes you think that I wanna watch somebody else's? You should be trying to let his real daddy watch him instead of me."

These were definitely some of the harshest words Chris had said to Falisha since they'd been together, and just as the anger subsided, sadness began to kick in. Falisha calmly walked over to the bed, picked Jordan up, and walked out of the room without saying another word.

Chapter 22

"Congratulations!" the whole office yelled out when Kim got to work. Tim, being who he was, had already got the word of Kim passing the bar exam. He had total confidence in her from the very beginning and had put a few things in motion because of it. "Get over here, kid," he said, pulling Kim in for a hug. "Come on in." Inside of his office, he went into his stash of booze and pulled out a bottle of bourbon. He poured two nice shots for both of them. Normally, it would have been a good time for a drink, but Kim declined, knowing what she had growing inside of her.

"Mark my words, you're gonna have a lot of law firms contacting you in the near future. I figure I'd let you know—"

"Tim, I'm not going anywhere, if that's what you're thinking," she interrupted. At least her staying there with Tim was her intentions, but Tim knew the reality of the situation and understood the legal game more than most. With high scores like Kim's, the word was going to get around fast.

"Just hear me out, kid," Tim began. "I have a $50,000 bonus for you just as long as you give me another year. All the cases you work with me, we'll split the retainer fee sixty–forty, my way. And last but not least, your office will be right next to mine," he smiled, pointing to Tony's old office.

Tim never said the words directly, but Kim understood this to mean that he was trying to make her partner and not just a lawyer. This was the best news Kim had gotten thus far, and she didn't believe that there was a better offer coming her way in the future. She wanted to sign on right then and there, but Tim didn't allow her to. Instead, he gave her two weeks to listen to what other law firms had to offer, and if she didn't like what she heard from them, then her place would be with Tim and his firm.

Tammy didn't expect that when she dropped the kids off at Chris's mom's house, that she would want to talk. It was a total shock, considering the fact that the last time they had a sit-down was two years ago. "That dang SpongeBob movie should keep them busy for a while,"

Ms. Elain said coming back down the stairs. She walked over and took a seat next to Tammy on the couch. "I really just wanted to know how you've been," Ms. Elain began. It's definitely been awhile since they had this kind of conversation.

"I'm doing better. The kids are healthy, I'm healthy, and we got a roof over our heads. I can't complain."

"I know that's right," Ms. Elain smiled. "You know I never got a chance to apologize for that dumb stuff my son did."

"Ms. Elain, you don't have to apologize for him. To be honest wit' you, I messed my own marriage up. I jeopardized what I wanted most for what I wanted in the moment. The love I had for Chris prevented me from being with someone else, but I'm about to make things—"

Tammy caught herself before she said too much. A lot had gone on since that day at Ms. D's house, and there were still some issues that needed to be addressed. Speaking on the topic, it reminded Tammy that she needed to be somewhere in the next hour.

"Ms. Elain, I'm sorry, but I have to get out of here," Tammy said, gathering her things from off the couch. She didn't want to seem completely rude. "How about you come over to the house on Saturday, and we'll have lunch?"

Ms. Elain saw that Tammy was in a rush, and she didn't want to hold her up. Agreeing to the Saturday lunch was all she could do before Tammy hugged her, then headed out the front door. Her business elsewhere was important and she couldn't afford to be late.

Chris sat on the couch smiling ear to ear, watching Falisha storm around the apartment as she was cleaning. Baby Jordan was off in the corner of the living room playing with some of his favorite toys. It appeared that he too was amused by his mother, laughing every time she walked past him.

"Aye, Falisha, come here," Chris said, right as she was passing by to go into the kitchen. She was going to ignore him, but Chris reached out and grabbed her wrist.

"Stop playing and come here," he smiled, pulling her down onto his lap. "How long are you going to be mad? I think I apologized like ten times last night. Come on, babe, let me see you smile," he chuckled, playfully poking her in the side.

Falisha didn't want to smile, but she did anyway, just to get him to let her go. She was still in her feelings about the other day.

"There she go. Now, that's my girl."

Falisha attempted to get up, but it only became a wrestling match, ending with Chris getting on top of her and pinning her arms to the cushion.

"You know what the best part of you being mad at me is?" he asked, leaning in and pecking her lips. She could feel his dick getting hard through his sweats, and it was only the thin fabric of her house pants separating her flesh from his bulge. Falisha wasn't getting aroused, though. She knew that all Chris was doing was trying to make up for what he said. It was game, the kind of game that she saw through. It had been a couple of days since Chris had been inside of her, and he wanted some, bad. Jordan had his own plans, as well, hopping up from his toys and wobbling over to the couch so he could play wrestling too.

"Cock blocker," Chris smiled, picking Jordan up and sitting his butt on Falisha's face.

This was exactly what Falisha was mad about now. Chris always had some ignorant shit to say out of his mouth.

A knock at the front door caught everybody's attention. Chris jumped up to answer it while Falisha started to play with Jordan. Chris was taken off guard when he opened the door and saw Lamar standing there. Before Falisha could see who it was, he stepped out into the hallway and closed the door behind him. He wasn't sure how Lamar even knew where they lived.

"What's good, brah? And how do you know where I live?" was the first thing that came out of his mouth.

Lamar looked at him like he couldn't believe Chris just asked that question.

"Do you know where your kids rest their heads at night?" Lamar shot back. It only made sense to Chris. He couldn't imagine not knowing where his kids were, at all times.

"So what can I do for you?"

"Look, homie, I just wanna see my son. Falisha playing a lot of games wit' this court shit. I'm kinda fed up wit' it to be honest with you."

The look Lamar had in his eyes said a million things, all of which Chris sympathized with. Lamar's eyes were starting to water up, and Chris knew it wasn't because he was scared; it was because of the love and emotion he had for his son.

"Nigga, you ain't strapped, is you?" Chris asked, looking down at Lamar's waist.

Lamar entertained him by lifting his shirt. Chris opened the door and nodded for him to follow him inside. Falisha jumped up from the couch after seeing Lamar and right before she

305

was about to give him a vicious tongue-lashing, baby Jordan reached out for his dad.

"Hey, li'l man," Lamar smiled, walking over to Falisha who had Jordan in her arms. She didn't want to let Jordan go for nothing, but the smile on Jordan's face was priceless.

"Come here, let me halla at you," Chris said, grabbing Falisha by the hand in an attempt to pull her in the other room so Lamar could have some alone time with his son.

"I'm not leaving my son alone with him."

Chris's voice was calm, and he showed no signs of worry when he whispered in Falisha's ear and said, "Please." She quietly protested for a minute, but eventually followed Chris into the other room. She didn't see how harmful it would have been to deny Lamar the opportunity to see his son, but Chris was going to explain in detail why a woman shouldn't keep a child away from his father, especially the type of father that really cares about his kid.

"And you better not be trying to boss me around neither," Tanya said as she, Kim, and Michael sat in Kim's new office.

"Ain't nobody gon' boss y'all around. You know I'ma be doin' my own research and motions,"

Kim shot back. Kim's phone began to vibrate on the desk, and on the screen an area code that was unfamiliar to her popped up. She looked at it crazy before picking up the phone. "Hello," she answered, looking over and shrugging her shoulders at Tanya. A man with a very deep voice like Barry White spoke back.

"Is this Kimberly?"

"Yes, this is she."

Just then, Tim walked up to the office door and posted up.

"My name is Jonathan Adams. I'm with William and Price Law Firm. Sources tell me that you was at the top of ya class, scoring a perfect score on ya bar exam. That's impressive."

"Thank you, but I don't understand the purpose of this call."

"Well, let me cut straight to the chase. Me and my colleagues are very interested in meeting with you. We think that you'll be a valuable asset to our law firm."

"I don't mean any disrespect, but I don't think I'm going—"

"All I'm asking you for is a meet and greet. If you don't like what you hear, then that will be it."

Kim looked over at Tim who was standing at the door smiling. He knew this was going to happen and warned Kim of it. He even knew that

William and Price was going to call her because when he scored high on his bar examination, they called him too. William and Price had a criminal division within the firm, but most of their bread and butter came from civil actions. It was rumored that the firm grossed over 200 million last year, more than any law firm in the United States. Tim gave Kim the nod, encouraging her to hear what they had to offer. He didn't want her to regret missing out on an opportunity.

"One meeting," Kim said.

"Fine. Pack ya overnight bag because a private jet will pick you up in the morning at Philadelphia International."

Tammy walked into Martez's Bistro, nervous as hell, thinking about how the conversation between her and Darious was going to go. She had only heard from him a few times since the incident at Ms. D's house, and that was just recently. She couldn't believe that he actually wanted to have lunch. Tammy looked around and was about to leave until she finally spotted him. Darious was sitting at a table in the far back of the well occupied restaurant. She took a deep breath and walked on over toward him.

"How are you?" Darious greeted, getting up from his seat and giving her a hug. The hug was unexpected. "It's good to see you."

Everything about Darious seemed different. He had a full, well-groomed beard, a low Caesar, and even his clothes looked different. "Never saw you in a suit before, except at our—"

Tammy caught herself, not really wanting to bring up anything about that horrible day. The fact was, the time Darious took for himself was well needed. He had time to think about everything that had happened in his life and reflected on ways to improve it instead of dwelling on the negative. That was the real reason why he was in good spirits right now.

"Yea, well, I think a lot has changed for me over the last couple of months. I guess that's why I wanted to have lunch with you. I got a job offer from a pharmaceutical company last week."

Tammy smiled as she was happy for him. What came next was a shocker.

"The job offer is in China, and depending on how things look out there, I may be making it my permanent home." Tammy tried to process what her ears were hearing. It got real quiet at the table while she rolled it over in her mind.

"China?" she asked with a confused look on her face.

"Yea, I know it's far, but to be honest wit' you, there's nothing left here for me. The best part of me is gone."

Hearing that, Tammy's eyes began to water, thinking about how she messed up in a major way. Hurting Darious the way that she did was probably the worst thing she'd ever done in her life.

"So I guess this is ya way of saying good-bye," she said, unable to hold back the single tear that fell from her eye.

"Nah, I was hoping you would come with me," he said, then started to laugh with a semiserious look on his face. Being away from Tammy for this long had made him reflect and only being honest with himself, he had to admit that he still loved her. For that alone, he knew he had to pose the question to her again, but this time in a more serious manner.

He shook his head before speaking again, "What if I don't want this to be our final good-bye? If I asked you to come with me, what would you say?" Tammy's eyes got wide. A part of her felt like maybe Darious was still joking, but the serious look on his face said otherwise.

"Darious, are you sure? Please let me know if this is a joke."

Chapter 23

Before Kim could actually get the cold out of her eyes, an Uber driver was calling her phone, letting her know that he was downstairs waiting. Brian had just got out of the shower and was coming into the room. He had an evil look on his face. "Yo, I know you wanted me to come with you, but I can't," he explained as he was getting dressed. "My man Chicken got killed last night, and I gotta take care of something." This morning was off to a bad start already, and Kim didn't have the time or energy to go into the reasons why she felt Chicken's death should make him wanna take some time off. Him stuffing a black .45 into his back pocket was a reminder what she was up against. "Look, I know you gonna knock this interview out of the park," he said, walking over and taking a seat on the bed next to her.

"It's not an interview, and I really wanted you . . ." Kim paused seeing that she was about to start fussing.

"How about this . . . When you get back tomorrow, we'll sit down and really put the wedding into third gear. Make a date, find a place, and do the invites," Brian said, kissing her on the cheek. "How does that sound to you?"

It sounded like some bullshit to her, but she didn't say anything, not right now anyway. The Uber driver was calling her phone again, and according to Jonathan, the jet was leaving within the next hour.

Chris walked into his mom's house, and as soon as he heard the kids upstairs playing, he tried to turn around and walk back out the door.

"Chris!" Ms. Elain yelled out before he could make it out the front door. He gave a playful fist pump, disappointed that he couldn't make it out the door fast enough.

"Wassup, Mom? I was just checking on you."

"Checking on me, my ass. That girl dropped these kids off yesterday and hasn't been back yet. She's not answering the phone, and when I drove to the house, she didn't answer the door neither," Ms. Elain vented. She loved her grandkids to death, but the medication she was on due to the recent hip replacement had her not able to function right, let alone watch after two lively kids.

"Mom, I'm trying to take care of something right now. Can you just watch them for a couple of more hours while I try to find Tammy?" Chris pleaded.

"Boy, as God is my witness, you got two hours. The next place I'll be making my way to is your place. Let that so-called girlfriend of yours really play house," she said with an attitude.

Chris jumped right on his phone as he was leaving the house in search of Tammy.

Today was the first time that Kim had ever flown on a private jet, and the ride to California didn't seem as long as she thought it would be. She had complimentary everything. Champagne, TV, and the Internet was more than enough to keep her busy. There was also a bed in the back, but the last thing Kim could think about was sleep.

When they landed at LAX, the jet peeled off the runway and pulled into a hanger. Three cars sat there waiting. A white 2016 Range Rover Super Charged, a white 2015 Lamborghini Huracan, and a white 2015 Rolls-Royce Wraith.

"Welcome to LA," a young white female greeted when Kim got off the plane.

"My name is Karin, and this is Rebecca," she said extending her hand for a shake. Jonathan was also there and reintroduced himself with a smile. Turns out he was only a recruiter for the firm but definitely served his purpose, assembling some of the country's best lawyers and bringing them under one roof. Karin and Rebecca had also been recruited by him a little less than two years ago.

"Now, look, I'm not gonna lie," Karin began. "William and Price have till the end of the day to convince you that getting back on that airplane tonight will be a mistake. So let's get right to it," she smiled, leading Kim over to the car she was driving which was the Range Rover. The drive from the airport to Pine Grove took a little less than an hour, but during the drive, Karin took time to explain what the law firm was about.

"Okay, good, he's here," Karin said, pulling into the driveway of a beautiful lakeside home. Still in awe from the private jet and the fancy luxury cars, this huge house had her even more mesmerized. She almost didn't see the short, white, gray-haired man standing in front of the home.

"It's an 8,000 square foot, five-bedroom, five-and-a-half bathroom home, nestled on about four acres of land," the old man said when Kim got out of the car. Even he had to turn around and take a look at the estate. "It's finally nice to meet you," he said, extending his hand for a shake.

Kim just knew that their firm had to be successful, seeing how he was living.

"I must say, you have a beautiful home," Kim spoke, only to get a chuckle from Mr. Price. She hadn't the slightest idea.

"No, sweetheart, this is not my house. This is *your* home, along with the car, as long as you choose to be a part of the greatest law firm in America," Price said, taking Kim by surprise.

"I don't understand." Kim had a confused look on her face. Mr. Price smiled, took Kim by the hand, and led her into the house. Karin followed close behind. Mr. Price was about to show Kim what life would be like should she work for him.

Lamar was getting tired of going back and forth to court, especially since he hardly ever came out victorious. Just like the last time, Falisha walked into the courtroom with a sleeping Jordan hunched over her shoulder. She had no intentions of letting Lamar get partial custody of her son, and after no consideration at all, she had even declined visitation rights.

"Don't come over here," Falisha checked, seeing the look in Lamar's eyes.

Anne tried to stop him, but her voice was unheard by him. He walked right up on Falisha, looked at his son, and then looked at her. He had a submissive look on his face, almost like he wanted to cry. Lamar had been up for nearly three days straight, trying to figure out what he could say or do to rectify this situation, and it seemed that all hope was lost. Falisha was hell-bent on making sure he had no place in Jordan's life, and it didn't look like the courts were going to help.

"Last chance to do the right thing," he spoke softly so only she could hear. It was as if he was taking his final stance in the matter. Falisha dismissed him without a second thought. A kiss to Jordan's head and a light tear falling from his left eye was all Lamar managed to get off before the judge walked into the courtroom.

"Your Honor, if I may speak," Lamar said as the judge was sitting down. Anne looked over at him and even tried to mumble for him to stop talking, but at this point, he was too far gone.

"Your Honor, I'm done with all of this. I been through hell trying to get some type of custody of my son, and every time I come in this courtroom, I leave empty-handed." Seeing the look on the judge's face, Anne tried to grab Lamar's arm to get him to stop talking, but to no avail.

"Effective immediately, I'm turning over all parental rights of Jordan Thompson to his mother," Lamar yelled.

Anne was stunned and tried to try to get Lamar to reconsider, but it was too late. Thoughts of Falisha and Chris playing house with his son, along with the irreconcilable relationship between him and Falisha, had brought Lamar to his breaking point. Even Falisha was shocked to hear him say that.

"Son, do you understand that you, being the father to this child—"

"I really don't care anymore. His mother wants him so bad, she has him now. I'm better off making another child with someone else. Someone who deserves to have somebody like me."

It sounded very harsh, but it was exactly how Lamar felt at that moment. The judge couldn't even respond as Lamar gathered his things and headed out of the courtroom. For an instant, it was completely silent. Everybody, including Falisha, was trying to figure out what just happened. It hadn't dawned on her until that very moment, when she felt a total sense of loneliness. She had broken Lamar, and the sad part about the whole thing was that Lamar, unlike many men, was a good father.

***

Brazilian cherrywood flooring, incredible grand foyer, sweeping staircases in the front and rear of the house, huge master bedroom on the main level with its very own secluded deck, a finished walkout basement for entertainment, sensational living room with a twenty-five-foot ceiling, a gourmet kitchen with stainless steel appliances, and a magnificent swimming pool that looked out to the lake . . .

"So you mean to tell me that all I have to do is work for you for the next year, and this house will be mine?" Kim asked, still in disbelief from the offer.

"The day you sign on to my law firm is the day when I will sign the deed to this property over to you, along with the title to the car," Mr. Price said.

With the cases he had lined up for Kim, she would have made enough money to buy this house three times over. The house and the car were only equivalent to $1.5 million, which he'd given to all of his lawyers that worked for him. Dressing it up this way always seemed to get him better results from newbies.

"What about Tim? I just can't leave him out to dry like that."

And that was truly how Kim felt. She almost felt obligated to stay with Tim's law firm.

"Rebecca," Mr. Price yelled out from the kitchen.

She walked in with a folder, placing it onto the marble countertop. Mr. Price opened it up, separating the deed, the title, and the one-year contract to work for William and Price. He pulled out an ink pen and put it on top of the paperwork. Kim couldn't believe he was giving her little to no time to think about it. She had to make a decision right now, and there was no telling if this opportunity would ever come her way again. Those were her thoughts as she looked down at the form.

Ms. D walked from the kitchen to the living room and was nearly out of breath before she could make it to the couch. Her energy had been getting less and less over the past few weeks between chemo and all the other medicines she was taking. Sometimes, she didn't know whether she was coming or going. The room started to spin, and as she reached out to grab the arm of the sofa, she collapsed, falling to the ground, but not before hitting her head on the wooden coffee table in front of the couch. The blow didn't knock her out completely, but it definitely caused some severe damage. The room continued to spin, and her eyesight began to blur. Ms. D tried to gain enough strength to reach up and grab her phone that was sitting on the couch.

"Oh, God, help me," she mumbled to herself. She looked for the inner strength within, but her limbs weren't moving. It was as if she was paralyzed from the neck down because she couldn't move anything.

Her vision continued to weaken as her eyelids became too heavy to keep open.

This must be it, she thought to herself. *This must be the end of the rope for me.*

Visions of certain events that occurred in her life when she was young and innocent began to flash through her thoughts. Life when she was a teen and when she became a young adult followed. She thought about the only child she gave birth to, her mother, father, her sister who passed away, and her brother who was still alive serving time in prison.

Now, Ms. D knew that this had to be the end for her. Her heart began to race uncontrollably, her breathing became weak, and her body was unable to go any further. She lay there on her back, looking up at the ceiling, and as her life slowly faded away, the last thoughts that went through her mind were the hopes that God would allow her into heaven.

The female eyewitness stood in the middle of Brian's living room, explaining how the whole shooting unfolded with his best friend Chicken.

"He tried to run, but the guy chased after him," the young female cried. "He shot Chicken right in the back of his head." After visualizing it, the female couldn't take it anymore and started to break down in tears, so much so that Brian had to wrap her up in his arms. He had to stop himself from crying, thinking about the way his boy died.

"I need you to listen to me," Brian said, forcing the young female to look up into his eyes. "If the police ask you anything about this, I want you to tell them you don't know anything. Can you do that for me?"

The girl nodded her head, but that wasn't good enough for Brian.

"I need you to say it," he told her, which, in return, she did.

He was well aware of the gunman who pulled the trigger and only hoped that he got to him before the police figured it out. After the young lady was escorted out of the house, Brian walked into the dining room and took a seat at the table.

His boys Peet, Teath, and Dez joined him, also taking a seat at the table. This was the last of his crew, and he wanted to make sure that he didn't lose anybody else.

"We gon' move on these niggas tonight. I'ma blow Fabian's head clean off his shoulders."

"I think tomorrow night will be better," Peet cut in. "That gives us a little more time to plan this shit out. I wanna make sure we get away. Eighth Street stay on point, and they keep shooters on the roof out there. Niggas stay strapped."

"Trust me, Fabian be slippin'. He's too dumb and too slow," Dez tried to counter.

Brian sat back in his chair and thought about what Peet was saying. He was right. Eighth Street was known for gunplay and running up with guns blazing could end badly for Brian and his crew. He wanted revenge, but not at the cost of his life.

"A'ight, we do this shit tomorrow night. Meet me back here tomorrow afternoon. And, Dez, bring that choppa wit' you," Brian said, then got up and walked everybody to the door.

Chris looked high and low for Tammy, but couldn't find her anywhere. He'd been to her house, her cousin's house, Carol's house, called her phone numerous times, and came up emp-ty-handed every time. He was now becoming frustrated, because every call that was coming through his phone was coming from his mother. She hadn't been off her feet since Tammy dropped them off, and for Chris, that was a major problem.

Chapter 24

Lamar sat on the edge of his bed looking down at the gun sitting in his lap. So many evil thoughts ran through his mind, all of which pointed to him killing Falisha, and Chris also if he happened to be there at the time. His phone began to vibrate on the nightstand, momentarily catching his attention. It was Anne, his attorney. "Yea, wassup?" he answered, holding the phone to his ear with one hand and grabbing the gun with the other. Lamar had taken all the professionalism out of their relationship. As far as he was concerned, Anne was just another part of a system that had taken his son away from him.

"I have some good news, Lamar, and I would rather tell you face-to-face. Are you home?"

"What kind of good news could you possibly have? I can tell you know I'm not stepping another foot into that courtroom," he replied.

"Well, I'm standing out in front of your house. Are you here?"

Lamar walked over to his window and looked down on the street. Anne was standing up against her car.

"Oh, OK. Give me a minute. I'll be right down," he said, ending the call. He quickly tucked the gun away, put on a tank top, and headed down the stairs. It had to be some real good news since she had come all the way out here he thought to himself.

"Hey, Anne, come in."

Lamar couldn't help but to take note of the outfit she had on. Anne always looked so professional, and today was no different. He loved the way the simple gray suit and white shirt she was wearing hugged all of her natural curves. Her beautifully manicured toes peeked through the black Jimmy Choo open toe pumps. In her hand was a charcoal leather briefcase, and she wasted no time digging inside and pulling out some paperwork.

"The judge granted our motion for you to have partial custody of Jordan. He got real emotional the other day when you walked out of the courtroom and came to the conclusion that if any man would fight for his kid as hard as you did, he deserved to be in that child's life," Anne reported, passing Lamar the custody papers.

The smile on Lamar's face was priceless. Not able to hold back his emotion, he said, "Anne, thank you so much," then pulled her in for a hug. Her small curvy frame disappeared as he wrapped her up in his arms. A kiss to the top of her forehead surprisingly turned Anne on. As she slowly pulled away from his grasp, there was a brief moment as they stared into each other's eyes . . . All of the attraction and desire that both had suppressed since he first walked into her office began to come to a head.

Anne reinitiated contact, grabbing his tank top and pulling his face down to hers. When their lips connected, the rest of her body began to melt. She pulled away, trying to fight the dangerous urge to stop while she had the chance. Lamar wasn't having it and grabbed her hand before she could walk away. He reached in and removed her blazer, all the while looking into her eyes. His tank top came off next, showing off his chiseled body, and once Anne saw that, she knew she wasn't about to just walk away. She just stood there, letting Lamar unbutton her shirt, and then undo her belt.

Before she knew it, Anne was standing in the middle of Lamar's living room with only her panties, bra, and heels on. He looked at her body, amazed at the curves and thickness. He

almost preejaculated at the sight. He wasted no
time lifting her up, wrapping her legs around
his waist, and walking her up the stairs. They
kissed passionately the whole way to the bedroom, and once there, Lamar laid her down
gently. His sweatpants dropped to the floor, and
Anne became even wetter from the size of his
long, curvy dick. As he removed her panties, he
hesitated, rubbing the head of his dick up and
down her center before pushing it in. She gasped,
then bit down on his shoulder as all nine inches
of him filled her canal. She only became wetter
with every slow stroke, and Lamar dug deeper
so he could hear her moans.

"Oh my God, you gon' make me come," she
whispered in his ear. Her pussy was so soft
and wet Lamar almost came as well. "Harder,
harder," she whispered, feeling the orgasm
coming on.

Lamar kept stroking harder and deeper, stuffing his tongue down her throat in the process.
He could feel her walls tightening up around
his dick, so he stroked harder and faster. Anne's
come splashed all over his dick, and as easy as it
would have been for him to join her, he declined,
wanting to make sure that he took his time with
touching every part of her body this evening.

***

Kim woke up in a large California king-size bed, slightly hung over from the events that took place the previous night after she signed with William and Price. Karin, Rebecca, and several other lawyers at the firm all threw Kim a last-minute party that turned out to be bananas. Kim got out of the bed, grabbing her phone off the nightstand, and walking out onto her bedroom's balcony. The view was amazing from where she stood, the kind of view she could easily get used to.

"Hey, baby," she greeted when Brian answered his phone. "I see you tried to call me last night, but I was busy."

"Yea, so when are you coming home? I miss you," he said as he wiped off bullets to load his weapon. Kim got quiet. This *had* to be the first question he asked.

"Boo, I'm not gonna lie to you. I took the job out here. I start next week."

Brian pushed the phone away from his face and stared at it. It was silent on both ends until Kim finally asked, "Are you still there?"

"Yea, I'm still here, but what do you expect me to say?"

"I expected that you would be telling me that you'll be on the next flight to California."

Brian wasn't feeling Kim at all right now.

"And how long do you expect for us to be staying out in California?" he asked with a curious look on his face.

It got quiet again, and this time, Kim looked out onto the beautiful landscape. After one year of her working for William and Price, the house and the Range Rover were going to be hers. The salary was going to be three times as much if she stayed and worked for Tim, plus the medical benefits extended to a husband and four kids. The more she thought about it, the more it became apparent to her that her decision to take the job was the right one.

"This is going to be our home for good, Brian. Me, you, and our—"

Brian hung up the phone before she could speak another word. He was so hot about the fact that Kim could make such a decision without consulting him first. He had nothing else to hear or say to her at that moment, and just in case she tried to call him right back, Brian turned his phone off altogether. His focus needed to be on the task before him. If he wanted to get the job done right, Kim and her BS were going to have to wait until later.

***

Lisa reached over and grabbed her phone out of the center consol. She actually had been waiting for this phone call.

"Damn, stranger," she answered seeing that it was Chris.

"I know, I know, don't kill me. I know it's been a minute since I checked up on you and Naomi," he said.

"Yea, whatever, boy. So what's going on wit' you?"

"Nothing much. I was calling because I wanted to know if you had seen or heard from Tammy. She's been MIA for a couple of days."

Lisa looked over at Tammy who was sitting in the passenger seat of her car.

"Nope, li'l brother. I haven't seen her, and the last time I talked to her was about a week ago," she lied. "You want me to call her?"

"Nah, nah, that's cool. I'll find her. You just give Naomi a kiss and tell her that it came from her uncle Chris," he uttered before ending the call.

Lisa smiled, looking over at Tammy. "Girl, how long do you plan on staying at my house?"

"I don't know. Why? You tired of me already?" Tammy shot back.

"Hell no. I'm about to make you my in-house babysitter if you keep messing around," Lisa joked.

Tammy really just needed some time to think. Darious offered her something that she never thought he would in a million years. The chance to move to China with him was mind-blowing, and though it was on the other side of the world, she was starting to consider it. The only thing that prevented her from making a decision right now was the kids. She didn't want to take them away from their father, not knowing when or even if, she would return back to the United States.

Eighth Street was booming, just like any other night, and there had to be at least 100 people out there scattered into little groups. The drug dealers were on the corner, neighbors were huddled up on each other's porches, kids were running up and down the street, and Fabian and his boys were sitting in the middle of the block doing what they did best: monitor all the money that was coming through.

"Yo, go buy the youngin's some ice cream," Fabian told one of his boys when he saw a Mr. Softy truck turning onto the street. All the kids swarmed the truck, knowing that Fabian would buy everybody a cone. It stopped right in the middle of the block. When the small window opened, an ice-cream cone wasn't the first thing that came out of it. Instead, it was the nose of an AR-15 aimed right in Fabian's direction. Without warning, shots started to fly. *Pop pop pop pop pop pop pop pop pop pop!*

Bullets flew over the top of the kids' head, right in the direction of Fabian, who was in Dez's crosshairs. Everybody scattered like roaches, including Fabian who didn't get that far. The AR-15 bullets chased him down, hitting him in his back calf muscle and making him fall to the ground. The ice-cream truck immediately took on heavy fire from the dope boys on the corner and the shooters on the roof.

"Drive, drive!" Dez yelled to Peet, who jumped into the driver's seat and peeled off. Bullets were coming from everywhere, knocking holes in the side of the truck. Dez jumped behind the ice-cream machine but a bullet made its way through the thin metal.

"Shit!" he yelled out, grabbing ahold of his side.

Peet took a bullet too to the shoulder, but he maneuvered the truck down the street like a pro. Everybody who had a gun ran down the street behind the truck, shooting at it repeatedly. Fabian tried to get to his feet, but the bullet took a nice chunk of meat out of his leg.

All of his boys ran in the opposite direction of
the ice-cream truck so he couldn't yell out to
anybody for help. Out of nowhere, a shadow
appeared to the right of him, and when Fabian
looked up, Brian was standing over the top of
him with a chrome .357 pointed right at his
face. Brian never said a word but instead, gave
him a slight grin . . . before pulling the trigger.
The hollow point bullet crashed through the
center of his forehead, knocking Fabian back
onto the concrete. Though he appeared to be
dead, Brian leaned in, placed the barrow of
the gun to the side of his head, and pulled the
trigger again. Then he laid the gun on top of
Fabian's chest and faded off into the night.

Being a part of William and Price had its
benefits, and one of them was being able to use
the private corporate jet. Mr. Price had actually
insisted Kim go back to Philly to retrieve her
valuables and rectify her affairs with her family
and friends. Only thing was, she needed to be
back in Cali by Monday so she could make her
first court appearance.

When she landed in Philly, she grabbed a
rental car and headed home. She got on her
phone and attempted to call Brian, but there

wasn't any answer. The second attempt went straight to voice mail. Kim was becoming annoyed real fast, so much so she sped off on the next exit, turning around to head for North Philly.

She knew Brian was home 'cause when she pulled onto his block, his car was double parked on the sidewalk. Two of his young boys were standing on the porch, and it looked like they both had guns tucked away in their waistband. They knew who Kim was, so they didn't even attempt to get in her way when she stormed up the steps. She almost passed out when she walked through the door and saw Brian lying on the couch with his clothes covered in blood. He opened his eyes to see her standing there with fear on her face.

"Baby, it's not mine," he yelled, jumping up from the couch. "It's not mine—look," he said, removing the shirt when he got closer to her. Kim wasn't completely convinced, scanning over his body.

"What da fuck is going on?" she snapped.

Brian walked her further in the room so nobody could hear their conversation. "Dez and Peet got shot tonight. Dez is in the basement getting patched up, but Peet had to go to the hospital," he explained. Kim looked to the sky and let out a frustrating sigh, figuring this was the reason why he didn't answer the phone.

"I can't take it, Brian," she said, walking over and taking a seat on the couch. "I can't do this anymore."

Brian walked over and took a seat next to her.

"You know, I was going to wait to tell you, but I might as well let you know. Brian, I'm pregnant," she said, looking over into his eyes. He had a shocked look on his face. "But if you plan on being out here in these streets, I'm not gonna keep it. I'm not gonna stress myself out and wonder when the morgue will call for me to come identify ya body."

"Kim, you knew what you was getting into from day one. I never hid my life from you, and now, you sound like you're trying to give me some type of ultimatum." This wasn't an ultimatum in Kim's eyes. It just was a choice he had to make. Kim saw a lot in her lifetime. Lisa losing Ralphy, Tammy losing Chris to prison, and now Falisha with her baby daddy drama. She wasn't trying to experience none of that.

"Look, I have a beautiful home, a nice car, and a great job back in California. I'm flying back tomorrow, and I swear, I want you to come back with me. I truly do."

"Come on, Kim, I just can't pick up and leave. I can't just—"

"Be at my place tomorrow morning at six o'clock," Kim said, cutting him off. "If you really desire to have a family to call your own, then I'll see you in the morning. If not, then go on with your life, but without me," she said, standing up. She didn't give Brian time to say anything, grabbing her things and walking out the door.

Lamar woke up to what appeared to be a female screaming out in front of his window. Getting up to investigate, he walked over to the window and saw Carol crying on her knees in front of Ms. D's house. He knew something was wrong. He quickly threw on some clothes and shot outside, only to fall to his knees as well when the medic was bringing Ms. D's body out on a stretcher. The white sheet covering her face made it obvious that she was dead. Cries from several other neighbors sounded out throughout the quiet street. Carol had been the one who found the body when she was coming over to take Ms. D to a doctor's appointment. This was a devastating blow. Not just for Ms. D's family, but for the whole of the community.

***

Jordan woke Chris up, smacking him in his face with a stuffed baseball bat. Anthony and Sinniyyah could be heard in the other room yelling and screaming about some toys. Off the bat, he was irritated, and since he couldn't get any sleep, neither was Falisha.

"Yo, get up!" he yelled, smacking her on the ass. "Yo, get up!" he yelled again when she didn't move fast enough. Falisha sat up in bed squinting her eyes. She had the kids all yesterday and was supertired.

"Get up and make us all something to eat," Chris demanded. Falisha looked at him like he was crazy.

"Why can't you do it?" she snapped back with an attitude. "I played house all yesterday."

Chris wasn't good with the whole child nurturing thing. He left all that up to Tammy, and this was one of the reasons he really missed her right now. She played her part when it came to her motherly duties.

Where da fuck is this girl at? he thought to himself.

In protest, Falisha finally got out of bed and headed for the kitchen. Chris, on the other hand, lay back down, but not before grabbing his phone off the dresser. He had a feeling that Tammy's phone was going to go to voice mail, but he tried calling her anyway. This time,

Tammy answered. "Where da fuck is you at?" he yelled into the phone.

His aggressive words didn't seem to bother Tammy one bit.

"I'm gonna ask you something, and I want you to be completely honest with me," she spoke in a calm voice.

"Fuck all that. Come get these kids. I got shit I'm trying to do," he snapped.

"Do you really love your kids? I mean, like, do you love them more than you love me?"

"What da fuck kind of question is that? Where da fuck are you?"

"Just answer the question and tell me the truth."

Chris scratched his head with a confused look on his face, more mad than anything that Tammy would be playing these types of games this morning.

"Of course, I love my kids more than I love you. That's because I don't love ya dumb ass no more. Look at the dumb shit you doing right now. How da fuck am I supposed to have love for—*Click!*—Hello, hello," Chris said into the phone, no longer hearing Tammy's voice. She had hung up, and when Chris tried to call her back, the phone went straight to voice mail again. It made him so mad that he threw his phone up against the wall, breaking it into little pieces. This definitely wasn't the way he had planned on that conversation going, and now he wondered if he had only made things worse. There was no way he and Falisha were going to make it another day with all three of the kids at the house.

Kim waited until nine o'clock, but Brian never came to her place. He didn't call, text, or anything, leaving Kim to believe that he had made his decision loud and clear. When she got to Philadelphia International, her phone began to ring. She hoped that it was him, but it wasn't. "Hey, girl," Kim answered seeing that it was Lisa.

The news of Ms. D's death buckled Kim's knees as she walked toward the jet. She found it hard to breathe for a few seconds, but when she finally got it together, she got on the jet and went straight up to the pilot. "Take me to Charlotte, North Carolina."

Chapter 25

Ms. D's funeral wasn't until Thursday, so that gave Kim, Lisa, and Tammy some time to catch up on life. They had lunch at the Crab Shack, one of their favorite places. "So when can we come out to Cali and chill?" Lisa asked as she cracked into a king crab leg. "I know it's nice out there."

"Yea, it's beautiful. I got a dream home, but y'all gon' have to give me a couple of months to get settled in, plus, I got work piled up to the ceiling, waiting for me to get back."

Mr. Price had to retrieve the jet for a business trip he had to take, but he gave Kim an extra week before she was needed back in Cali. When she did get back to Cali, it was going to be all work and no play, at least for the next month.

"So what about you. How have you been?" Kim asked Tammy, still feeling sad about what happened to her.

"I'm doing fine. I just got a lot on my mind right now."

"This bitch is on the run right now," Lisa cut in jokingly. "She done left Chris with the kids for almost a week now," she chuckled, thinking about him taking on that kind of responsibility. Tammy had to laugh herself. "He gon' kill her when he catch her." Lisa laughed with a mouth full of food. Kim didn't want to ask about Falisha while Tammy was there, but Lisa was on a roll. "And that crazy-ass Falisha won't let that boy see his son. I'm telling you, that girl got the devil in her. Even with a court order, she's denying him visitation."

Kim shook her head, taking in all the juicy gossip. She could never get tired of it, sitting there getting the full scoop from them. It was times like this she missed being in Charlotte. For the rest of the afternoon, they all just enjoyed each other's company. They talked about all that had been going on since Kim had been gone, and they also talked about Ms. D. The only thing that wasn't brought to the table today was Kim's pregnancy, and she wasn't ready to tell anybody else about it because she wasn't sure if she was going to keep the baby.

Brian took a deep pull of the marijuana, then exhaled it through his nose like a dragon. The recent murders of Fabian and Chicken had

Eighth Street and Twenty-third Street and Diamond on edge. No one had plans on letting up, and Brian had it in his mind that he was going to kill any and everybody who tried to get at him.

"Did you call her yet?" Dez asked, knowing Brian had been a little stressed about Kim moving to Cali.

"Yea, I tried to call, but she don't wanna talk to me right now. It's crazy 'cause I miss my bitch," he said, taking another pull of the weed. "You know, she told me that she was pregnant."

"Wow, bro, that's big," Dez replied, squinting from the pain of trying to move his arm. "So let me ask you this, and don't take this personal, my nigga. If you got a bad bitch out in Cali with her own shit, a good job, and wit' ya seed growing inside of her, why in the fuck are you still sitting here with me?"

"'Cause I'm hood bound, my nigga. I don't know nothing else but these streets, and for me to go out there, I feel like I would be out of place."

"I'ma keep it real wit' you, my nigga. You sound like a damn fool. But guess what? I'ma let you sit there and think about that dumb shit you just said out ya mouth," Dez concluded, taking the blunt from Brian. He grabbed the compact .45 off the table and tucked it into his sling. He looked back at Brian, and the next few words he spoke out of his mouth were so powerful. First, he pulled the gun back out so Brian could see it. "I gotta be strapped walking to the corner store. If you think this way of life have any significance to it, how about you keep this shit and let me go out there with Kim?" Dez proposed sarcastically before turning around and walking out the door. It was a gut check, no doubt, and something Brian would have to process in his mind for sure.

"Get da fuck away from my door, Lamar!" Falisha yelled, all the while trying to comfort Jordan who was crying.

"I got a court order to see my son!" he yelled back through the entrance. They'd been going back and forth like this for the past ten minutes, and the neighbors were starting to get a little irritated behind it. Falisha had no intention on opening up the door, especially since Chris wasn't there to monitor the visit.

"I'ma call the cops and tell them you trying to rape me. Ya ass is gonna go to jail today!" she threatened.

Lamar looked to the sky, clutching his teeth and balling up his hands. He was frustrated no doubt, but more hurt than anything. He began to speak in a low tone in the corner of the door.

"I swear, I don't know why you're doing this," he began.

Falisha put Jordan down on the couch, then walked over to the door to hear what Lamar had to say.

"All I wanted to do was be a good father to our son and a good man to you. Where did I go wrong?" Lamar felt like he wanted to cry, thinking about all that he'd been through with Falisha. She could care less about how he felt. She too was dealing with some unresolved issues, one being the fact that Lamar cheated on her with Kim in the beginning of their relationship. She regretted the fact that the only reason why Lamar chose to be with her was because of the pregnancy. It wasn't because he loved her as he claimed in the beginning, but rather by force. It ate at Falisha and scarred her for life. She would never be able to forgive him for that, and as long as she breathed the good gift of air, she was going to make his life a living hell.

"Just leave, Lamar, before I call the cops," Falisha spoke at the door.

Though he did have a court order to have partial custody of his son, the judge specified that a hearing was to commence in order for the custody issue to be explained more in detail.

Until then, there was nothing he could do about
it, and instead of getting in trouble with the law
and messing up any chance he had of getting his
son, Lamar walked off.

Brian was awakened by the mailman who
dropped several articles of mail through his
door. Getting up from the couch, he walked
over to the door. The first envelope that stuck
out to him was one with Kim's name on it.
Curious, he opened it first. Inside was a one-
way plane ticket from Philly to LAX. Kim had
bought the ticket when she was at Philadelphia
International, then dropped it in the mailbox
while she was there. No letter, no note, just a
plane ticket. Brian looked at it, thinking about
what Dez had said to him. The only thing was,
he really wasn't trying to leave Philly.

Despite all the drama he was going through,
he loved his city and a lot of people in it. He
didn't want to start over or leave his boys behind.
His feelings were similar to Caine in the movie
Menace II Society, except that he was leaning
more to the left. Getting him out of the hood
was like a mission impossible. Ultimately, Brian
crumbled up the ticket and threw it in the trash,
then grabbed his gun and got ready for another
day in the concrete jungle.

***

Lisa couldn't believe Tammy didn't show up to Ms. D's funeral. Not only didn't she show up, she didn't even call anybody to say that she wasn't going to make it. Tammy knew Chris was going to be there, and she didn't want to deal with his foolishness, plus, she still had a lot of thinking to do.

"So look, I'm trying to get everybody to come over to Ms. D's house for dinner," Lisa said as she, Kim, Lamar, Falisha, and Chris were walking away from the burial site.

Kim thought about the last dinner they had at Ms. D's and how messy things got. "I wish you would have said something to me about this a few days ago," she responded, finding her way out.

Falisha was next, crying that she had better things to do. Lamar jumped right in on the opportunity.

"How about you let me see me son?" he said in a slight tone. Falisha looked at him and smiled, knowing that she had Lamar by the balls when it came down to Jordan. "Don't you think that if I wanted you to see my son, I would have brought him here?"

Kim felt sorry for Lamar and decided to say something.

"Come on, Falisha, let that man see his son."

Falisha cut her eyes over at Kim. At this point, Falisha had forgotten that if it wasn't for Kim, she would probably still be in jail right now. Nobody was safe.

"Mind ya fuckin' business, bitch. If you wanted him to see his son so bad, you should of kept the one you aborted," Falisha barked.

"Awe, shit, here we go again with this shit. Can't you come up with something better?" Kim shot back.

Lisa put her hand over her forehead and let out a frustrating sigh. They weren't twenty feet away from Ms. D's burial site, and they was already arguing.

"Are y'all seriously going to do this right here, right now?" Lisa asked.

"Why not? This is where she started it," Falisha said, cutting her eyes over at Kim.

Chris tried to check Falisha, but she wasn't having it. He too was in her crosshairs.

"Fuck you, Chris," she snapped. "You think you got all the sense. Go look for ya baby mutha. I know you still love her. I know you still want her. You must think I'm a damn fool." She turned back to Kim. She wasn't done with her yet.

"And take ya boogie ass to California. Don't nobody want you down here anyway."

Chris threw his hands in the air, pretty much done with Falisha.

"You know what, Falisha? You bitter as hell. You got looks but no brains, and that's the reason why you can't keep a man. And for the record, you've always been jealous of me. But guess what? I'ma pray for you. God knows you need it," Kim said, then walked off, not allowing Falisha to respond.

Lamar stood there for a moment, fighting the urge to put his hands on her. Reluctantly, he walked off too, and so did Lisa, leaving Falisha standing there by herself. Ms. D was probably in her grave shaking her head with a smile on her face thinking, *This evil girl done struck again*.

Brian walked up the steps to go into the house, but as he was turning the key in the lock, he felt somebody walking up behind him. He went to reach for his gun, but it was too late. He could feel a gun being jammed into his side and a hand pressed up against his back. "Open the fuckin' door," a voice spoke in a low tone. Brian did what he was told and opened the door. He was pushed inside, almost falling to the ground. The gunman was on his heels, so Brian couldn't do too much of anything. He didn't want to try to pull his gun for fear that the shooter would kill him.

"What do you want, my nigga?" Brian asked sternly, trying to maintain his hardness.

"I wanna see you die, you bitch-ass nigga," the man replied, clutching the gun tighter. Brian could see it in the man's eyes that he meant what he said about wanting to see him dead. A fresh RIP tattoo was on the gunman's arm, so there was no wonder the motivation behind this encounter. Brian just couldn't understand how the gunman got up on him that fast.

"Yo, I didn't kill ya man," Brian lied, looking him in the eyes.

"Even if you didn't pull the trigger, you was the reason why." The gunman backed off of Brian with the intention to shoot him, but when he pulled the trigger . . . The gun clicked.

The gunman quickly cocked the gun back and pulled the trigger again before Brian had time to do anything. Again, the gun just clicked. Brian saw the opportunity and didn't want to let this chance pass him by. He jumped up from the couch, but the gunman cracked him right on the top of his nose with the side of the gun. It damn near knocked him out. *Crrrraacckk!* The gunman hit him again, this time with the butt of the gun on top of Brian's head. The second blow didn't knock him out either, but it dazed Brian long enough for the gunman to take flight out the door. Brian finally shook it off, but it was too late to try to get up and chase the guy. Plus, his nose was leaking blood all over his clothes. He grabbed his gun from off his waist, then went to lock the door. All he could think about was how easy it was for one of Fabian's boys to creep up on him and kill him. It was something he'd never expect to happen, not at his home, anyway. But it did, and now it was time for Brian to respond accordingly.

Chapter 26

One week later . . .

When Chris walked into the apartment, it looked empty. He walked into the bedroom, and every piece of clothing that belonged to Falisha and Jordan was gone. He didn't know exactly what it was, but a noise in the living room caught his attention. When he walked back into the living room and looked down by the front door, an envelope was on the floor. It wasn't there when he first walked through the door, so somebody must have slid it under there just now.

"What da hell," he mumbled, opening the door to see if somebody was out there. The hallway was clear and quiet. He thought that Falisha was behind it, but when he opened the envelope and started to read the letter, he darted back out the door, down the hallway, and into the parking lot, hoping he could have caught her. But she was nowhere to be found. Slowly walking back into the apartment building, he began to read the letter.

Dear Chris,

I know you're probably wondering where I've been and why haven't I tried to reach out and contact you and the kids. Well, I really just needed some time to myself so I could carefully make the decisions that I'm about to explain to you. First, let me say that through everything you put me through, I still have love for you. You're the father of my children, so how can I not love you? I guess that's the main reason why I chose not to take your children from you. I know you're probably thinking, "What the hell is this chick talking about?" Please let me explain. I'm moving far away, Chris. Darious has decided to take me back. He forgave me and offered me a chance to move to China with him. I can't lie, I'm still in love with this man, and if it takes me moving to the other side of the world to be with him, then that's what I'm going to do. As far as the kids are concerned, I think that it's time they get to know their father. So I'm leaving them with you and your family. At first, I thought about taking them with me, but again, I still got love for you, and I know how hurt you would have been if I took Anthony and ya princess away from you. Also, me and my husband need some time to put our life back in order. Once I get my life

*in array, I'll make a way to have them come.
Believe me when I tell you this, leaving them
behind is the hardest thing I ever had to do. But
at the same time, I truly think that it was the
best choice. I really hope that you find what it is
that you're looking for in life, and I really wish
you the best. Know for sure that I will always
love you. Take care of yourself and our children.*
   Tammy

Chris found it hard to even stand, taking a
seat on the stairwell. For her to leave like this,
it was a devastating blow. Chris always thought
that he had time to fix everything between them.
He thought that the love they had for each other
would prevail over all. His thoughts were wrong,
and, in fact, he had run clear out of time. Tammy
was gone, and she wasn't coming back. And now
it was time for him to step up and be daddy for
real.

When the taxicab pulled up to Kim's house,
Brian looked at the driver as though he had
made a mistake. A quick check of the address
that he got from Tim confirmed that this was
indeed Kim's home. Just in case, he instructed
the cabdriver not to leave until he returned.

"Damn, girl, you really done it this time," Brian mumbled to himself, walking up the short flight of stairs to the front door. Even the doorbell sounded fancy when he hit the button.

Kim had just grabbed a pint of butter pecan ice cream from the freezer and was heading back up the stairs when the bell caught her attention. She thought that it was Rebecca stopping by with the brief for her to look over. When she opened the door to see Brian standing there, her heart dropped to her stomach. Her eyes immediately began to water, and after putting the ice cream down, she jumped right into his arms. Brian paused for a moment, placing his hand on her stomach, wanting some confirmation that she was still with child. Unbeknown to him, Kim had already made up her mind on her flight back to California that she was going to keep the baby, with or without Brian being in her life. The thought of going through the whole abortion process again was enough to solidify her reason for keeping it.

"What made you change ya mind?" Kim asked, leading Brian into the house.

He almost didn't hear the question as he looked around the stunning home.

"Damn, this house is nice," he said, following behind Kim. "You said this is paid for?"

Kim walked him into the living room where they sat down on the supersized sectional. "What made you changed ya mind?" she asked again, wanting to know what was going on with his thoughts.

Brian turned to look at Kim. There were a few life-changing moments that brought him to this stage in his life, but the only real reason that mattered was family. To be more specific, *his family,* the one he wanted to start with Kim. Dez's advice also played a crucial role. It made Brian take a look at all the opportunities he had that most men in the city of Philadelphia didn't have. He had a little money saved up, a good woman that loved him, and a way to get up out of the hood. He couldn't ask for much more than that, and Kim could have not been any happier than she was at that very moment.

Tammy looked around the airport at all the waves of people walking around trying to make their flights. Darious startled her a little, walking up behind her and wrapping his arms around her waist. "I'm not gonna lie. I didn't think that you was going to come," he said, turning her around to face him. He looked around with a curious stare, wondering where the kids were.

"It's just me. I think we need some time of just you and me. I want to start this off right this time."

"Are you sure about that? You know I always understood that you were a package deal, and I would never accept you without accepting them. They are part of our life, a part that I love." Darious knew how much Tammy cherished her children and didn't want to burden her with making the type of decision that would separate her from them.

"You know I'll take care of them like they were my own."

"I know you would, Darious."

Boarding for the flight to China was announced over the intercom, prompting them to head for the boarding gate. When they got up to the woman who was taking the tickets, Tammy looked around one last time. Darious stopped too, seeing she was a little hesitant.

"Are you sure?" Darious asked again, getting her to turn and face him.

"Are you sure this is what you want? Are you sure that you can honestly forgive me for everything I've done to you in the past, and still love me the same?" Tammy asked back. She was moving to the other side of the world, and she wanted to be totally sure that he wouldn't have any regrets.

"Baby, I love you, and though you hurt me, I never stopped loving you. The time I took for myself really gave me a perspective on the things that's most important to me. And you are that thing. I married you for thick and thin, for better or worse till death do us part. I know it's not gonna be easy, but I'd rather weather the bumps in the road with you than without you," he explained.

Tammy stood there, and as the woman asked for her and Darious's tickets, she looked around the airport one final time. For some crazy reason she thought that Chris was going to pop up out of nowhere with the kids and beg her to stay. A movie-type ending where Chris made a last-ditch effort to try to get her back before she left forever. It never happened. Chris never showed up, and because of that, Tammy knew she was ready to start her new life with Darious for the second time.

Falisha tossed the last duffle bag of clothes in her car, while periodically looking over at Lamar's house and hoping he didn't come outside and catch her. Baby Jordan was in the backseat strapped in his car seat, and if Lamar saw that, he wasn't about to let Falisha leave.

Tomorrow was the day of the hearing to see what type of provisions the judge had for Lamar and his partial custody order. Being as evil as she wanted to be, Falisha decided to take Jordan and go on the run. She had some family in New York and was going to try her hand in the Big Apple. She didn't want Lamar to have any type of custody of Jordan and was willing to move as far away as possible to make sure that it never happened.

"Falisha, I need to talk to you!" her mother yelled from the porch. Falisha didn't have time for the speech her mother was about to give her pertaining to her running off like this.

"Mom, I'll call you when I get to where I'm going!" Falisha yelled back, opening the car door. Then she noticed a set of headlights turning onto the street. It was a black, older model car she wasn't familiar with and really didn't pay it much mind, especially since Lamar's front door had just started to open up.

Lamar and Anne stepped out onto the porch, smiling and laughing in a very intimate way. When Falisha saw that, her blood began to boil. Lamar looked over, connecting eye contact with Falisha who was now getting out of the car. He knew that there was about to be some drama, and Falisha didn't seem to care anything about Jordan who had now awakened.

The car that turned down the street had cut Falisha off before she could cross the street. It came to a complete stop right in front of her. The tinted driver-side window began to come down, just a couple of feet away from her. A large chrome revolver was pointed out of the window, and the last thing Falisha saw before the first shot was fired was the evil stare Fox had on his face. He had got word from his lawyer that someone had been speaking to the feds about him. First person that popped up in his mind was Falisha, and he was going to make sure that she never became a government witness against him.

The first bullet hit Falisha in the gut, knocking her backward onto the ground.

Instinctively, Lamar ran back into the house to retrieve his gun. Anne dropped to the ground and took cover behind the bricks. She could hear several more shots being fired before the car sped off down the street at a high rate of speed. Lamar came back out of the house to the screams of Falisha's mom who was running across the street to her daughter. The car had just turned the corner and for a moment, Lamar was about to get into his car and chase behind it.

Seeing Falisha laid out flat on the sidewalk stopped him in his tracks. Her clothes were stained with a lot of blood that came from the multiple bullet wounds to her body. He walked over, looked down at her, and knew that she was dead. One of the bullets hit her in her head, killing her instantly. Little Jordan was in the backseat of the car crying, and it was Anne who rushed to his side. She quickly took Jordan into the house before he could see his mother's dead body. Lamar was frozen in a state of shock, looking at Falisha's mom cradle her daughter's lifeless body.

There were a lot of mixed thoughts running through his head that were confusing. He watched the mother of his son get murdered right in front of his eyes, and a part of him wished he could have done something about it. But on the other hand, and as bad as it may have seemed, he was relieved that he would no longer have to fight for the right to be in his son's life.